SEXTING THE SILVERFOX

AN AGE GAP, SINGLE DAD ROMANCE

K.C. CROWNE

.

He's the irresistible single dad who owns half this city.
And thanks to one ill-fated drunk text...
My colossal crush is no longer a secret.

I should have known better.
I'm a freaking teacher for crying out loud.
Supposedly the epitome of responsibility.
Yet there I was, detailing my wildest fantasies about a man twice my age.
He was never meant to read it.
But he did.
And he wanted more.
So much more...

Jason:
A drunk text from a stranger left a large stiffness in my trousers.
What's REALLY wrong with this picture?
I'm a single dad. She's half my age.
And her defiance makes my blood boil.

One thing's crystal clear: I won't rest until I claim Audrey.
Taste her full lips. And devour every inch of her heavenly curves.

But I'm not the only one who wants her.
The Bratva thinks they own her.
They have no clue.
I'm not your ordinary billionaire. I'm ruthless.

I'll protect Audrey. And our baby
growing inside her.

CHAPTER 1

AUDREY

My heel taps a rhythmic protest on the checkered marble floor.

One hour lost in the wilderness of corporate indifference and I'm dangerously close to being late for work.

Mr. Winchester, the billionaire real estate tycoon, had insisted on personally attending to the plights of us less fortunate Emerald residents.

You'd think a billionaire real estate mogul would have enough lackeys on his payroll to delegate such menial tasks. Instead, here I am, wasting precious moments of my life, mentally crafting a vibrant tapestry of complaints and legal threats.

I've yet to lay eyes on the man, but my mind paints him as a modern-day Ebenezer Scrooge, albeit one who likely invests heavily in hair restoration—because clearly, any excessive fluff up top must be compensating for other...shortcomings.

I stifle a chuckle at my own mental imagery.

His secretary appears to be both stressed out and abrasive toward anyone who dares to interrupt her workflow. Her fingers tapping away at the keyboard as though her very life depends on it.

For the love of sanity, someone hand that woman a tequila shot. By my observation, she's under a lot of pressure.

As a kindergarten teacher, I've learned to pay attention to the details in human body language. From kids to adults, we're all the same. Nervous tics. Fleeting glances. Flaring nostrils. The changes in one's breathing pattern. There are many ways in which our own bodies betray us.

I'm transfixed by the hypnotic allure of her long and nimble fingers, the red nail polish glistening under the soft reception lights, wondering when I'll get a chance to paint my own nails. My students keep me so busy, and we often get our hands dirty with our daily activities that it feels like a waste of time and a waste of pricey nail polish at this point.

I observe an elderly gentleman coming out of Mr. Winchester's office.

"Thank you, Jason," the man in a grey suit says. "I'll be in touch with the next quarter's reports."

"Take care of yourself," drifts the reply, a voice smooth enough to be criminal.

It's not until the secretary's relentless typing ceases that I realize it's my turn. Her gaze catches mine, an odd mix of curiosity and irritation.

"Oh, it's my turn?" My voice drips with dry humor. I've waited long enough; my patience has passed its limit.

"Yes," she confirms, ushering me forward. "Mr. Winchester will see you now."

I don't plan on letting him off the hook.

Everybody's time is valuable, billionaire net worth or not.

"Thanks," I shoot back, confidently strutting past her desk. I let her callous attitude slide.

Stepping into Mr. Winchester's office, I'm unexpectedly brought to a standstill, my breath catching as I take in the figure before me.

For the first time in my twenty-three years, a man has rendered me utterly speechless.

Jason Winchester shatters all my expectations.

Even while seated, his presence is commanding—broad shoulders and muscular arms barely contained by a dark blue suit that hints at the raw power underneath.

Those eyes...

His piercing blue eyes strip away my defenses, leaving me exposed and vulnerable.

His hair, rich brown with whispers of gray at the temples, is styled with an artful nonchalance that suggests casual luxury. The thought of running my fingers through his hair, over the rough shadow of stubble on his chiseled jaw, sends a thrill of anticipation down my spine.

Jason Winchester, in his mid-forties, exudes a devastating charisma that dominates the room, his very essence an intoxicating blend of authority and allure.

My eyes travel down to his left hand. No wedding band. Fuck yes!

As he watches me, one eyebrow arched in curiosity, I suddenly realize my gaze has been locked on him for far too long.

This time, it's my own body that betrays me, reacting in ways I hadn't anticipated.

"Miss Smith, I presume?" His voice, as smooth as aged whiskey.

"Yes, that's right," I manage, pulling myself back to the reason for my visit. "Our meeting was scheduled for an hour ago."

Jason's lips curl into a faint smile, reminiscent of a tiger surveying its prey.

"The takeover of The Emerald complex has demanded a considerable amount of my attention. I appreciate your patience."

Everything about his voice and body language scream 'no fucks given'.

I almost laugh. His indifference is palpable.

"Keeping someone waiting, particularly a tenant, is not only disrespectful—it's poor management," I reply, allowing Audrey the Assertive to surface, although I have no idea where she's coming from—his heavy gaze causing the knot in my stomach to tighten.

"Please, have a seat. I'm listening," he counters coolly, every word measured, his attention seemingly genuine but I sense the performative undertone.

He surveys me, an unspoken challenge in his gaze as the wind howls its wintry fury outside. My trek here, through the frigid weather, seems to matter little to him.

"Here's the deal. I don't care who bought the complex, who's in charge now, or what your reasons are for keeping me waiting. What I do care about is that for the past couple of months, we've not had enough heat or hot water," I tell him, my tone clipped with frustration. "I'm damn tired of taking cold showers. I pay a lot of money for an upscale apartment in the heart of old Chicago. The Emerald is supposed to be a premium complex, yet I'm freezing my ass off on a daily basis. It's mid-winter in Chicago!"

"I see."

"I've complained repeatedly and have spoken to everyone in the administrative office. I also emailed anyone else I could find who might be able to help, and I am aware other residents in the complex have as well since I'm not the only one dealing with this problem."

"Go on." He leans back in his chair, apparently listening to me, though I beg to differ.

"And I've been given the runaround and nothing else. When did your company buy the complex? Three weeks ago? Four? I've lost track because I've been too cold to think of anything else. This situation is unacceptable. All I am being told is, 'Sorry, Miss Smith, we'll send somebody to check it out.' And so they send the building's maintenance guy who then tells me it's a supplier issue. When I call the supplier, they tell me it's a building issue. And so on and so forth. In the meantime, it's the middle of January, and I'm still freezing my ass off."

He nods a couple of times. "Anything else?"

His apathetic tone is pushing my buttons.

Here I am, on the verge of losing my shit while he sits here, infuriatingly composed, watching me with his striking blue eyes. I'm already amped up, so I keep going, listing every issue I've ever had with the building, sparing no details.

Out of breath, I'm finally satisfied.

"Excuse my rant but I figured as the new owner, maybe you'd care to finally do something about this shit show."

"I expect nothing less," he says.

It's amazing how infuriating a man can be without saying a word. Jason Winchester has barely spoken. Yet beneath my winter coat, I am shivering and simmering at the same time.

Every time our eyes meet, I get a jolt somewhere inside my chest, and I feel the heat spreading downward.

After a pause that seemed to stretch into eternity, he finally speaks. "The previous owner's neglect has not gone unnoticed, which is why I'm taking the time to meet with tenants personally. I fully intend to rectify this... shit show, as you've aptly described it. However, these changes won't happen overnight, and I can see you've endured quite enough. Here's what I propose: I'll arrange for you to stay in one of my Lake View penthouses, free of charge, while we address the heating issues in your building."

"Your penthouse?!?" I ask, not sure I heard him correctly. "Are you kidding?"

He doesn't seem fazed, only amused. "No, I'm not. It's inhumane to have you staying in a place with no heat and barely any hot water in the middle of a Chicago winter."

"Well. I can't possibly stay in a stranger's home, and Lake View is too far from my work. That's just not a viable option."

"Audrey, rather Miss Smith," he begins, and I notice a slight change in his tone. "Whatever the issue is with The Emerald Residence, it won't be resolved overnight. Besides, I now have to replace the entire building staff over there since they clearly haven't been doing their jobs."

"Hold on," I say, my blood suddenly running cold. "That's a lot of people, and at least half of them are good folks. They work hard, and they have families to support. You can't do that."

"Well, you can't have it both ways now, can you?" he asks, smirking. "What's it going to be, Miss Smith? You came to me with a problem; I have offered the only solution I have available for you at this time. My penthouses are momentarily unoccupied, and I don't mind letting you stay there while your place gets fixed. But I still have to do something about the building management, either way. No matter how you look at it, someone is going to lose. Would you rather it be you? Again?"

I think of Sammy, who manages the janitorial team; Rosa, who handles the day-to-day logistics; and Manny, who has been nothing but kind and patient with me when his own bosses had him telling me to call this number or that number. They don't deserve to lose their jobs because the building owners are absolute crap. He's talking about firing the wrong people, and it's completely unfair.

I shoot up from my seat. "It's not fair," I snap, my anger getting the better of me. "It's not ethical. And it's not what I came here for, Mr. Winchester. I expect my heating problem to be fixed within the next forty-eight hours, or I will have no choice but to let my lawyer handle it from there!"

Little does he know I can't afford a lawyer since every penny I have is tied up in my apartment, and my kindergarten teacher's salary won't even cover a single consultation with an attorney.

He says nothing, which makes me feel helpless and vulnerable.

"Thanks for nothing," I mutter as I stand up and turn to leave.

"Hold on, Miss Smith."

I turn around just in time to see him get up and offer me a business card. "What's this for?" I ask.

"I think you'll need it."

He walks over and hands it to me. Our fingers touch for the briefest of seconds, and it's enough to make my vision temporarily hazy as I stare at the card. "We'll see about that," I scoff.

He's confident and somewhat cocky, but I try to leave with my head held high.

However, by the time I reach the elevator, I'm trembling like a leaf in the wind, and not because of the cold. I've been rattled to the core by this man, and I have no idea why.

It's as if my own brain and body have turned against me.

I was supposed to keep my cool at all costs.

How did I go off the rails so quickly?

How did I practically throw a tantrum in front of a seductive man, twice my age—insanely attractive and infuriatingly cocky?

CHAPTER 2

AUDREY

At home that evening, I reflect on my apartment, which has given me one minor headache after another until becoming a giant migraine that I simply could not get away from.

I'm wearing my warmest jammies and woolen socks, a hoodie, and a plush bathrobe on top. My nose is red and cold, but I've managed to warm up a little with a bowl of chicken ramen noodles, extra spicy.

The flimsy plug-in radiator does the trick if I sit close enough to it. Not too close, though, because then I'll get calf burns. I can't leave it on for more than a few hours, either. It'll overheat, and that will become another problem. I can't get a second one because the electrical wiring can't handle it. The apartment is fully electric, so I don't even have a gas stove to turn on. There is just no better way to warm up than the current setup.

Cursing under my breath, I gather the nerve to boil some water to add to my lukewarm bath. I have to be quick about it because as soon as I start taking my clothes off, the cold rushes up my spine, making my teeth chatter.

I could've stayed in New York, I tell myself as I sink into the hot water.

The water temperature will be perfect for a few minutes, tops, so I make the most of it.

But no, I wanted freedom.

It was a hard choice to make, but two years later, I still don't regret it. I am free. I chose my own path, and I built my own life. I only wish I'd done more research on this building before putting most of my money into it. My brothers would laugh their asses off if they saw me now.

So that's what you ran away for? To freeze your ass off in a fancy-schmancy apartment in Chicago? the eldest would say.

Shut up; it's better than what Dad had planned for me, I think.

And it is true. This is better. Yeah, it's cold, and I'm living off a teacher's salary. I've got a few friends, but none that I trust enough to allow them deeper into my life. I've got loads of books but practically no social life.

I'm still a virgin, and I have a hard time trusting most men. But I am the master of my destiny, and I am doing fine without them. "Frickin' hell, it's cold!" I cry out as I jump out of the tub and hurriedly pat myself dry.

It only takes me five minutes to warm up because I'm wrapped in three layers again—socks and all. I pull the radiator closer to my bed and turn on the TV, while my thoughts race. It's been a hellish week, probably the worst one since this whole heat debacle began.

My mind wanders back to Jason Winchester.

He's a complete stranger, Audrey, I think, berating myself, and I proceed to open the bottle of red wine I'd brought with me to my bedroom. There's no other way for me to truly get warm and stay warm until I fall asleep.

I need to forget Jason. He's rich and powerful, and he was trying to use that to silence me.

"Keep this whiny sucker in my uppity penthouse until we fix her heat so she won't bother me again," I mumble, downing the first glass of wine too fast, but hell, I deserve the distraction

By the third glass, I've completely loosened up and am warming up nicely under my blanket while the TV plays a rerun of one of my favorite sitcoms. I'm not paying much attention to what's happening on the screen, though. I'm too busy pondering the choices that brought me to this point. Again, no regrets, but dammit, the universe could show a bit more kindness from now on. I've been good; I've been patient and hard-working, devoted, and always looking to better myself.

By the fourth glass, I'm back to mentally analyzing each of Jason Winchester's features. The way he sat behind his desk like a king surveying his kingdom, pride gleaming in his hazel eyes. That half-smile, the way his lips slowly parted whenever I got angry or started talking too fast. The way his gaze bounced from my mouth to my eyes enough times for me to identify a pattern of curiosity that I couldn't quite understand.

Soon, my thoughts become blurry. I imagine him getting up from behind his desk and coming so close to me that I can smell his sharp cologne. It seduces me and makes my skin tingle all over. I imagine his fingers running through my hair, his lips tracing an invisible line along the side of my jaw until he finds my lips.

Liquid heat gathers between my legs as a scene unfolds in my mind's eye. Jason taking off his jacket and shirt. I can almost imagine the ropes of muscle stretching across his torso, those broad shoulders and strong arms taking hold of me. I melt in his embrace.

He takes me from behind, bending me over his desk.

"Oh, wow," I mumble, my eyes popping open as I realize how far down the rabbit hole I've actually gone. I grab my phone and stare at his number for a while. I saved it, just in case.

I replay images of how Jason might claim me in my head. In his office. On his desk. In his chair. I imagine him pulling my hair as he slides deep inside me. I can almost feel him, my body responding to his touch. The jolt of electricity as he bites my shoulder then pulls back and has me straddling him on the sofa. I ride him hard ...

I need to get thoughts of him out of my head, so I decide to type them in my phone. I'll delete them later, but for now, I need these thoughts out of my brain.

You are the most infuriating and most attractive man I've ever met," I type. "You make me want things ... terrible things ... dirty things .... You'd grab my hair and fuck me like a savage, hard, from behind. Bend me over the table and slap my ass. Spread my cheeks and lick me first. Eat me out. Make me cry out your name. Pinch my nipples until they sting, then fuck me hard again, over and over. I want to ride you until the morning, then do it all again the next day."

There's plenty more where that came from, and I'm already feeling better, but my wine glass is empty, so I reach over for the bottle on the nightstand. My phone slips out of my hand. "Shit!" I hiss as I almost drop the glass, too.

I set the glass next to the bottle instead, deciding I've had enough wine for the night. I need something else. Something I dabble with when it's dark and lonely. I find my phone and leave it face-down on the nightstand.

Closing my eyes, I imagine Jason again. He's a clear image before me. My idea of him is precise. I replay the moment we met but I change the outcome. I say something to piss him off, and next thing I know, he's stripped me bare in his office. There are people outside waiting, and I voice my concern.

"They can't hear us," he whispers in my ear, then nibbles on the lobe before trailing wet kisses down the side of my neck. "But still be quiet."

"Yes, sir," I whisper back.

He kisses me then, and my hand slips under the covers and under my clothes, finding that hot, wet spot between my legs. I'm soaked and so heavily aroused by the mere thought of this man it's almost frightening.

I let him fondle my breasts, squeezing and massaging as I touch myself, just like this ...

My fingers slide in, and I imagine it's him. Stretching and probing me.

My clit swells, tension gathering into a tight ball in desperate need of release. He's big and thick as he goes in. He thrusts deep, hands firmly gripping my ass. I moan harshly into the cold silence of the night as Jason rams into me over and over again. I'm rubbing my tender nub, faster and faster.

"Ah!" I cry out, pleasure rippling outward from between my legs. The tension is suddenly released, a thousand lights exploding as I can almost hear him coming with me in the fantasy, deep inside me, filling me with his essence. Conquering me. Making me his.

Damn, that felt good. I needed it.

When I wake up, it's Saturday. Late morning, judging by the light pouring in through the window. My head hurts.

Ugh.

My mouth is dry. It's as if I swallowed a heap of cotton in my sleep. I'm also hungry and cold.

Dammit.

I remember where I am, my unheated home. The fabled and revered Emerald Residence apartment complex, where each unit goes for well over two hundred grand. I put all the money I had when I left New York into this place, only to end up freezing my ass off.

"Home, sweet home," I groan and drag myself out of bed.

I need a few minutes to get my feet to move properly, but a splash of ice-cold water on my face snaps me back into the present with sparkling cruelty. I brush my teeth and do my usual rushed morning routine.

I check my phone and find a new message from Jason. How the hell did he get my number?

I freeze at what I see. That message I drafted.

"Oh ... my ... God ..."

My knees give out, and I sit on the edge of the bed as I struggle to catch my breath. Heat spreads throughout my body, as I realize what happened. When I fumbled and dropped my phone, I must've accidentally sent that text. It was supposed to be a draft; nobody was supposed to see it!

Oh, God. Oh, God.

He got all of it. My little snippet of therapy. All the things I wanted him to do to me. Every dirty thought I could think of. He read it.

My mind wanders into utter silence as I manage to focus my eyes on the screen for long enough to read his reply.

Go on ...

Go on?

Paralysis takes over. I can't move. I can't speak. I can't even think. I can only stare at these two words in pure shock, my jaw practically unhinged.

Go on.

He wants me to ... go on?

CHAPTER 3

JASON

Audrey Smith is something else.

I knew it from the moment she walked into my office. Despite her visible discomfort from the cold, it suits her. Her long, blonde hair was slightly curly and pulled into a messy bun. Her cheeks were flushed, her full lips tantalizing. Those icy blue eyes still haunt me. I don't think she's aware of how gorgeous she actually is underneath those heavy knit sweaters and thick overcoats.

As soon as I saw her, my heart jumped, and my pants became tight. I had to work overtime to keep a cool and composed attitude. Audrey's problems are legitimate—she's not the only one dealing with heating failures at The Emerald, and I know I bought a fucking mess from that hedge fund—but somebody had to save those buildings and restore them to their former glory. I had money to spare and I was in need of a project.

I simply didn't imagine I'd meet someone like her in the process.

I tried to focus on listening to what she had to say. Hell, I was actually quite pleased with how I handled that entire conversation, and I almost managed to put her out of my mind until last night. She didn't mean to send me that text— I'll bet everything I've got on it. Audrey Smith doesn't strike me as a dirty-minded vixen. She teaches kindergarten, for fuck sake.

I knew it had to be a mistake, yet I couldn't resist the temptation to respond. My cock jumped as I read the words. I had to do something about it, so I kept reading them until I got a brief but hefty release. It's been a while since I rubbed one out while thinking about a woman I've only just met.

It's late afternoon, and I'm already sipping whiskey.

In my defense, it's been a long week, and the fact that Audrey insists on popping back into my thoughts every other fucking minute isn't helping. I should be focusing on something else, but her words keep flashing across my brain unbidden, and I'm distracted all over again.

What the hell is wrong with me?

I have abandoned all trust in women after what Ramona did. I would've given her the world. We had *it all*—the romance, the relationship, the passion. After everything I went through, Ramona was supposed to be my happy ending, and I was determined to be hers. So, I gave it my all, and I married her. I gave her my name. We created a baby, and we were going to raise Lily together, like the best friends and partners I believed we were.

Except Ramona had other plans, plans that included cheating with my best friend and leaving me to raise our daughter alone. I've been doing the best I can for the past couple of years. I love Lily more than anything in this world, and I would do anything for her. But it's been a lonely and exhausting road, at least on an emotional level. Lily is almost five now and is starting to ask more questions about her mother. I don't yet know how to explain certain things without vilifying Ramona in the process.

I hear the door open, signaling that Lily and her nanny, Rita, have returned.

Instantly, I light up from the inside and set my empty glass on the table. I manage to put everyone else out of my mind, Audrey included, and slap on the softest smile I can muster while I go into the entryway to greet them.

"Daddy!" Lily shouts as soon as she sees me, then rushes into my arms.

I scoop her up and shower her with kisses. She giggles and hides her face in my chest. Rita laughs as she puts Lily's coat and boots away.

"Welcome back, munchkin!" I tell my daughter, then give Rita an appreciative nod. "How were the piano lessons?"

"Good, actually," Rita replies. "Her teacher says she's a natural. She would like to keep working with Lily."

I couldn't be prouder as I look at my daughter and revel in her excitement. "I like it," my little girl says. "I like playing the piano."

"You do? Why?" I ask.

"I like the songs. They make me happy!"

"Gosh, you should've seen her, Mr. Winchester. She was so nervous at first," Rita says. "But Mrs. Fogarty is kind and patient, and she works with kids Lily's age on a daily basis so she knew exactly how to handle Lily's jitters."

"Maybe I'll join you for your next lesson," I tell Lily. "Can I?"

"Not until I'm ready," Lily replies, frowning slightly.

"Ready for what?"

For a moment, I'm reminded of how much she looks like me. Her brown hair is long and curly like Ramona's and frames her pale, round face, but everything else is bits and pieces of me. The hazel green eyes. The smile. The way she scrunches her nose when she's thinking hard about something. Lily is her own person, though, and all I can do is make sure she has every opportunity to grow and become the best version of herself for as long as I draw breath.

"I want to do the ... the ..." Lily pauses, failing to remember something, so she looks at Rita for guidance.

Rita has been working for me since Lily was two years old. She picks up on my daughter's cues with lightning speed every time. "'The Moonlight Sonata,' I believe, is what Mrs. Fogarty said," Rita replies.

"'The Moonlight Sonata,'" Lily repeats after her.

She looks adorable in her green tartan dress and white stockings. Like a Victorian doll but with a spunky Winchester attitude. I wish I had a bigger family to give her. I'm all she has, and she's all I have. We'll have to do for each other, at least for a while, but Lily doesn't seem to mind.

"So, you won't let me come to any of your piano lessons until you can play 'The Moonlight Sonata' for me?" I ask her.

"Yes."

"Aiming for perfection," Rita says with a wink.

"Fair enough. But I expect you to tell me everything about what you're learning along the way," I tell Lily. "And I hope you'll keep practicing on our piano as well."

I bought the Steinway & Sons in our living room specifically for her. As soon as Rita suggested piano lessons and Lily said yes, I immediately went ahead and ordered one. It's been with us for a week, and it looks good in the room; I just can't wait to hear my daughter play it.

"I will, Daddy!" Lily promises.

Rita comes over and takes Lily into her arms. "Come on, time to get changed and ready for dinner."

"You should go home," I tell Rita. "I can cook or order something in."

"Nonsense, Mr. Winchester, it's my pleasure," Rita retorts. "You do enough as it is."

"Well, so do you. It's the weekend; you shouldn't have troubled yourself."

Rita puts on a warm smile while Lily plays with the locks of her greying hair. "I have been working with you long enough to recognize that there are moments, even on the weekends when you could use more time to yourself, so I urge you to take advantage of my presence and go and pour yourself another drink," she says. "You deserve it."

"You're too kind."

"Maybe. Or maybe I simply understand how hard you work on a daily basis," Rita replies. "Now, if you'll excuse us, this little one needs to change so she can help me with dinner."

"Thank you, Rita."

"What are we eating? Spaghetti and meatballs?" Lily chimes in, her eyes wide with excitement. "Please?"

"All right, all right," Rita feigns exhaustion. "Spaghetti and meatballs it is. You're lucky I went grocery shopping yesterday."

I laugh and plant a kiss on my daughter's cheek before I leave her in Rita's care. The penthouse is big enough for them to move around in without us crossing paths, though Lily will find every moment she can to either come over to check on me or to call me into the kitchen so I can help them with something. Not that I mind; I welcome the momentary respite.

For a few minutes there, my mind felt clear.

Rita can read me so well. I believe she can tell when I'm about to tune out. Maybe she can read it on my face. She is one of the most intuitive people I've ever come across, and it's certainly one of the reasons why our professional relationship is working out so well. That, and she treats and loves my daughter like her own flesh and blood. I couldn't ask for more.

Once I'm back in my seat by the window, I pour myself another scotch and go through the stock exchange dashboard to see where we're at. Most brokers are off for the weekend, but I do plenty of speculation on my own whenever I get the chance. S&P is looking good this afternoon.

A sudden text message pops up.

"Audrey," I whisper. My breath gets stuck in my throat. My thumb won't move, but I am eager to open the message. My heart is racing. Does she regret what she wrote last night? Did I make an even bigger fool of myself by replying?

I'll never know unless I open the damned thing.

I won't apologize for that text, it reads, and I can't help but smile.

A sense of relief washes over me. I can almost see her, with her messy hair and wide eyes, trying to look defiant. I don't like the idea of her living in a cold apartment, though. I don't like the idea of her being in any kind of discomfort.

I wouldn't want you to, I reply, then lean back into my chair.

I have no idea where this conversation will lead, but I know I want to know more about her. And I most certainly want to put that list of hers to the test.

CHAPTER 4

AUDREY

I've become so enthralled with this text message exchange that I've almost forgotten how cold my apartment is. It's late on Saturday night, and I'm not shivering on the sofa. I'm too busy giggling at each of Jason's messages.

They get naughtier by the minute, and I realize I don't even need alcohol to loosen up and respond in kind anymore. Every ball he sends my way, I show up to serve without hesitation.

He brings out the devil in me.

How cold is it over there? he asks.

We were talking about strawberries and whipped cream a second ago, I shoot back, my thumbs moving remarkably fast across the onscreen keyboard.

I am warm and getting warmer under my blanket, feet burning in woolen socks. I think about undressing, but that's not a good idea. It's the arousal that's messing with my senses, and the last thing I need is to catch a chill.

Jason's mind is even dirtier than mine, though I am genuinely fascinated with the way in which he stimulates me, physically and mentally.

True, but the thought of you naked reminded me of your heating issue. Are you naked? Jason replies.

My face feels red-hot, and I'm squealing like a horny teenager as I read the words aloud. *Mr. Winchester, how dare you ask me such questions?*

You wanted me to bend you over my desk last night. I didn't think you'd be such a prude the next day, comes the reply.

He's got a point. We've been at it for the past couple of hours. Every serious topic we try to broach inevitably goes back to that list of things I want him to do to me, but his persistence is ridiculously sexy because he always drops the bomb when I least expect it.

Even now, he manages to completely disarm me without being anywhere close to me. This man's magnetism goes way beyond his physical presence.

It shouldn't feel this good. I don't really know who he is, aside from what I've retrieved from a couple of different online search engines. Former Army, divorced, single dad, billionaire, invested a lot in hedge funds and crypto, then started buying up properties all over Chicago, renovating and flipping them for insane amounts of money. "Jason Winchester Turns a Profit Whenever He Blinks" was the title of a finance magazine article.

I know more about him than he does about me, however. I am always careful about my past and what information I give out. There are moments when I still look over my shoulder, but I haven't had any reason to worry thus far. It's been two years, and they haven't found me. I just hope they've given up and understand that I wanted it that way.

I'm not a prude. I just think there should be limits, I text Jason, trying to get my bearings while actively ignoring the arousal pooling between my legs. *Besides, I'm dressed beyond any man's ability to undress me at this point.*

That sounds like a challenge.

No, sir. It's just cold enough to warrant three to four layers of clothing, I write back.

He goes quiet. I'm not sure if I like it. Maybe he's busy. He's got a kid, after all. A life.

Eventually, the TV captures my attention.

I lose track of time before the next message comes in.

So, tell me what you're wearing then, Jason writes.

I double over laughing, damn near dropping the phone again, but I manage to regain my composure and text him back.

That is such a cliché! Is this how you get girls these days? Does that even work?

No, I am genuinely curious to know what clothes you've got on. You said it's still freezing cold at your place.

You'll need a strategy and a lot of patience to undress me; let's leave it at that.

Not good enough. What are you wearing, Audrey?

Is he serious? I won't know unless I play his game. I shouldn't, but my fingers are already itching. Jason is surprisingly good at obliterating my inhibitions. Granted, I am a bit inexperienced, and given my strict upbringing, every single word that I've written to this man could easily qualify as a capital sin.

My ears burn hot with an enticing mixture of shame and arousal. I don't really know what to do, but the only thing that makes sense is to reply to his message and follow his lead.

This is going somewhere, and judging by the knot in my throat, I might end up liking it, maybe a little too much.

A fluffy pink bathrobe I got myself as a present last Christmas. A Lakers hoodie and a set of pink and white flannel pajamas, the kind you'd wear at a ski chalet in the Alps, huddled around the fire with a hot chocolate in hand.

Marshmallows included?

It's not hot chocolate without marshmallows.

What else?

What else what?

What else are you wearing?

I take a deep breath and continue texting.

A white lace bra and cotton briefs. They're grey. I'm sorry I didn't match my underwear.

No socks?

Yes, socks. Wool. But the soft kind, not the scratchy kind.

I stare at the three dots on the screen as he replies. They keep flashing, but no response comes. Time passes in the heaviest silence while I breathlessly wait.

Ten minutes later, my phone rings.

Jason's name flashes across the screen.

"What the hell?" I croak. I feel hot. I'm dangerously curious so I pick up. "Hello?"

The very voice I wanted to hear pours into my ear, sending fire flowing through my veins.

"I'm outside."

"Outside where?"

"Outside your apartment."

For a moment, I fail to register the words.

Outside my apartment. Meaning, he's at my door. My head turns, nearly snapping my neck in the process as I look to the door.

"What do you mean you're outside my apartment?" I ask, my voice barely a whisper.

"Did you think we'd just sext all day without a physical conclusion, Audrey? Or do you want me to leave?"

My legs move before I can do anything about it. "No, no, hold on."

What in God's green earth am I doing?

It doesn't matter. I'm already doing it. My conscience is muffled underneath layers of spicy fantasies that are about to come true. After two years of quiet solitude, every fiber of my being demands this. I leave the sofa and pad across the floor. Opening the door slowly, I sense my breath leaving me as I see him standing there.

"You weren't kidding about layering up," Jason says, an amused twinkle lingering in his eyes while his voice echoes through both of our phones at the same time. I turn mine off and laugh nervously.

"Nope."

His gaze captures mine, and the silence that follows becomes unbearable. All I can do is exhale sharply and stare at him. Tall, dark, and handsome. Those specks of silver in his hair, those fine lines drawn at the corners of his mouth, those delicious-looking lips that stretch into a hungry smile.

"I take it you don't want me to leave," Jason says.

His voice is lower, filled with unspoken desires. Brimming with simmering anticipation. I nod slowly and take a step back, welcoming him in. "I apologize for the cold. The building's new owner promised to take care of it," I reply with a playful eye roll.

"I think I know the guy," he replies as he cautiously comes in. "Usually follows through with what he says."

"I sure hope so."

He chuckles softly as I close the door and turn around to face him. He's donning a pair of khaki slacks and a burnt orange shirt underneath a brown leather bomber jacket. I have a mind of running my fingers over the woolen lapels, but he takes it off and tosses it over the back of the nearest chair before I can, his eyes never leaving mine. "You are positively insane, Audrey, do you know that?" he asks.

"Why?"

"Undress for me, please."

"Wait, what?"

But Jason isn't here to take no for an answer. Nor do I wish that to be my answer. But everything is moving a little too fast, and I want to enjoy the moment for as long as possible. "It's cold, and I would like to keep you warm through the night. I can't do that if you're wearing three layers of clothes."

"Is this part of your pledge to support the building's residents? Going from door to door to warm them up?" I can't help but laugh lightly, my hands already busy removing my plush bathrobe.

"No, I just want to look at you. I've been thinking about this from the moment you walked into my office," Jason says.

"You have?"

"You aren't even aware, are you?"

"Aware of what?"

"Of the effect you have on a man," he answers.

My cheeks suddenly feel hot again but my fingers continue the effort to get me out of this suddenly heavy hoodie.

Jason curses under his breath as he takes his shirt and pants off. This feels so strange and yet wonderful at the same time, like we are doing a precautionary analysis of each other. It's cold, and we're trembling, but his body is a sight to behold. Jason is a strong man, splendidly fit and toned, just as I expected him to be. I can't take my eyes off his muscular torso, his rippling pecs making me lick my lips.

Finally, I'm out of my hoodie, but I still have my jammies on.

At this point, my gaze slides downward, settling on his thick thighs while he takes every inch of me in, quietly, methodically, his lips slowly parting as his eyes find mine again.

"Don't rush," he says.

A secret fantasy of mine is about to come true, and the excitement is enough to heat me to my core as I unbutton my pajama top and let it fall to the floor.

"Why am I the crazy one?" I ask, a tremor persisting in my voice.

"We're both crazy," Jason replies. "I'm crazy for coming up here, and you're crazy for letting me in, Audrey. We're complete strangers."

"Well, not really *complete* strangers anymore," I mutter. "You know a thing or two about me. I know a thing or two about you. And we're about to get naked in front of each other."

He nods in agreement, then comes closer, and just like that, the air between us disappears, replaced by heated passion, as he cups my face and pulls me into a rushed, ravenous kiss. The entire world shifts and ultimately dissipates around us as I lose myself in the moment. His tongue slips through and plays with mine, twirling and probing, testing my defenses—of which there aren't any left.

"What a surprise you turned out to be," Jason whispers against my lips.

"I've clearly lost my mind. That has to be the reason why I'm—" But he doesn't let me finish as he kisses me again. A flame ignites in my chest, determined to consume everything in its path.

I moan as he deepens the kiss. I can taste the hint of whiskey on his lips and I wrap my arms around his neck, as his hands roam freely. It seems rushed, but it isn't. It's a methodical exploration of my flesh as his fingers register every inch of me. They dig in and squeeze, delicately touch and fearlessly grab, as they move lower and lower.

My head falls back, and I gasp as he takes hold of my breasts, kneading them through the white lace fabric of my bra while I hold onto his strong shoulders. I feel his cock nestled against my belly, bulging and hard as a rock.

Within seconds, we shed the rest of our clothes. There's no need to waste time on fruitless foreplay; we're both already heated up from hours' worth of raunchy texts. I'm so wet I can feel the arousal trickling down the insides of my thighs.

He kisses my neck, sending thousands of electrical tendrils shooting through my limbs and down my spine. I gasp when his mouth finds my breast, lips closing around the nipple, while one hand slips below and cups my pussy. "Holy hell," he growls. "You've been waiting for me for hours, haven't you, Audrey?"

"Yes," I rasp as his fingers slide between my wet folds.

I let my hands wander, exploring the hard muscles stretching down his arms. The bulky biceps, the strong forearms. I can't get enough of him, so I scan his chest, too, fingertips lingering in lazy circles around his hardened nipples while he takes good care of mine.

"Spread your legs for me, Audrey," Jason says.

I do as I'm told and he slips a finger inside me. "Ah!" I moan as he probes my entrance, reveling in the sound of erotic wetness. I've been ready since I met him. So ready.

"Hold on," he says, pausing for a moment.

I'm about to cry as he pulls back. This can't be it. This can't be over.

But Jason isn't anywhere near done with me. He guides me across the living room and around the sofa. "Bend over," he commands me. "It's how you wanted it, Audrey. And that's how you're getting it."

Nodding slowly, I lean forward and place my hands on the back of the sofa, keeping my legs spread wide for him. He slaps my ass, and I yelp in surprise.

"I gave you an order, Audrey. What do you say when you wish to comply?"

"Yes."

"Yes, what?" He spanks me again. The sting is subtle yet powerful enough to make my knees shake and my pussy clench. I'm aching for him. I'm aching to be stretched and filled and fucked for the first time in my life, and I will do anything he wants.

"Yes, sir!" I moan again.

"Good girl," he mutters, and I listen as he settles behind me.

I should tell him. He should know that I've never been with a man before. "Oh, God!" I manage as I feel his tongue sliding between my slick folds, tasting and licking everything in its path. "Oh..."

"You taste like heaven, baby," he says, then proceeds to shamelessly eat my pussy.

Kissing. Licking. His lips close around my swollen clit while I grip the sofa tighter. A ball of lightning unfurls in my core as I feel an orgasm building up. I can barely breathe as he suckles my tender nub and slips two fingers inside me—the movement beckoning me to slowly rock my hips, back and forth.

Jason is crouching beneath me, the back of his head against the sofa, while his hands take hold of my ass and prompt me to grind against his face. He continues to go down on me, hungrier with each passing second, while simultaneously finger-fucking me out of this world.

The pressure is too much to bear. I reach the edge of madness and unravel. I come hard, gasping and crying out in sweet agony as the ripples dismantle me from the inside out.

My knees are weak and barely able to hold me as I continue to ride the wave while Jason stands and positions himself behind me. My mind is numb but my body is alive and kicking. Jason's index and thumb catch my chin, turning my head so he can kiss me.

I taste myself on his lips.

"It's my first time," I whisper, shivering in the settling night.

Outside, the city sleeps beneath the cold winter snow. Inside, despite the dropping temperatures, I can see the condensation building up on my living room windows. The stiff silence has me worried and I open my eyes to find Jason staring at me in disbelief, his cock twitching anxiously, nestled between my buttocks.

"What did you say?"

"It's my first time being with a man."

"Are you serious?"

"Is that a problem?" I manage, suddenly afraid he won't want me.

Jason's gaze softens for a moment but then he kisses me again. It feels different this time, however. It reaches deeper into my being with a sense of reassurance, of something more powerful and infinitely more intense. The wonder of discovery burns brighter as he pauses to look me in the eyes. "Relax," he says.

"I want you inside me, Jason. All of you."

"All of me."

"Yes, all of you. Just like I said in my text," I insist. The passion between us demands absolute abandonment. I don't need silk gloves and princess treatment. "Take me. Hard and deep."

He smiles, gently caressing my face, then kisses me again before he probes my entrance with his rock-hard cock. Slowly, he slides in, one inch at a time, and I hold my breath as I feel everything, as my pussy stretches to welcome him.

He is huge and thick and it hurts, but in the best possible way. It quickly becomes addictive just to have him inside me.

"How does it feel?" Jason asks. "Fucking hell, you're so wet, Audrey. You were made for this, I swear."

"It feels incredible," I say, my voice uneven as I tilt my hips back.

He groans and thrusts himself all the way in.

The shooting, sharp pain is brief. I whimper for a moment, quivering as he holds me firmly by the hips and then gently moves. The motion takes on a rhythm of its own and before long, the discomfort fizzles out and pleasure takes over. Raw, decadent, all-consuming pleasure as I welcome this man with each thrust.

"Audrey," Jason manages. "I'm going to make you come again. And I'm going to fuck you hard, do you understand me?"

"Yes, sir."

As if suddenly activated, one hand moves between my legs. He massages my pussy, fingers eager to work my clit into another frenzy. It's already flushed and overly sensitive, every stroke sending waves of pure fire to ravage my senses, while his cock slides in and out of me with growing intensity.

"Touch yourself," he says.

I squeeze my breasts, massaging the soft flesh, then tease and pinch my nipples the way he said he likes it. He glances down, over my shoulder, fucking me harder and deeper while simultaneously stimulating my clit. I can feel the second climax coming, vicious and determined to shatter me into bits and pieces.

"Yes!" I cry out, the sound of skin slapping skin causing my mind to go haywire.

We become wild animals in the middle of a January night, with no inhibitions, no remorse, not a care in the world except for this particular union, for the sizzling heat between us. Our bodies become one as Jason pounds me into oblivion, fucking me and stroking me while I beg for more.

"Come for me, Audrey. Come for me now."

"Oh, Jason, yes!" I scream and shiver as I explode, bursting like a volcano as he gives me everything he's got. I love the sound of his beastly grunts, the way he bites into my shoulders and thrusts himself deeper, harder, until I clench tightly around his cock and glaze him with my essence as he releases himself, filling me with his seed.

"Fucking hell," he manages, but I'm too busy still enjoying every damn second.

All I can do is kiss him desperately, then shamelessly ask for more.

"You were made for me," he whispers, holding me close.

"Jason, I need more."

"Good because I'm not going anywhere just yet."

"The bedroom is that way," I reply and nod to my left.

He takes my hand and leads me there. My heart flutters, my pussy still quivering and pulsing, as I brace myself for what's to come. We fit together like two pieces of a puzzle. He fills me to perfection.

But something tells me it'll end badly.

CHAPTER 5

JASON

I haven't been able to get Audrey out of my mind for the past couple of days.

This enticing creature originally walked into my office with a frown, and now her ragged moans in the heat of passion echo in the back of my head. It was a whirlwind. Neither of us expected it, but we played along. We played hard all through the night. We would've continued had I not had my daughter to come home to.

We haven't put a label on whatever this is between us. I didn't want to bring it up, and neither did Audrey. I can't believe it was her first time. I'm still reeling from that. How did she stay a virgin for this long? She's twenty-three.

A woman like her should've met her match by now. Any man in his right mind wouldn't think twice before conquering and claiming her. And considering how quickly the flame burst between us, how did I get to be the lucky one to introduce her to lovemaking?

I can't remember the last time a woman had me hung up like this, constantly thinking about her. My skin remembers hers like warm silk. My fingers itch, desperate to explore her again. I'm practically walking around with a constant hard-on.

I don't know what to do with these emotions except keep them hidden under a tightly closed lid until I figure it out.

"Mr. Winchester, your four o'clock was rescheduled to tomorrow," Shay says. She's one of the better secretaries I've had the pleasure of working with over the past few years. People are fooled by her posh and pristine exterior because once she's pissed off, the streets come out, and may the Lord have mercy on any poor fool who thinks of crossing her. "Figured you'd want to know in case you wish to leave early."

I didn't even hear her come through the door. The memories of my night with Audrey keep flooding my brain. I'm not even sure what I'm working on at this point, nor do I want anyone to notice my distraction, so I give Shay a faint smile.

"Thanks. In that case, you should leave at four as well," I say.

"Greatly appreciated, sir."

The door closes behind her, and I'm on my own again. I groan with frustration as I slide back into thoughts of Audrey, slowly shaking my head. The apartment *was* freezing cold. I can't let Audrey live like that for much longer. She's proud, though, and wouldn't accept my help. A strong, independent woman, that one. But my honor demands that I do something about it.

From what I gather, the issue is stuck somewhere between the supplier and the building maintenance. I've got people looking into it, scanning and checking The Emerald's financial accounts, but there are other problems within the complex besides that.

Old wiring. Shoddy pipework. It's an old set of buildings that should've been gutted and renovated when they turned it into The Emerald. Except they didn't do any of that. They just cleared out the dirt and the grime that plastered the holes and slapped on a couple of coats of paint or a tasteful wallpaper to hide the problems. That was it. Well, that and installing some sleek-looking appliances and updated countertops that made the apartments seem expensive enough to justify the asking price.

Audrey had no idea what she was moving into, much like the other equally affected residents. It makes me angry because I take pride in my work. None of my properties are like The Emerald. I don't do shoddy. I fucking hate shoddy work because a house or an apartment is more than just a unit for sale or for rent. It's a home.

A knock on the door has me sitting up straight.

"Come in," I say.

My heart stops for a moment as Audrey walks in. A smile blooms on my face, mirroring hers as she carefully closes the door behind her. "Hope you don't mind," she says, keeping her voice low. "Your secretary wasn't at her desk."

"Not at all," I chuckle softly, surprised to see her. "What brings you here?"

She frowns then, and the mood suddenly goes south.

"I have an issue, Jason."

"What's going on?"

"The internet is acting up now. I mean, it's bad enough there's still next to no hot water or heat in the apartment, but now the internet is down, too."

"Are you serious?" I ask, trying to find a quick solution in my head.

She can't keep the smirk off her face, and I know then that she is lying.

"You said I could come to you if I had a problem," Audrey shoots back, careful to lock the office door before she slowly and deliberately makes her way over to my desk. "A busted internet connection seemed like a problem."

"Fair enough."

"I thought it was worth a shot."

"What are you really here for then?" I ask as she comes closer.

Audrey rolls her eyes, holding back a chuckle. "Well, you said we need to go over that list of things ..."

"List of things?"

"Things I want you to do to me." Her gaze darkens as it locks onto mine, and heat spreads through my chest. She takes off her coat and tosses it over the guest sofa, then gracefully sits on the edge of my desk, mere inches away from me. So close, in fact, that her floral perfume fills my nostrils, and I breathe in the promise of spring. "Now's as good a time as any."

"Miss Smith, you are positively shameless," I say, but I'm already taking my hands off the wheel and flowing with the lava river that ignites on the inside. "This is my office. My sanctuary. My workplace."

"And this here looks like a sturdy desk," she shoots back with a wink.

I lean forward, and I can see her nipples hardening, struggling against the fabric of her bra and her dress. My money's on lace. Nothing padded. I lick my lips and look deep into her eyes; her hitched breath making every muscle in my body tighten. "I had no idea you had this side to you when I first responded to your accidental text," I say.

"I had no idea, either, but you bring it out of me," Audrey replies.

"I believe bending you over this desk was on that list."

My cock jumps when she responds with a quiet nod, her gaze never leaving mine as I get up from my seat and move closer. My heart beats a million miles per minute, and her instant response only serves as fuel for the flames.

"We can't let anyone hear us," I warn her.

"Then you should probably kiss me."

I grab her by the back of the neck and crush my lips to hers. It's a desperate kind of kiss, mindless, reckless. Her lips are soft, her tongue eager to play. I taste her sweetness as I wrap my left arm around her waist, pulling her in close so I can feel every curve of her body glued to mine.

I move my other hand over her thighs. They are warm and creamy, and I squeeze and pinch, loving the whimpers slipping from the back of her throat when I reach her pussy. "Fucking hell, Audrey," I growl against her lips. "You're not wearing panties."

"No, sir, I am not," she giggles.

She is already so fucking wet. My fingers slide through her wet warmth, probing and exploring as I marvel at how reactive she is. I kiss her again, then quickly pull back, determined to have my way. Judging by the eager look on her face, she is game for whatever is coming, biting her lower lip as she watches me remove my leather belt.

"Bite on this," I tell her. "No one can hear you."

"Yes, sir," she says.

Her obedience makes me grow even harder and become even more enthralled. She bites on the belt, and I take a moment to just look at her. Blonde hair cascaded down her back, glossy lips pressed over the dark brown leather, pearly teeth. I'm about to let my inner beast out because she's so gleefully asking for it, not to mention so fucking sexy.

"Look at me," I say, standing in front of her. Our eyes meet again, lust burning in a pair of blue pools. "Hands behind your back. Don't move."

She nods and does as she's told while I get on my knees and spread her legs before glancing up for a hot second. It's a splendid view from down here, with her dress rolled up over her hips, desire glistening in her eyes, and sheer arousal trickling down the inside of her thigh. I take charge and slide three fingers inside her.

"Hmph!" Audrey holds back, biting down on the belt as I go hard and fast.

I close my lips around her clit and suckle it. I press my tongue against the swelling nub while finger-fucking her into a rapidly onsetting orgasm. Audrey's legs shake, but I don't stop. I probe and thrust, curling my fingers with each retreat while teasing her clit. I can feel her pussy clenching, her core bracing for release. I'm dying to fuck her senseless, but I need her to come first. I need to feel her explode.

"Come for me, Audrey."

With her hands behind her back, she's close to losing her balance. But she soldiers on, grunting and biting into the belt until she finally comes. Hard. I drink every drop, licking her clean while my fingers squeeze every single ripple of her devastating climax. Before she has a chance to recover, I get up and turn her around.

"Now, let's give you what you came here for," I say before pushing some of the papers off my desk to make room for her. "Bend over. Keep your hands behind your back."

"Mmm..."

She's mine. Right now, she's mine. Body and soul.

Her ass is a glorious peach shape, her legs spread, and pussy dripping with desire. I pull my cock out and spear her with my full length. "Oh, fuck," I mutter as I feel her stretching, enveloping me, taking every goddamn inch. She's perfectly hot and wet and deliciously tight.

I keep one hand clasped around her wrists. The control I have over this nymph is inebriating and dangerously addictive. And she loves every second of it. I take a moment to bask in her liquid fire, pussy still throbbing from that orgasm.

And then I start to move.

In. Out. Slowly but surely, a rhythm is established. She perks her ass up for me, moaning against the belt as I go deeper. Deeper. Each thrust filling her to the brim. Each thrust stretching and consuming her. She's so sensitive right now, coming into her own and unraveling all over me.

I slap her ass, grinning like the devil upon hearing her muffled whimpers, then start fucking her like there's no tomorrow. She glances back at me, teeth sinking into the leather as desire glimmers in her gaze. She loves it.

Pressure mounts in my lower belly, and my whole body bucks.

The desk creaks slightly with every thrust, but I don't care. Audrey is taking it like a good girl, and I pound into her.

"You like getting spanked, I see," I grunt and go harder.

Faster. Harder, still. I feel her clenching, tighter and tighter. She groans loudly as she comes again, and I lose the last of my self-control, filling her up. My climax shatters my senses.

I lovingly caress her hips, let go of her wrists, and remove the belt, then cover her with my body, kissing her cheek. Audrey's pants of raw pleasure are music to my ears. She's so soft, so warm, so fucking perfect.

"You're a menace to my sanity," I whisper.

"I can't get enough of you," she replies.

"Good, because I'm not done with you yet," I reply.

Her eyes widen with anticipation. Pure joy radiates through each of her pores as she stands up and turns to face me.

I'm breathing heavily. My blood still simmers. I'm hungry for her, still. Hungry, thirsty, everything at once and overlapping. Yet it's the playful glow in Audrey's eyes that ignites a new and even more devastating fire inside of me. "What are you up to?" I ask, my voice low and humming with arousal.

"Can I show you?"

"By all means."

Decisive in each movement, Audrey gets down on her knees before me. Instantly, my cock reacts. I expected a few more minutes before I would be ready for round two, but she is a marvel.

I watch her as she wraps her fingers around the base and starts gently stroking the shaft.

I grow harder and bigger in her hands. Thick veins pulsate with every motion, sending heat signals through my body and making my pulse reach galloping speeds once more. Audrey's lips part as she looks up at me. "Fucking hell," I hear myself mumble.

"I've wanted to do this since the day I first saw you," she says, then licks the tip.

Her tongue is subtle but capable. Within seconds, I've lost all common sense, and so has Audrey. She takes all of it in, deep-throating me with hunger and eagerness.

It was supposed to be a one-time thing, or at least that's what I told myself. It is clearly way more than that, yet neither of us has the ability or the sense to stop. It's too good. Audrey relaxes the back of her throat and I slide all the way in, noticing her eyes as they tear up, and still, she won't stop.

She's fucking insatiable.

She's fucking perfect.

I am so fucking screwed.

CHAPTER 6

A one-off.

That's what I told myself the first morning after Jason and I were together, after I gave myself to him, wholly and completely.

I've actually lost count of how many moments we've had since then, hidden from the world and lost to our lovemaking. It's been weeks, and we're only getting hotter, brighter, hungrier for more. We have been able to keep things strictly physical, and for that, I am grateful. I wouldn't even know where to start as far as relationships go. I never had anyone to talk to about these things.

My heart aches. I wish I had Mom around, but she left this world long before I was old enough to even comprehend the idea of love, relationships, or marriage. I was left with my overbearing father and two older brothers, all three determined to "keep me pure" until I was wed.

I never really questioned my upbringing, but I couldn't agree with what Dad had planned for me, deciding certain things for me, regardless of what it would cost him. So, I ran away. It was a dangerous and perhaps foolish thing to do, but I've been breathing a lot easier since I left.

Sometimes, I wish I could go back and do things differently. They never listened, though. I had no one to talk to, no one who would understand me. At least here in Chicago, nobody knows me. I'm just a bubbly kindergarten teacher who was somehow able to afford an apartment in The Emerald Residence.

"Mrs. Ashel!" I call out to my next-door neighbor just as she comes down the front steps while I'm walking up.

It's Sunday morning and judging by her blue tartan outfit and lacquered beige shoes, she's on her way to church. A widow and former schoolteacher herself, Mrs. Ashel and I have gotten along great since the first day I moved in. As soon as she saw me come in with my keys and nothing but a suitcase to my name, she helped me get the lay of the land and get settled.

Upon seeing me, Mrs. Ashel lights up like the sun.

"Oh, Audrey, sweetheart, there you are! How are you holding up?" she asks, her milky blue eyes worriedly searching my face.

"I'm all right, thank you. How about you? You haven't heard anything from the building manager yet either, huh?"

She shakes her head in dismay. "No, but my son wants me to move in with him and his wife until the problem is resolved. They're coming by tomorrow morning to pick me up."

"Thank God, you can't keep living like this."

"Neither can you, honey," Mrs. Ashel replies. Underneath her matching blue tartan hat, she keeps her grey hair in tight curls, spending at least an hour every evening to make sure they hold up overnight. "What did the owner say? You mentioned you'd gotten in touch with him."

"They're still investigating the issue, but I understand there's been a misappropriation of funds. That's just one of the causes, mind you. There's more, but they're working to get the heat back on before the end of next week. Jason said they've already signed contracts with a new supplier, but they need to get a team onsite to check the installation requirements first."

We're outside the building in the middle of a cold February morning, but I'm used to it. My home isn't much warmer when I think about it, but I do look forward to hugging my little heater once I get upstairs. I spent the night at a hotel with Jason. I would've liked to have spent it at his place, at least, but we agreed not to let things get too personal between us.

"Well, that's good news then!" Mrs. Ashel exclaims. "It means I won't be bothering my son and his family for more than a week."

"Mrs. Ashel, you could never bother anyone," I reply, my gaze wandering up and down the street.

It's not busy at this hour, so I have a clear view of the block from where I'm standing. For the past week or so, I've felt a constant urge to look over my shoulder, though I don't think it's warranted. Two years have passed since I left; I can't imagine they are still looking for me. Besides, I would've seen something, a sign of their presence. They're not exactly the subtle type.

But this feeling has been getting more and more persistent, especially when I'm on my own and especially around The Emerald. Maybe it's just the ongoing discomfort of my heat situation.

"Audrey, I've been on my own for years now, and I do all right. My husband would be proud. I certainly am, especially in my old age. Going to stay with Eric does make me feel a little helpless."

"But you're not helpless," I reply. "The whole building is facing the same problem. I'm pretty sure our entire floor is currently temporarily unoccupied for the same reason."

"Yet you're still here."

"That's because I don't have any friends or family in Chicago," I chuckle dryly. "But don't worry, I'm going to be fine. What's another week in this freezing hell, anyway?"

"Hold on, who's Jason?" Mrs. Ashel asks, her slim brows furrowed tightly.

"Jason."

"You said you spoke to Jason?"

"The new owner," I say, smiling. "My apologies, we're on a first-name basis. Jason Winchester. His company owns the building. A good man, I'll give him that. Very ... hands-on, you could say."

"Jason Winchester," Mrs. Ashel repeats his name, slowly nodding as her gaze wanders off to the side. "Oh, there's that dang car again."

I glance across the street and immediately spot the car she's talking about—a black sedan with tinted windows. The driver's window is rolled down, and I can see the man's profile quite clearly from where I'm standing. He doesn't seem to notice us, though; he's too busy scrolling through his phone.

"Who's that?" I ask.

"No idea," Mrs. Ashel replies, "but I saw him around here the other day. A week ago, too. Always parks right there and always at these early hours."

My stomach does a flip. Doubt is quick to infiltrate my thoughts as old worst-case scenarios threaten to rear their ugly heads and ruin my day. It can't be one of theirs. They wouldn't send an emissary. They'd come here themselves, and they would definitely make a spectacle of the whole thing. Subtle isn't their style.

"Maybe he's somebody's driver," I surmise, my voice lower than usual. I can't take my eyes off the guy. The more I look at him, the more uneasy I get. I can't put my finger on the problem, yet I cannot ignore this sensation, either. "Or a prospective buyer."

Mrs. Ashel scoffs. "I have a mind of going over there and telling him to forget about this place unless he wants to live in the equivalent of a Siberian winter."

The mere mention of Siberia sends my mind off to Russia, a trigger for me. Suddenly, I see the man in a completely different light. My uneasiness doesn't seem as ridiculous as before. His profile looks familiar for a reason—he reminds me of people I grew up around.

Pale-faced with a strong jawline and thick cheekbones. Short, brown hair. He wears a black turtleneck and a black leather jacket and seems to be deeply engrossed in whatever he is reading on his phone.

As soon as he looks up and notices me, I freeze. My heart stops, and I feel like a deer caught in the headlights. The helplessness I once felt as a child comes back to haunt me, to twist my senses, summoning a reaction I worked so hard to suppress in the years since I left New York.

There's a twinkle of recognition in his eyes.

Or maybe I'm losing my mind.

"Audrey, are you okay?" Mrs. Ashel asks.

I am unable to respond, caught in this man's brief gaze. His glance is fleeting, lasting for maybe a couple of seconds before he goes back to scrolling through his phone. Yet the impact it has on me lasts longer. Thoughts are swirling in the back of my head with no sense or meaning, filled with that same unpleasant familiarity.

"Audrey," Mrs. Ashel says again.

"What?" I snap out of it and look at her. "Sorry, my mind was somewhere else," I add with an awkward smile. "I'm sure it's nobody important. This is a busy street, after all, and there are a lot of residents on this block. Someone's always here visiting somebody."

"I miss the good old days when this was just a small, quaint neighborhood," she grumbles, readjusting the purse on her shoulder. "The '70s and '80s may have been messy, but I'm telling you, honey, this neighborhood was nowhere near as packed as it is today."

"That's the price of progress, Mrs. Ashel," I reply with a casual shrug.

Chills run down my spine as the black car's window rolls up. Moments later, it's gone, yet the empty space it leaves behind fills me with a subtle feeling of dread.

I wish I could figure out what it is that's got me so twisted on the inside. I keep telling myself that I just need more time to get over the past. I may have left it behind, but there's always a chance it could catch up with me.

"I need to go upstairs and warm up by the radiator," I say, suddenly freezing and no longer willing to be out in the open like this. "I'll see you when you get back. Have a great service at church."

"Of course, honey, you go on up and get warm," Mrs. Ashel says, gently squeezing my hand before turning away.

I watch her as she walks up the road, her heels clicking on the pavement. Most of the snow is gone, but the freezing temperatures remain. At least it's a dry end to this wretched season because the last thing any of us needs is to figure-skate across the street to the nearest 7-Eleven. Mrs. Ashel is a sweethcart. Always kind and generous. Always worried about me. Always brings me a slice of whatever she bakes over the weekend.

It dawns on me for the umpteenth time that I haven't made any true friends in this city. It's been two years, but I'm still worried. I try telling myself that I'm safe here, that I've been safe the whole time. My family is in the past, where they belong. And while it breaks my heart, it's for the best.

I decide to put the dark thoughts aside as I rush into the building to get warm, or at least try to.

What are you wearing?

Jason gets a kick out of texting me the same message every evening. It's become our little inside joke, and I enjoy describing in full detail every layer of clothing that I've got on. The heat is supposed to be up and working again by tomorrow. I'm counting the hours at this point, nestled on my sofa with a glass of mulled wine and a thick blanket wrapped up around me. The TV is on, but I'm not paying attention.

I'm too busy enjoying my usual back-and-forth with Jason. He's at home and just put Lily to bed. I'd love to meet her. I'd like to know what she's like. There's a good chance that getting to know her will give me a clue about the inner workings of Jason's life and his character. He has been nothing but honest with me, but our children are our mirrors, whether we like it or not.

My baby blue jammies, I write to Jason.

My fingers are cold, even though the radiator is literally at my feet.

I know those. They're cute. What else?

My bathrobe. And a blanket.

That's not enough. Get another blanket. Or, better yet, let me come pick you up and take you over to Lake View.

My heart tightens ever so slightly. I know he just wants me to be comfortable, but I can't get over this reticence; it's illogical. We've been together, sort of, for almost a month now. Jason has repeatedly offered to have me stay in Lake View, and I have consistently rejected him every time.

It's too far from work, I say it again. *But thank you. I'm okay. The heat is back on tomorrow.*

Your stubbornness annoys and turns me on at the same time, he shoots back.

Next time I see you, it'll be at my place, I tell him. *And I won't be wearing anything.*

You'll open the door naked? What will Mrs. Ashel say?

She'll be wearing her birthday suit, too. I wouldn't be surprised if everybody in this building goes buck naked to celebrate having the heat back on, I reply, a grin on my face as I type.

Thanks for the mental image of a naked Mrs. Ashel.

Honestly, though, I type and giggle at the same time, *thank you for being so involved with The Emerald and everyone's concerns here. I wish all landlords were like you.*

It's my pleasure. I take pride in doing my job right. Off to bed, Audrey. The kids count on you first thing in the morning.

I check the time and gasp. Jason is right; it's almost midnight. I have to be up before six in the morning if I want to get in that first coffee before I head to work.

Always looking out for me. Sweet dreams, Jason.

He replies with a kissing emoticon.

A knock on the door startles me.

Something doesn't feel right. I know it's not Jason. He'd tell me if he was coming over. And besides, we just said good-night to each other. "Who the hell comes knocking at midnight?" I mutter to myself and slowly get up from the sofa.

Another knock.

I practically jump out of my skin. I hold my breath, taking cautious steps toward the door when the third knock comes. It's louder this time, a whole fist banging against the door. It's hard and menacing, and it's making my nerves jump.

Suddenly, the past rears its ugly head in the rearview mirror of my consciousness as I struggle to keep it together. Could it be? No, I've been careful. It doesn't make sense.

The fourth knock is downright aggressive.

I'm frozen on the spot, mere inches away from the door. I'm not breathing anymore. But my heart beats fast and loud, echoing in my ears, drumming relentlessly as I stare at the shadow stretching in from the building's hallway. I can see him through the bottom crack of my door, standing there, knocking over and over. I dare not step any closer. Whoever it is, he might hear me. I just turned the TV off, and there's not a single sound coming out of my apartment.

As far as anyone is concerned, I'm not home.

Another knock brings stinging tears to my eyes, quickly followed by a letter sliding under the door. I watch the shadow pull away and hear heavy footsteps receding. The longest minute of my life passes. I'm still holding my phone, the grip so tight that my knuckles have turned white. My palm is sweating. I slip the phone into my bathrobe's pocket and pick the letter up with shaky fingers.

"Oh, fuck," I mumble as I unfold the single piece of white paper.

The letters are clear in their black ink.

The message quickly sears itself into my very soul.

For two years, I thought I was okay. At first, I looked over my shoulder a lot, making sure that no one was following me before I ever turned the corner to my street. I made sure I didn't pick up a tail whenever I went in and out of the subway. For a while, I even waited in the downstairs lobby after walking in just to see if anyone might come in after me. No one ever did.

Once the coast seemed clear, I slipped back into living mode.

I got a job teaching kindergarten. Slowly but surely, I made a couple of work friends—the kind who didn't ask too many questions and didn't insist on my attendance at various cordial events. We had the occasional drink after work, but that was it.

The words in the letter are written in Russian. I keep reading them, hoping that somehow, they'll transform into something different. But the meaning is blisteringly obvious:

We've found you; now it's time to come home.

CHAPTER 8

JASON

Something has changed between us.

I can't quite put my finger on it yet, but Audrey sent an email to the building manager asking about the intercom system for The Emerald. It's supposed to be working, or so I was told. The technician we sent down yesterday confirmed it.

Audrey wouldn't go into any detail regarding the subject but our phone and text conversations have gotten briefer over the past couple of days. She's become distant.

I'm starting to think something happened to upset her, but when I ask, all she says is that I don't need to worry about it and that everything's fine. She said she's seen suspicious people lurking around, and she's concerned about the elderly residents' safety since there's been a string of home invasions happening on this side of Chicago over the winter.

I'm tempted to bring in a different security team altogether, but I need to confirm that her concerns are valid, as she's the only one who's brought it up out of a couple of hundred residents.

"Daddy, what are we doing here?" Lily asks.

I've just picked up my daughter from kindergarten and decided to stop by The Emerald to check up on things. I don't like this gap that's growing between Audrey and me. It's been bugging me more and more. I know we haven't exactly put a label on it, but I've come to miss her when she's not around.

"Oh, we're just visiting one of my buildings, honey, and we might even run into a friend," I tell my daughter as I scoop her out of the booster seat and carry her across the street.

"Your girlfriend?"

I stop on the edge of the sidewalk to look at Lily. For a five-year-old, she can be annoyingly observant sometimes. She also has a knack for dropping conversational bombs when I least expect it.

"What makes you think I have a girlfriend?" I ask her.

"I can tell."

Her eyes are wide and fierce with knowledge. It's as if there's a whole other world inside my daughter, and she doesn't have the mental capacity at her age to accurately explain what goes through her head. I've always felt she's way smarter than most five-year-olds, but there are moments when Lily leaves me speechless. All I can do is smile softly and put her down so we can both go up the front steps.

"She could be my girlfriend if you like her," I say.

"I think I already like her."

"How so?"

Lily thinks about it for a moment, then straightens her yellow winter jacket and looks up at the building. "She lives in a nice place. And she makes you smile a lot."

I grow more and more intrigued. "What makes you think that I smile a lot because of her?" If only I could tap right into her cute little brain, perhaps I'd understand my daughter better.

"That's what Rita says," Lily replies. "It's why you're on the phone a lot. You didn't do that before."

It hits me all of a sudden how observant Lily can be, even when I'm not aware of any changes in my pattern. But she noticed, and she asked her nanny about it. She didn't ask me. Should I feel bad about that? Why didn't she feel she could talk to me about this?

"We talk a lot," I tell Lily. "I think you'll like her. She teaches kindergarten."

Lily gasps and gives me a troubled look as we go into the building. "Wait, is it Miss Pemberly?"

"Miss Pemberly?" I reply, momentarily confused, until I remember Miss Pemberly is Lily's kindergarten teacher. "Oh, no, honey, no. Audrey works at another school."

"What's wrong with Miss Pemberly?" Lily asks, frowning slightly.

My Lord, she cracks me up. "Nothing is wrong with Miss Pemberly. Besides, I'm pretty sure she's spoken for. I thought I saw a ring on her finger."

"Yeah, but you're way better," Lily decides. "Her boyfriend brings her lunch every day, but you could buy her the restaurant!"

I can't help but laugh.

My humor softens as I look up and see Audrey coming down the stairs. I'm about to smile and wave and introduce my daughter when I notice that Audrey appears to be in a terrible mood. She doesn't even see me until she reaches the bottom of the stairs.

"Oh, Jason!" she gasps, freezing for a moment.

"Hi, Audrey," I say, measuring her reaction carefully. "Is everything all right?"

She stares at me, then at Lily, and as soon as their eyes meet, Audrey's demeanor brightens up. "You must be Lily. It is such a pleasure to meet you," she says. "I'm Audrey."

"Hi, Audrey," my daughter replies and firmly shakes her hand, measuring Audrey from head to toe like a human scanner. "You're my dad's girlfriend, right?"

"Wow," Audrey laughs nervously, then looks at me. "Um, what?"

"We were just in the neighborhood," I say. "I wanted to show Lily around. Granted, I also hoped we'd run into you so you two could meet. I figured it was about time."

Why is my heart beating so fast? Lily's opinion about Audrey matters, but I find that Audrey's opinion of what's going on between us matters just as much. I want her to want more out of this because *I* want more out of this.

It's been a while since I've felt this way about someone. It's scary as hell. I'd rather re-cross an Afghani minefield than endure the awkwardness of this moment.

"That's sweet," Audrey says, giving Lily another smile. "What do you think of The Emerald?"

"I like it. It's pretty," my daughter replies. "You're pretty, too."

"Oh, thank you," Audrey says and laughs lightly.

But I can see the shadows in her cool blue eyes. The concern. The unspoken worries that swirl through her mind. She's working overtime to make herself seem calm and breezy, ever the friendly neighborhood girl. Something is definitely going on with her, and I intend to get to the bottom of it one way or another.

"Audrey, what's happening?" I ask, my voice low.

"What do you mean?" she asks, trying to play her part for a little longer.

"Talk to me. I'm here," I say. "Whatever it is that's bothering you, you can tell me."

She shakes her head slowly. "I'm okay, I promise. Just tired. I need to head out, but I'll see you another time."

"Hold on," I stop her from walking past us and whisper in her ear while Lily curiously looks up at us. "I think we both know by now that what we have is more than a mere fling. You can talk to me; you can tell me anything. I think I've proven myself worthy of your trust by now."

SEXTING THE SILVERFOX | 67

"Jason, I'm fine," she manages, but tears are rushing to her eyes. "I'm just going through a stressful period, that's all. You don't need to worry about a thing."

"Fine," I sigh and take a step back. "You know where to reach me if you need to talk. Please, remember that."

"Thank you," Audrey replies. "And I hope to see you again, Miss Lily! Bye!"

Lily waves her goodbye while I stand at the bottom of the stairs, watching as Audrey hurriedly walks away, a trail of doubt and darkness lingering in her wake. I don't believe a word she just said, and that's because Audrey is a good woman and, therefore, a terrible liar.

I know when she's not being truthful because it's simply not in her nature, but the fact that she feels the need to try and deceive me speaks volumes.

"Daddy?" Lily asks, her warm hand still squeezing mine.

"Yes, honey?"

"She's not okay like she said ."

Again, I'm compelled to glance down at my daughter in genuine surprise. "How on earth do you pick up on these things?" I wonder aloud.

"I don't know," Lily shrugs nonchalantly. "She just looked not okay."

"I thought so, too," I agree.

"So, can you fix it?" she asks earnestly.

"Fix it?"

"Yeah, like you fix me when I'm not okay."

"You know what, sweet girl? I'm going to do everything I can."

Everything.

CHAPTER 9

JASON

Once Lily is asleep, I leave Rita in charge while I drive back to Audrey's place. It's past midnight, and the streets are mostly clear. I like the city when it's dark; there's barely a soul around, and it's quiet other than the occasional car or taxicab rushing by.

I'm alone with my thoughts as I try to figure out what it is that has me so bound to Audrey in the first place.

I don't get easily attached, yet I am slowly becoming addicted to her.

I don't mind it. I find I rather enjoy the feeling, but it makes me feel vulnerable. I haven't felt that way in a long time, and it's usually accompanied by hurt. Lily and I have been fine on our own, dealing with everything together, one day and one step at a time. We've made it work, especially with Rita's help. It's a formula that has made sense for nearly five years now, and I don't want to spoil it. I don't want to destroy this subtle balance.

But after seeing Audrey earlier, I'm worried about her.

I pull up outside her building, observing it for a while before I get out of my car. Audrey's living room and bedroom window face the street, and I can see the lights are still on. I glance up and down the road and see nothing but an endless row of parked cars, most of them black and expensive. It's a prosperous neighborhood. It's always been a place for the crème de la crème of Chicago to live, and it's a shame the previous owners of The Emerald didn't have a clue about how to keep up this once-illustrious property.

It still needs more work, but I think it will start paying for itself in a couple of years. I'm a patient man in terms of business. Where Audrey is concerned, however, I feel restless, so I go into the building, using my skeleton key to enter. To my astonishment, when I reach Audrey's apartment, she is sneakily stepping out with a large suitcase in tow.

"What the...?" I mutter and startle her so much that she jumps.

"For fuck's sake!" she snaps as her hand goes to her chest, then instantly cools down as she recognizes me. "You scared the crap out of me, Jason. What are you doing here?"

"I think the better question is, what are *you* doing?"

She's dressed like an undercover cop: she's bare-faced, her blonde hair is tucked under a grey ballcap, and she's wearing a heavy overcoat over a black tracksuit. And then there's the large suitcase she's lugging. She could fit a good part of her wardrobe in there, and I see a couple more bags waiting just inside the door.

She's leaving.

The thought of it hits me like a ton of bricks. My chest hurts, and I need to catch my breath before I say anything.

"I'm going away for a couple of days," Audrey mumbles, averting her eyes.

"Is that so?"

She gives me a sour look. "It's not like I owe you an explanation, Jason. It's my life, and it's my business."

"I never said it wasn't. But you seem to forget who you're talking to, Audrey. I think I deserve a little more credit because I'm not buying what you're trying to sell me here, honey."

For the longest minute, Audrey's gaze drops into what I can only interpret as a painful combination of fear and shame as she struggles with the decision to tell me the truth. She knows I won't settle for anything less.

The mere fact that she's literally about to skip town tells me there's a side of Audrey I've yet to see, which only intrigues me further. And seeing her like this only makes my desire to protect her grow stronger by a thousandfold. Something has scared her badly enough to push her into packing her bags and leaving town in the middle of the night.

"I'm sorry," Audrey says as she finally looks up at me, her eyes filled with tears. "I've been trying to keep it together, to work it out on my own. I don't think the building manager took my emails seriously."

"I certainly did. They added more security staff to the nighttime shifts," I tell her.

"It's not just that. Men are watching this place, going up and down each floor. One of them knocked on my door the other night. They were persistent. I can feel their eyes on me whenever I come in and out of the building, and I don't want to be paranoid, but I simply don't feel safe anymore, Jason. I don't know what else to do except to get away from here for a few days."

I take it all in, quietly paying attention not only to what Audrey is telling me but also to what she isn't telling me. Because I can sense she's leaving important details out of her story. There is definitely a secret that she's working hard to protect, but I don't want to yank it out of her. I need Audrey to feel comfortable enough to tell me without any pressure or coercion.

"Can you describe these men?" I ask. "Are they the same guys every time? I can have my security team comb through the CCTV footage."

"Yeah, I can describe three of them. There may be more. Mrs. Ashel said she saw a couple of them, too, on different days. But she carries a mace spray in her purse and walks around with the confidence of a UFC fighter."

"Audrey, starting tomorrow, I'm going to add more security measures to the building," I tell her. "Whatever I can get my hands on that is sold on the civilian market, that is. Biometric identification technology, special access codes, anything and everything until you feel safe in your own home again."

"But that will be a huge expense for you," Audrey mutters. "What's the point of buying a building if it brings more costs than profits in the long term?"

"Actually, the expense itself is a short-term issue. Long term means I have happy and comfortable residents who want to stay longer, especially in the leased units," I shoot back with a confident smile, already doing the math in my head about how I'm going to flip certain funds around in order to cover such an upgrade. It's worth it, though. If it brings Audrey some peace, it's worth it. "That being said, you're not going anywhere."

Audrey gives me a startled look. "I am. I'm not staying here tonight."

"Sorry, I wasn't clear enough. You're not going anywhere on your own. You're coming home with me."

"What? No, I don't want to impose. Jason, I'll be fine."

"I'm not taking no for an answer."

"Oh, for—"

"Out of the question," I insist with a playful smile. "Spend the night with me. Lily's already asleep. You'll be somewhere safe. You'll be with me."

"Jason ..."

"I'm not asking you to move in with me."

It's not exactly the worst idea I've had since I met her. I'm not the type to rush into anything, but there's something about this woman that beckons me to do more, to work harder, to be better than I was before.

"Just for tonight. Maybe tomorrow night, too, or until we figure out who these men are and what business they have here. That's all."

For a split second, I notice a fleeting twinkle of fear in Audrey's blue eyes. It's different from before, and it resonates with something inside of me, a suspicion that I've had for a while that's been lying dormant in the back of my head, a suspicion that Audrey is afraid I'll find out something about her past, something she doesn't want anyone to know.

Whatever it is that she's holding back, it could connect to this stalker issue.

"Fine," Audrey finally concedes. "I'll spend the night if it'll shut you up."

"There are other ways for you to shut me up, babe," I shoot back with a chuckle.

She playfully smacks me over the shoulder. "Get your mind out of the gutter."

"That's hard to do when I'm around you."

And just like that, a resolution has been reached, albeit temporarily. The uneasiness lingers in my chest, but at least she's not running away to an unknown location. At least I get to keep her close and figure out what it is that's got her wound up so tightly.

Besides, the more I think about it, the clearer it becomes that whatever this is between us, it's growing, fast and steady, smooth and organic. There's no pressure, no label, no expectation on either side, yet we are growing closer. Our bond gets stronger with each passing day.

I don't know what to make of it, but I do know that I don't want it to end.

Once we're back at my place, I give Audrey some room to unpack a few of her things so she can make herself as comfortable as possible. Fortunately, this penthouse is huge, and the master bedroom alone is the equivalent of half of her apartment. There's room for everyone and everything.

I check on Lily in the meantime, content to find her asleep. I am thankful that Rita agreed to stay the night.

After gently kissing my little girl and pulling the covers over her, I move into the kitchen and open a bottle of wine to serve next to a hastily prepared cheese platter. Not that I'm particularly hungry, but judging by the faint shadows under Audrey's eyes, I'm guessing she's been too nervous to eat properly over the past few days.

She's just coming out of the shower by the time I bring the platter and the wine back to her bedroom. She stops in the en suite bath's doorway, wrapped in a plush green towel, her blonde hair pulled up in a loose bun on the top of her head, her eyes wide as she stares at me.

I only glance at her, too busy keeping an eye on the tray and the wine until I reach the small round table by the window. I set everything down and breathe out a genuine sigh of relief.

"Wine and cheese," Audrey says with an appreciative smile. "You sure know how to impress a girl, Mr. Winchester."

"If I told you that all I did was grab some stuff out of the fridge and set it onto the plate, would you be as impressed?" I reply. "I shouldn't even admit this, but I grabbed the first bottle of wine that I saw in the cooler. I have no idea what it is."

"Oh, that's right, you're not much of a wine drinker," she giggles.

I have a hard time looking away from her. I love the way she moves. Those long legs with thick thighs, toes sinking in with every step that she takes across the fluffy carpet. Her gaze turns curious as it wanders over the cheese plate, and when hunger glistens in her eyes, I know I hit the right spot with this move.

We sit down to eat and enjoy a glass of crisp California Rosé.

"I may not be much of a wine drinker, but I have to admit, this is a fine bottle," I say after the first sip. "I keep a few bottles in the cooler for any guests who might fancy it, but that's about it. Oh, and Rita uses some of it for cooking."

"Rita is pretty much a staple around this place, isn't she?" Audrey asks as she gets busy with a piece of mature cheddar. I watch as she dips it into a small porcelain bowl filled with chili honey before popping it into her mouth, but my attention is soon distracted by the smooth curves of her shoulders and the way in which her breasts struggle against the wraparound towel. "Nanny, chef ... what else?"

"Honestly, Rita has been like a second mother to both Lily and me. Of course, she is compensated accordingly. I never skimp on the bonuses, either. She's a loner by nature, though, and so she enjoys spending time with us. She's close to retirement, but she doesn't want to ever stop working."

"I think I can relate to that. I love what I do, too, and hardly see myself retiring from it."

I nod once. "Rita's the same. She loves Lily like her own daughter, and she's been with us through thick and thin. I do a lot of the cooking, too, but there are certain dishes that Rita enjoys making for us. I have a maid service for the cleaning, however. I want Rita to focus on Lily, first and foremost."

"It's very sweet and kind of her," Audrey muses, her gaze briefly lost somewhere over the Chicago skyline. "Devoting so much of her time, so much of her life to you and your daughter. Doesn't she have a family of her own?"

"Her husband, Marvin, and I were in the service together," I say. "He was my commanding officer, actually."

"What happened?"

"He was killed in action," I say slowly. "I couldn't save him. He sacrificed himself so the rest of us could escape an ambush on the outskirts of Kabul. We were lured there. It was a mess. When I got back, I felt compelled to do everything in my power to make sure Rita was well taken care of."

"So, you brought her to work for you," Audrey replies.

"Yes. Marvin's pension barely covered the mortgage and monthly utilities," I say. "While Ramona and I were married, Rita had a full-time job looking after the house and making sure Ramona didn't get into too much trouble, but that was an impossible mission."

Audrey knows the story or the gist of it anyway. I never share too many details about Lily's mother because I hate putting any more energy into that woman and her selfish ways than I need to. She broke my heart, and I thought I'd never be able to love anyone ever again. She left me with a daughter to raise and then dared to sue for custody. We settled for supervised visits twice a year, given her unsavory history and on-and-off relationship with narcotics.

"I'm glad you had someone like Rita looking out for you and Lily when things got rough," Audrey says and exhales sharply. "And honestly, I'm impressed by how gracious you are when you mention your ex-wife, especially after the troubles she caused."

"I'm more concerned about taking care of the people who chose to stay in my life than worrying about someone who ran out of it. I'm too busy raising my daughter and making sure she'll grow up to be a better human than most of us," I reply and refill my glass.

"That's a healthy mindset," she says.

The conversation delves into various other aspects of my life since she won't tell me much about hers, not without a poke or a prod from me. But I'm content to see her calm and relaxed as opposed to the gunpowder keg I stumbled upon earlier.

The wine is working its magic, and the cheese platter is a decisive knockout to the point where Audrey's gaze softens as she leans back in her chair, satiated.

"Thank you, Jason," she says after a long silence.

"For what?"

"For all of this, for just being you," she replies, half-smiling. "For not asking too many questions, for giving me room to breathe, for ... making me feel safe again."

Ah, the magic words that every man wishes to hear from the lips of his woman. It fills me with a different kind of energy, strength surging through every fiber of my body as I get up from the table and take her in my arms. Audrey surrenders instantly, melting in my embrace as I kiss her lips softly.

"You're going to have to tell me everything at some point," I tell her in between tender pecks. "You can't keep me in the dark forever."

"I know. I need a bit more time to find the right words to explain," she sighs. "Not tonight, though."

"No, not tonight. Tonight, I'm making love to you."

She looks up, losing herself in my eyes for a while. "Making love?" Her voice is but a whisper fluttering in the dim bedroom lights. An echo wedged between our fastening heartbeats.

"You have to admit it, Audrey. This thing we've got going on, it's not strictly physical, is it?" I ask, already seeing the answer deep in her gaze. "It's something else, it's something more. I'm okay with not rushing into anything, but I can't lie to myself, and I don't want you lying to yourself, either. Whatever happens next, it's going to be the two of us together. As long as you'll have me, anyway." I pause and kiss her cheek. "Will you have me, Audrey?"

"Oh, yes," she replies without hesitation.

My mind unravels as I let her take over. We kiss hungrily, ravenously, desperately clawing at one another. Our hands roam up and down, feeling and touching and squeezing everything in their path. Her towel is the first thing to land on the floor while she manages to get me out of my shirt before I start trailing wet kisses down the side of her neck.

I take my sweet time kneading and kissing her breasts, reveling in the smooth firmness of her flesh as I close my lips around her nipples, suckling and licking each until all I can hear are her gasps of raw pleasure. I bite into one, my teeth nipping tightly enough to tear a whimper from her throat, then decide it's time to take things to the next level.

"Do you trust me, Audrey?" I ask, peering into her hazy eyes.

She's so hot, so turned on, she'll let me do whatever I want as long as I give her that sweet and devastating release. I've come to know her so well; it's as if I'm rereading my favorite book, one page at a time, dissolving into the story all over again.

"Yes," she says. "I trust you, Jason."

"Good. Come here," I say and guide her over to the four-poster bed that dominates the room. I sit her down for a moment and ask her to wait while I fetch a pair of fuzzy cuffs and slim, velvety ropes from the closet in my master bedroom. I return to the room, quietly closing the door behind me and locking it. She watches me with a mixture of concern and curiosity, making me laugh. "It's for your pleasure, I promise. We'll stop if you want to stop, Audrey. You're in control. You will always be in control."

She nods slowly. With gentle motions, I cuff her wrists and loop the ropes through before tying them to the bed posts, making sure her arms are comfortably loose and stretched out. I take a moment to admire her gorgeous, naked body. Those nipples perk up under my gaze, and it makes my pants feel a lot tighter, but I'm determined to make her crumble tonight in the best and most decadent way possible.

"This is weird," she says.

"Are you okay, though?"

"Yes."

"Good," I reply and lean in from the side of the bed to kiss her.

Our tongues play, joyfully swirling before I go back to teasing her breasts some more. I listen to her ragged moans as I gradually shift my attention downward. She's helpless. She can't touch me, and it's tormenting her, but I make up for it by kissing every inch of her creamy skin, squeezing and pinching along the way until I settle between her parted legs.

"Oh, Jason!" she groans as I slide my tongue over her swollen clit.

She's wet and more than ready for me, her pussy glazed with glistening arousal. I lick her folds and suck on her nub, feeling it grow in my mouth while I insert one, then two, fingers inside her. Audrey loses control when I slip in a third, her hips swaying as a rhythm is built between my hand and her pussy.

"That's it," I growl, my cock twitching painfully against the fabric of my pants as I finger-fuck my woman out of this world. "Come for me. Give me everything you've got."

"Fucking hell!" she whimpers as I press my tongue onto her clit.

I can feel the pulsating ripples as she explodes, my fingers curling with each retreating motion. I feel her clenching tightly before she lets go of herself, wholly and completely, writhing in the sweetest agony. Her whole body shudders under the sudden release, the throes of ecstasy making her come hard.

"That's it, baby," I coax her, finger-fucking her even harder as I tease her clit even more, with greater intensity and without a shred of mercy.

Audrey lets out a muffled cry, clearly aware that we are not alone in the penthouse. She is struggling and falling apart at the same time, unable to stop herself from riding an unending wave. She comes again mere moments after the first climax, every muscle taut and stretched as I work her into a mindless frenzy.

"Oh, fuck, oh, fuck!" she moans as I drink her whole.

She's at my mercy, coming and trembling and losing her mind, her pussy trickling sweet juices. Little does she know this is just the beginning.

I pause, and Audrey gives me a confused look as she watches me get up and pull back. I slowly take the rest of my clothes off, one item at a time, and I can tell she's getting anxious, in desperate need of more of me, for all of me. I place an object I had hidden in my back pocket on the bed out of her line of sight.

Her pussy is ready, her lips parted as she licks them, hunger glowing in her blue eyes. Audrey can't stop herself from smiling. "I need you to fuck me as you've never fucked me before."

. . .

I love this dirty mind of hers. I love to see her inhibitions fly out the window as soon as I put my hands on her. I love how she brings out the beast in me, never afraid, never concerned, but always eager to figure out where her limits are. And I'm always delighted when she's able to meet me on the threshold between sanity and madness.

Without hesitation, I climb on the bed and spear her with my full length.

"Oh my God!" Audrey gasps.

I am still, my cock throbbing as it's wrapped in her warm wetness. I want to enjoy every second of this, though I'm not sure how long I can hold back.

"Wrap your legs around me," I command her.

"Yes, sir," she replies and promptly locks her ankles behind my back. "Oh, wow, that feels so good."

I move, ever so slightly, into a first thrust. Her eyes widen when I reach behind me to retrieve the small, ring-shaped vibrator. "You didn't think I was going to let you off easy tonight, did you?" I chuckle softly.

"Make me come again then," she replies, equally excited.

Slowly but surely, we build ourselves into a frenzy. I keep the vibrator on my left thumb and pressed against her clit as I slide in and out of her. I feel my cock in its wonderful torment, registering every inch of her tender pussy as I fuck her harder, deeper, faster. I feel her tightening, clenching as the vibrator does its job.

"Look me in the eyes," I tell her, and our gazes become locked as I continue to pound into her.

She takes it like a good girl, moaning and writhing under my body, the vibrator wedged between us as I bring her closer and closer to the edge of sanity. I lose myself, fucking her as she requested, until she explodes all over me, and I completely let go.

I fill her with my seed, each thrust deeper, and she welcomes all of it, quivering and quietly moaning.

Eventually, I release her wrists, and she embraces me, kissing my face and running her fingers through my hair while I lay on top of her, not wanting this perfect moment to end. Her body is soft, her thighs still firmly wrapped around me.

"We're not done yet," I casually tell her.

There's something about this woman that revs my engines in record time. I'm already getting hard, eager to get lost inside her again. But the look she gives me, along with the low tone of her voice, dripping with arousal, is what sets me on fire.

"Cuff me again, Jason. But this time, take me from behind," she tells me.

"Fucking hell, you're growing into this, aren't you?"

She likes this darker side of me. It turns her on, and she is able to lose control, to abandon herself to me simply because she can, because I make her feel safe enough for her to release every wild dream, every forbidden fantasy.

"Fuck me hard, Jason."

Jesus, this woman is going to be the death of me.

CHAPTER 10

One night turned into a week, and then a week turned into a month.

I have no idea how it happened, but Jason and I have been more or less living together since he took me away from The Emerald. He drives me to work, picks me up, and then drives me back and forth between home and his place so I can retrieve things that I need.

We go out once in a while. We go shopping for groceries or whatever else our hearts desire. We spend most of our time together, and I'm loving every second of it.

Lily is a treat. She's been the kindest, sweetest little girl, and I'm genuinely surprised by how quickly we've bonded. Rita takes good care of us, but I can't sit back and let her do all the work. Jason has started to attend Lily's piano lessons, and more often than not, he'll bring her back to find Rita and me working our asses off in the kitchen, making a scrumptious dinner for four.

We talk and laugh for hours, and I love spending time with Jason's daughter. It's weird how I've settled in so quickly with such ease and comfort.

I'm afraid it won't last, however.

Jason's security team scoured through the CCTV footage from The Emerald. They managed to get some stills from the tape, but the stalkers knew to dodge the cameras, so there wasn't anything conclusive—nothing that could be processed through facial recognition software by the appropriate authorities.

On the other hand, there haven't been any sightings or suspicious activity reported at The Emerald for about two weeks. It appears the coast is clear.

I cling to the hope that those bastards figured out that I skipped town and gave up. I'd hate to have to leave this place, this city. I definitely don't want to leave Jason. Lily and I have grown so fond of one another and Rita and I have grown close as well. I love my kindergarteners, even the spoiled ones, and my coworkers are great.

My heart soars with the purest energy whenever I'm with them, shaping their minds and teaching them to become better humans. It's why I became an educator—to provide the world with curious and educated minds.

We need a brighter future and mine seems a tad shady at this point.

As I browse through one of the drugstore aisles, looking for some cough medicine, I look up to see Jason by the haircare section, picking out some shampoo and conditioner. I love how he takes such good care of himself and his family. Unlike most men of considerable means, Jason still handles the little things. Groceries, household items ... you name it, and he buys it himself. I finally got him to order some stuff online, though, to make it easier for him and Rita.

The more I look at him, trying to decide between shampoo brands, the fonder I grow of this man. I've yet to find the courage to tell him the truth, but he hasn't pressured me, either. That just makes me love him even more. *Love*. Oh, God, what a dangerous word that is yet it speaks the truth of how I feel. I'm in love with him; there's no denying that anymore.

"Can I help you?" one of the attendants asks me. I didn't notice her approaching; I was too busy fawning over my man. "Are you looking for something in particular?"

"Oh, sorry, um, yeah," I reply, keeping my voice down. "I need a pregnancy test."

The girl can't be older than twenty, dressed in the drugstore's branded white and blue T-shirt and a pair of jeans, her brown hair pulled back in a tight ponytail and a pleasant smile permanently adorning her pretty, tanned face. She glances down at the shelves. "Sure, we have a few options. They're right over here," she says, pointing the way as I follow her to the other end of the aisle.

"Thanks, I'll take it from here," I mutter and give her a gracious nod.

She nods back before going to help other customers while I grab the first box I recognize and head straight to the counter with it, careful so that Jason doesn't see me. I haven't shared my recent concerns with him, but my period is late, and I've been feeling a tad weird lately.

At first, I put it all on account of stress. Having to leave my apartment, fearing that my family might've found me in Chicago, adjusting to my new living situation. But the morning sickness hit me like a ton of bricks today as soon as I opened my eyes.

I need to be sure.

Once I pay and get my receipt, I slip the box into my coat pocket and go back to browsing through the cosmetics section. I don't like keeping secrets from Jason, but given the uncertainty of my situation, I don't want to tie him down in any way.

I haven't heard from my brothers or my father, but the note that was slipped under my door still haunts me. Someone from my old life knew where to find me.

"What are you up to?" Jason asks from behind, startling me.

I pause and take a deep breath. "You have a knack for sneaking up on me, don't you?"

He laughs lightly. "Yeah, but there's nothing like a good jump to get the heart rate going, right?"

"We're in a playful mood, I see." I giggle and get up on my toes so I can kiss him. He welcomes my lips and reciprocates with gentle sweetness, then shows me his small shopping basket. "Ah, there's the loot."

"Got everything we came in here for," he declares. "Found your conditioner, too."

"Should we get that cough medicine for Lily while we're here? I saw it in the other aisle."

Jason shakes his head. "Rita said she was going to give her the ginger, lemon, and honey concoction another day before resorting to medication. Lily's throat is getting a tad better, I must admit."

"Fair enough. If we can cure it the natural way, even better."

"Ready to go?"

I nod, masking my anxiety as best I can as I accompany him back to the counter. Once we're in the car, I sink into the heated passenger seat, giving myself a moment while Jason loads the trunk. We've been on quite the shopping spree all afternoon. There will be a lot to unpack when we get home, but Lily will be more than happy to assist.

Dammit, I love this feeling too much. I shouldn't have gotten so attached. But it's not like I could help it.

Jason is such an incredible man. Sexy, adventurous, and dominant in bed. A considerate gentleman in all aspects and a wonderful father. A great businessman with a mindset on growth and development. A patient and attentive boyfriend. I really hit the jackpot when I first stumbled into his office, angry and freezing.

"Something is going on with you," Jason concludes as he gets behind the wheel, giving me a long and curious look.

I try to laugh it off. "What? No, babe, I'm just exhausted. I can't believe I'm saying this, but this whole shopping session really knocked the wind out of me."

"No, I can tell there's more. I know there's a lot you haven't told me, and if you want to add whatever this is on top of everything else, I'm fine with that," he replies in a calm voice. "Just be mindful, Audrey, that there's only so much you can sweep under the rug before you find yourself overwhelmed and unable to cope."

"Jason, I promise everything's fine."

He looks at me for what feels like forever. There's something about the intensity of his hazel eyes that seems to drill deep into my soul. It's as if he can see everything, but he can't quite identify it. Therefore, he doesn't know how to confront me about it.

He knows I'm keeping secrets, and I'm aware that I'm constantly testing his patience. Jason deserves better from me, but if I tell him the whole truth, I am terrified that he'll pull away to protect himself and his daughter. I don't want to lose him or what we've built.

His family will always come first, as it should, and I respect that.

"Whatever it is, Audrey, I'll say it again—you can talk to me about it," Jason says. "In the meantime, buckle up."

"Yes, sir."

A smile tests the corner of his mouth as he turns the key in the ignition. He loves it when I say that, both in and out of the bedroom.

A couple of hours later, I leave Jason with Rita and Lily in the living room. They're going to be busy with the PlayStation for a while, which means the coast is clear for me to take the pregnancy test.

My heart is the size of a flea as I lock myself in the bathroom and follow the printed instructions to the letter. Hell, I'm so nervous that even my bladder fails to cooperate. It takes a few minutes but I manage to get it done, then spend another two minutes just staring at the stick.

I'm pacing the bathroom, going through each of my symptoms—the mood swings, the growing hunger, and cravings for food I normally wouldn't be that fond of, and unexplained fatigue.

Shaking my head slowly, I wash my face and pat it dry with a towel, trying to think of worst- and best-case scenarios, depending on the test result.

The blood rushes to my head as the lines gradually appear. Pink and bright. A decisive yes. A clear confirmation of something I never even considered but should have.

"Fuck," I whisper.

I'm pregnant. No doubt about it.

Whatever scenarios I tried to consider before are all gone. My mind is a blank canvas, and fear is swift in its attack on my senses as I struggle to keep it together. My breathing is erratic, and I'm struggling to keep my composure. Tears flood and sting my eyes. This should be a joyful moment, one that makes me feel happy, not terrified.

Deep down, I am happy. I am. I've always wanted a family of my own. Children to raise with the man I love. A man who loves me back. A man who makes me feel safe and nurtured, cherished and valued. But my past, my family ... they have a way of spoiling everything.

I'm going to be a mother.

Technically unplanned, but we didn't exactly avoid it, either.

This is supposed to be cause for excitement and glee, not fear and anxiety.

I hear footsteps, and I rush to throw the test in the trash bin.

"Audrey, are you in there?" Jason's voice makes my heart jump.

"Yeah, I'll be out in a second."

"Are you okay?"

"Yeah, just ... you know, girl stuff."

I hear him chuckle, and then his footsteps recede. My mind suddenly works like lightning as I pull the trash bag out of the bin and head out to the chute in the kitchen, gliding past Jason and the living room without a care in the world.

"Audrey, what's the matter?" Jason asks, rushing to catch up with me.

I give him a faint smile and drop the bag in the chute, firmly shutting the latch immediately afterward, then breathe a heavy sigh of relief. "Nothing, babe. Like I said, girl stuff."

"Okay ..." he pauses to carefully analyze my expression. I suppose the time he spent in the military gave him an acute sense of character and an ability to identify certain things through body language. I'm not a good liar, as he so often likes to point out, so I'm worried. I force a smile as I look up at him. "I'm going to give you one last pass today because we're both tired, but starting tomorrow, we will try a different approach. How does that sound?"

"I feel like one of my students," I mumble, my cheeks catching fire.

"Not without reason, though," he replies with a wry smile.

I look to the side and notice Rita and Lily watching us from the living room. I could tell him the truth right now. All of it. I could just spill everything from beginning to end and drop the pregnancy bomb in there, too, while I'm at it. But the fear of losing him, Lily, and Rita takes over, paralyzing me. I want to be around them for longer. I'm not ready to say goodbye yet.

I'll have to leave eventually, if only to keep them safe. I understand that now.

There's no way I'll truly be able to relax and be happy with such a big, ugly shadow hanging over my head.

"Fine," I say, nervously wringing my hands. "I've been meaning to talk to you, anyway."

"Honesty is the best policy," he says, still smiling. There is warmth in his eyes, kindness. So much patience. I know I haven't exactly been the best girlfriend, keeping so many secrets from him.

"You said The Emerald is clear, right? New security staff, additional security measures in place, no new suspicious activity?"

"Right," he mutters, giving me a curious frown.

"Well, as much as I enjoy spending all this time with you and Lily, as grateful as I am for your support, your hospitality, your ... everything, maybe it's time for me to go home. Since it's been deemed safe, that is."

My heart seizes in my chest as I await his reaction. I worry he might get upset, but then again, we've been together for less than two months. Moving in on a more permanent basis shouldn't be happening anytime soon.

"I'll support whatever decision you make," Jason says, his tone calm and gentle. "While I love having you here, I don't want you to stay if it isn't what you want to do."

"Don't get me wrong, I love being here, too, but—"

"You've got your own place, your own life," he interjects. "I get it. And it is perfectly normal and understandable for you to want to be back in your own space. But just so I'm clear, we're not breaking up, correct?"

"God, no!" I blurt out, making him laugh, a lie that makes my heart hurt.

"Seriously, it's okay," he says, coming closer. He cups my face with both hands and pulls me in for a tender kiss. "I'll take you back to your place tonight after dinner if you want."

"Thank you," I whisper against his lips.

I feel awful. It's the first step I'm taking in what will probably be a painful separation process. I've never done anything like this before. No man has ever captured my body and my soul the way this man has, nor have I ever been so attached to someone.

Pregnancy is a massive issue, and I'm terrified of where all of these pieces will fall in the months to come. I may have to sell the apartment and take off again. The coast may be clear for now, but my family could try to get to me again.

I left New York behind for a reason, and I can't, I won't allow that reason to barge into Chicago and destroy Jason and Lily's life because of me.

CHAPTER 11

AUDREY

I 'm back home in my haven, my place of warmth and comfort. My safe space with three locks on the door.

Nothing seems out of order; everything is just the way I left it. I'd missed my plush, soft sofa with one too many throw pillows and cozy blankets. My cluttered coffee table with its out-of-date magazines that I keep going back to when I need some fashion or beauty advice. My electric tea kettle and tea collection that I keep in a designated cupboard. My warm bed with its memory foam mattress ... not that Jason's isn't superior in every possible aspect, but I'm used to my stuff, my place.

I'm used to being on my own, though sharing a space wasn't bad when I really think about it.

I liked spending so much time with him. He's a heavy sleeper, as am I, which made our nights tranquil and sweet when we weren't riled up and rolling in the sheets. He enjoys cooking, and when he's in the kitchen, there's barely any room for Rita or me to help out, though Lily let it slip once that he had been cooking a lot more since I moved in.

And he's just so gosh darn sweet. Jason likes to take care of me, of my every need, but not in a way that suffocates me or makes me feel incapable of taking care of myself. He's the kind of man who adds value to a woman's life, not one who inhibits it.

"Is it wrong that I already miss him?" I mutter to myself as I unpack my bags and fill the laundry basket for tomorrow's household chores. It's close to midnight, but I am restless. Thankfully, we stopped by the supermarket before he brought me home, so there's plenty of food for me to stuff my sad face with.

Sadness. I can't lie to myself about it. Leaving his place felt like a separation, and I've got a feeling he senses something's off. I spotted a tinge of worry in his hazel eyes that wasn't there before.

Sitting at the kitchen counter in front of a bowl filled with ham and mushroom pasta, a layer of grated parmesan heavily sprinkled on top, I try to put my thoughts in order. My emotions are an endless blur of anxiety and anger, aching love and fear.

It was too good to be true.

The more I mentally list the things I love about him, the harder it is for me to pull away. I'm struggling to find anything I dislike where Jason is concerned, so that's not a feasible strategy for me. I guess I'll have to simply pull the plug and be done with it. I'll leave the apartment before having a real estate agent list it at a good price, hopefully above market value.

Until then, I'll rent something smaller elsewhere.

"I could change cities again," I surmise, delving into a generous slice of tiramisu cake. I wash it down with cold, sparkling lemon water. Pretty sure it's the baby's preference —I'm not a fan of lemons myself.

Reality starts to sink in. Who will want to hire a pregnant lady? Post-natal care, the time I'll be away from the job on maternity leave, doctor's appointments throughout ... it's a hard pill to swallow, but it's the truth.

I could try to hide the pregnancy for as long as possible, at least until I'm hired. But it would put me at risk later down the line, saying goodbye to any form of severance package.

Besides, my moral code won't allow me to deceive anybody like that.

I love my job here in Chicago. Rosa Parks Elementary may not be the elite preschool like Willow Academy in New York, but it's lovely—warm and cozy, kind and welcoming— and all of my kids feel included, seen, and valued.

I love every minute that I get to spend with them, even the less pleasant moments when I have to double-check if Patrick's trying to eat glue again or if Sammy is still pulling Lacey's pigtails. They're just kids. They are genuinely easy to handle once you understand that every emotion that they experience is simply too powerful and hard to handle for their still-developing brains.

I'll miss every one of them.

I could leave after the baby is born, I tell myself, while at the same time wondering if I could fit a second slice of tiramisu into tonight's lonely midnight snack.

The baby. Our baby. Jason's and mine. Even though I know it's cruel to leave him out of the loop and unaware of his child, I can't risk tethering him to me with my family snooping around trying to find me.

But moving to another city with a newborn is a challenge on its own on top of everything else. It's a logistical nightmare. I'd need to get a job as soon as I land. Who will I trust to take care of my child while I'm working? Wherever I decide to go, I won't know anybody there. Shaking my head slowly, I forsake the second slice and start washing the dishes.

It's nice to feel the hot water pouring over my hands. It relaxes my nerves while I struggle to declutter my thoughts.

Every idea crossing through my mind stems from a reaction based on fear. Running away. Keeping more secrets. Not telling Jason about the baby. I would say it's unlike me, but it wouldn't be the first time I'd be running away.

A car horn's honk blares somewhere out in the street, breaking the silence of the night. I go over to the window and look out. Two cars almost kissed at the intersection; it looks like the traffic lights aren't working. The streetlamps are on, their amber glow casting long shadows against the buildings. A couple of midnight joggers bolt by. A taxi. Nothing out of the ordinary. Nothing suspicious. Nothing that should rile me up.

Yet the knot in the pit of my stomach persists.

CHAPTER 12

JASON

I believed Rita when she told me in confidence that there was something off about Audrey lately. I believed her because I noticed it, too. Audrey is growing more distant. Canceling dates, citing work reasons. We haven't been texting as often as we used to, either. The few hours we do get to spend together have been noticeably more intense. It's as if she relishes every moment for as long as she can before we have to part ways.

And every time I bid her farewell, I feel this nerve tugging in the back of my head, this concern that it could be the last time I see her. Audrey was ready to skip town once; I wouldn't put it past her to try it again.

"You seem upset," Rita says, coming back from Lily's bedroom.

"How's my munchkin doing?" I ask, trying to change the subject as I stare at a bottle of whiskey left on the coffee table. I took it out earlier, planning to down a glass or two before hitting the sack, but I've been dealing with one work-related call after another. I don't exactly welcome business calls after I leave the office, yet I admit I needed the distraction tonight. "Is she asleep?"

"Sawing logs as we speak," Rita replies, half-smiling. "That was smart, signing her up for soccer. I didn't think she'd have that much energy left after school, but I guess I was wrong."

"She is the atomic child," I chuckle softly. "Besides, she may be a piano virtuoso, but I want to make sure she never neglects her physical well-being. A healthy mind in a healthy body is unstoppable."

"Oh, I wholeheartedly agree. Besides, you should've seen her running around, trying to get the ball from the other kids. Of course, it was absolute chaos trying to organize five-to-seven-year-olds on the soccer field. It was also hilarious. But you got your money's worth because I'm pretty sure Lily won't be up before six in the morning."

"Good. She'll get used to it. Would you like a drink, Rita? I'd like one, and that bottle keeps eyeing me tonight," I sigh heavily as I grab two tumbler glasses from the bar and take a seat on the sofa.

Rita nods once and settles in the armchair beside it. "What's bothering you, Mr. Winchester?"

"Honestly, I keep going back to your concern about Audrey," I say as I pour the whiskey, staring at the golden liquid for a while before speaking again. "You're right, she's ... off. She's been off for a while."

"She's not the kind to easily open up to other people," she replies and takes a long sip of whiskey while I swirl mine in its glass. "Which tells me she was badly hurt in the past by people she trusted and cared for the most. That's not an easy thing to get over. I recognize that wary look in her eyes. It's hard to miss."

"Fair enough. But I haven't given her reason to doubt or fear me."

"True. I don't think it's about you, though, Mr. Winchester. I think it's about her and about how much she's willing to do for this relationship," Rita says. "Audrey did mention that you are, in fact, the first man that she has ever been with. She's been on her own up to this point, and that alone should tell you everything you need to know in order to better understand her."

"What do you mean?"

"She's scared, Mr. Winchester. Something happened to her, something so bad that it made her leave her hometown. You know she's not originally from Chicago, right?"

I give Rita a startled look. "Audrey never mentioned that. But then again, I never asked. I just assumed she was from here." I pause and briefly go over our past conversations, realizing that I did most of the talking and sharing. "Honestly, she's not mentioned much about her past. Especially anything about her family other than the fact that they were very strict and that they could be cruel and cold-hearted. She's got a dad and two brothers, but they're estranged. Her mother died when she was little. And that's about it. Suddenly, I'm seeing it in a whole new light. Wow."

SEXTING THE SILVERFOX | 103
SEXTING THE SILVERFOX | 103

"It's all right," Rita says. "Audrey is either ashamed or afraid of her family, that much I can tell you."

"Again, I have to ask, how do you know?"

She shrugs softly, taking another sip of her whiskey. Her brow furrows for a brief moment. It's not often she drinks hard liquor, but she has chosen to indulge me tonight. "I've come across a lot of people over the years, Mr. Winchester. I've seen suffering of all kinds, and I'm positive that Audrey is simply trying to keep the past in the past, as far away from her present and her future as possible."

"You would've made one hell of shrink, Rita, I have to say," I groan, leaning back into the sofa. For some reason, as much as I've been eyeing this whiskey ever since I got home, I'm still not tempted to bring the glass up to my lips.

"I'm just a good listener. People tell you things without actually saying anything. You know that, as well, from your time in the service."

"True, but I was looking out for traitors and insurgents. I didn't have to scan my girlfriend's body language."

"I think her heart is in the right place. Perhaps she just needs more time to learn to fully trust you. I'm sure she wants to trust you. I've seen the two of you together. Audrey is emotionally invested; she has profound feelings for you. And I can tell that you adore her, as well. But you both have different kinds of baggage that you're bringing into this relationship. Yours is more straightforward. Hers, well, it needs a bit more unpacking."

"I would like to be able to help her unpack," I mutter, setting the glass back down on the coffee table. "I have a constant, nagging feeling that Audrey might try running off again. If only I knew the reason. Why is she keeping one foot out the door?"

Rita thinks about it for a moment, glancing out the living room window. Somewhere below, a sea of taillights echoes in a red glow against the glass panes. "I presume you've already checked Audrey's history?"

"There's not much to check. Up until two years ago, she hardly existed," I reply. "I should dig deeper. Maybe hire a PI or something."

"Wouldn't that be an invasion of Audrey's privacy?"

"It could be, yes. But what other choice do I have? Every time I ask her something about her past, every time I try to learn more about her, Audrey just shuts down. She finds a reason to leave early, and I end up sulking and feeling like a fool for asking perfectly reasonable questions. You're right, Rita. I do have feelings for her, and I love how well she gets along with Lily. To be honest, it's been a while since I've felt this way about a woman, but a man in my position ... there are things I absolutely need to know before I can allow the relationship to progress."

"I understand. Perhaps be discreet in your investigative endeavor?"

"Oh, definitely," I nod with confidence. "I'll get one of my former Army buddies to—" I pause as an alarm goes off on my phone. "Hold on."

Rita stays quiet while I check the screen.

My heart starts racing as soon as I tap on the blaring notification. My skin tightens all over, beads of sweat blooming on my temples as I go over the live CCTV footage coming in from Audrey's building. A few moments pass before I'm able to spot the issue, but as soon as I see it, I jump from my seat.

"Mr. Winchester, what's wrong?" Rita asks, understandably worried.

"I installed a silent alarm system in Audrey's apartment, just in case anything happened," I tell her, my voice low and uneven with uncontrollable emotion. "If anybody broke down the door, for example, I'd get an immediate alert on my phone. I didn't put any cameras in her place—that would've been an invasion of her privacy—but the alarm system is rigged to the entire building, and it also gives me access to The Emerald's CCTV feed."

"Okay, so what happened? Is Audrey all right?"

"I'm not sure. CCTV footage just caught two big fellas, clad all in black with guns, heading up the stairs," I explain. "I have to go."

Rita gasps. "Oh my gosh! Do you need me to call 911?"

"Please, and patch them straight to my cell number if they need any more details. Advise them that I carry a licensed weapon. Tell them who I am and what I'm wearing, just in case, okay?"

"Yes, Mr. Winchester."

I grab my keys and fly out of my penthouse and down the stairs, rushing to my car, struggling to keep a clear mind while consistently aware of two armed men in Audrey's building.

Fucking hell.

I drive like a bolt of lightning through the city. To my aston-ishment, I haven't picked up a single cop along the way. Then again, it's late, and the streets are mostly empty. Besides, I'm expecting at least a few squad cars to pull up to The Emerald as soon as I get there.

The engine roars as I floor it.

The wheels screech in agony as I take a tight left turn with a smoking drift at the last couple of inches, reaching The Emerald just in time to catch a glimpse of two shadows slip-ping into the side alley next to the building. I jump out of my car and start running after them as I hear Audrey's screams muffled by the two men dragging her away.

Sirens wail in the distance. I spot the getaway car parked just behind a large industrial dumpster on the right side of the narrow alley.

"Hey!" I shout after the men.

They're too busy struggling to keep Audrey subdued to immediately hear or notice me coming. Something happens within me that I haven't experienced since serving on active duty since that wretched night outside Kabul. My stomach churns but my blood pumps red hot and fast through my veins, heat loosening my joints while the instant shot of adrenaline courses and makes my heels a lot lighter.

Immediately, I take note of the surroundings.

The cops are definitely on their way, but they're still a couple of minutes out. Minutes I can't afford to lose. The street outside The Emerald is empty. The alley is dark and dirty, used mostly by the delivery trucks servicing the pastry and coffee shops just across the street.

I notice that the getaway car is a dark blue sedan with Minnesota plates. Likely stolen.

The two men are big and burly, dressed in black jeans and black leather jackets, black balaclava masks covering their heads. From their hands, I see they're both white. I remember that they're armed, but they're busy with Audrey, who's making herself incredibly hard to subdue despite being half their size. My heart clenches when I notice she's in her pink jammies.

They must've broken into her apartment while she was asleep or just about to doze off; otherwise, she probably would've had more opportunity to make more noise. Maybe the neighbors would've heard her. Someone would've come out of their apartment or called the cops.

"HEY!" I shout again, louder this time, my gun in my hand and ready to fire if I have to.

I swore I'd never fire another bullet outside of active duty.

One of the men spots me and says something to the other, something I can't understand. It's in Russian. What the hell have you gotten yourself into, Audrey?

She hears my shouts. "Jason, NO!" she screams through the black bag that covers her head. Her wrists are bound with cable ties, but her legs are free, and she is squirming and simultaneously kicking as much as she can, making it harder for the men to control her. "They have guns!"

I'm aware of that, but I don't care.

I can only focus on my mission, which is to get her away from her captors alive and unharmed. The first guy takes charge of Audrey while the other one stops and turns to face me. Before he can reach for his gun, however, I charge him and tackle him with my full body weight.

"Argh!" he grunts as we both land on the cold, hard pavement.

He throws a punch, and I give him back two, but he elbows me in the jaw, and my head starts spinning.

I end up on my side.

He shoots back to his feet, groaning from the pain but trying to kick me in the stomach. I roll away and pull my gun out. The first guy notices me drawing down on him and tosses Audrey against the car, taking out his weapon as well. Everything happens so fast that I'm not even sure where my reason ends and my instincts begin.

POP.

He fires a shot and misses.

POP.

I fire one back, and Audrey screams as she drops on all fours, dodging a potential stray bullet as the Russian prick takes more precise aim the second time around. But because I'm constantly moving, he misses me.

POP.

The guy I tackled stumbles away when I briefly point my gun at him. He barks another order in Russian, and the two of them quickly get into the car and drive off, their tires screeching while Audrey is left behind on the ground, crying and screaming her head off.

Blue and red lights flash brightly behind me, and the sound of sirens fills the air.

The police are finally here.

"Audrey!" I gasp and holster my gun as I rush over to her.

She's shaking like a leaf, dirty, scratched, and bloody. I pull the bag off her head to find her with puffy, crying eyes and quivering lips, a look of horror having drained the color from her face. "Oh, Jason ... Oh, God ..." she manages.

"Fucking hell, Audrey, are you all right?" I ask, scanning her from top to bottom.

"Yeah. I think so. How'd you get here so fast?"

"It doesn't matter. Who were those guys? What happened?"

Boots thud across the pavement. Uniformed police officers swarm the scene, pouring into the alley with their guns out. A flurry of orders and instructions are being shouted, muttered words that make little to no sense to me. The cops have questions, and Audrey immediately shuts down, her gaze lost somewhere in space.

Shock is setting in.

I have questions, too. So many fucking questions, I don't even know where to start.

But I am also shaken to the core. My fingers are trembling, and my body burns hot from anger and fear; I feel dangerously close to snapping.

I almost lost Audrey tonight.

Who were those people? What did they want? And how the hell is Audrey involved with them?

CHAPTER 13

AUDREY

I hate lying, although I've been doing it a lot lately, like tonight. Tonight, I lied like my life depended on it because, in many ways, it does.

Jason is angry and befuddled, but he is also worried sick about my safety and well-being. If I tell him the truth now, he may never want to speak to me again. Nothing horrifies me more than the idea of losing him, especially now with the pregnancy. I've decided he needs to know about that, at the very least.

But tonight is not the time to drop that bombshell on him, which only adds to my guilty conscience about keeping such an important issue from him. What a hot mess this has become, and I couldn't have predicted any of it.

Wrapped in a thick blanket, I lean against one of the squad cars with its flashing red and blue lights. My teeth chatter as I try to focus on what Officer McKinley is asking.

He's taking copious notes while his colleagues cordon off both ends of the alleyway with yellow tape and collect bullet casings, prints, and any other evidence they can gather.

"Miss Smith, you're sure you don't know those men?" he asks again, eyes narrowed with what I assume is a natural tendency to treat every victim with a smidgen of doubt.

I shake my head vehemently. "I swear, I have no idea who they are."

"Audrey, they broke into your apartment specifically. Yours isn't a ground floor or even on a lower floor, which would normally be the target of choice for burglars," Jason says. A paramedic is treating our scratches and scrapes with gentle dabs of a stinging antiseptic. Jason winces from the discomfort, then gives me a hard look. "This was a targeted attack."

"I don't know who they are or what they wanted from me," I insist. "All I remember is being half asleep when they busted through the door of my apartment."

"So, you have no Russian-speaking friends or enemies?" Officer McKinley asks.

"No. I'm a kindergarten teacher, for Pete's sake."

And the daughter of one of the most powerful Bratva leaders in New York, but that's for me to know.

I couldn't bear the shame of Jason learning the truth. They say we don't get to choose our family, but in most cases, we have the option to walk away. I *ran* away two years ago, and I've been living in a shadow of fear ever since.

What worries me the most is that I truly have no idea who those two brutes were. The one with the scar on his temple seemed familiar because he looked like the literal stock photo of any Bratva family member—a big, burly Russian dude with some form of disfigurement and a dead-eyed glare that made me fear for my life.

I know my family's people, and they certainly wouldn't come after me the way those bastards did—with guns and balaclavas, not with using force and threatening me with death.

My best guess is that somebody figured out that Fedorov's daughter is in Chicago, and they decided to take me in the hope of being able to use me as leverage against my father. I'm not okay with that. I've worked too hard to build a decent, quiet, uneventful life.

"And you're certain they were speaking Russian?" the police officer asks Jason.

"Yes. Positive. Judging by the way they moved, the way they dressed and used their weapons, I'm inclined to believe that at least one of them has some kind of military experience," Jason replies.

"But so do you," McKinley says with an admiring smirk.

Jason offers a subtle nod in return. "Yes, sir."

"Army?"

"Rangers."

"You fellas pack a punch."

"I'm not invincible, though," Jason sighs. "Had I not been carrying a weapon, none of us would be here right now."

The police officer gives me another curious look. "And what is your connection to Mr. Winchester here?"

"She's my girlfriend," Jason answers before I can say anything.

The words roll off his tongue in a way that sounds so natural, so sincere, I could literally cry. He just told the cop I'm his girlfriend.

His lying girlfriend. Oh, God, Audrey, you're going to burn in hell for this, and you need to figure out a way to make it right before it's too late.

"Yeah," I mumble in agreement as Jason puts his arm around my shoulders.

I welcome his careful embrace and feel my whole body gradually warming up and relaxing against his. But the relief comes with a sense of guilt. I don't deserve his kindness, not with the little bit of truth I've actually told him. It was one thing to keep my past private; secrecy isn't the worst crime one can commit in a relationship. Lying, on the other hand, is infinitely worse.

"Have you considered the possibility that the assailants were trying to hurt you, Mr. Winchester, by getting to Miss Smith first?" McKinley asks.

"It's highly unlikely," he tells the officer. "I don't have any ties to Russians or the mob."

"The Chicago Bratva is known to be quite influential. They have their fingers in many pies, to the point where a lot of business owners don't even realize that they're in bed with them until it's too late," McKinley says.

"No, it doesn't make sense," Jason replies. "All of my businesses are legal and my own. I don't have any partnerships established anywhere with anyone else. I vet all of my employees and contractors carefully, given my own Army background. I do my due diligence and pay all of my taxes. I promise you, Officer McKinley, everything is above board with each of my trusts and companies. We even check the donations coming through my foundation. Not once have we found anything that could be flagged as out of the ordinary or less than legal."

But McKinley raises a skeptical eyebrow. "It could be that you pissed someone off and don't know it. Have you purchased any new properties lately? Maybe you inadvertently muscled into Bratva turf."

"Just The Emerald," Jason replies. "However, this whole neighborhood is clean in that sense. Besides, wouldn't they have reached out to me first? The news about my company buying the complex came out months ago. If they had a problem with the purchase, surely they would've sent someone to talk me out of it."

"No one came, huh?"

"No," he sighs deeply. "This is incredibly confusing."

Not to me, it isn't. It has nothing to do with Jason or his businesses. This is about me. About my God-given last name and the blood that flows through my veins. Jason's life was in danger tonight. For better or worse, I was raised in that environment—I'm used to looking over my shoulder.

I know what to do if someone tries to kidnap me or if someone succeeds in taking me prisoner. I know how to leave DNA behind in case I'm killed. And as horrendous as that sounds, it's what I was taught at a young age.

Other girls grew up with Barbie dolls and ballet classes. I grew up with a strict Russian nanny who never hesitated to spank me whenever I did anything that went against the Fedorov family code: Our Bible was a carefully implemented survival manual in case rival Bratvas ever tried to come after me or my brothers.

I'd hoped I was able to leave it all behind me when I left New York. Clearly, I was wrong.

"How are you feeling?" Jason asks me.

I didn't even notice McKinley moving away from us. He's busy liaising with the other officers as they bag bullet casings and lift fingerprints from the dumpster. I remember telling them that one of the assailants leaned into it at some point during the struggle.

"I'm better, thank you," I mumble, my cheeks burning as I stare at my trembling hands. "I can't stop shaking, though."

"That's the adrenaline. It'll wear off," he says. "You do know you're coming back home with me tonight, right?"

I can't fight him on this. The Chicago Russians know where I live. They're not going to leave me alone; that much is painfully clear. But I can't live like this. I'm not quite sure what I'll do next, but Jason is right—I can't stay at my place anymore. Knowing that hurts my heart on a deeper level. This was my home, my safe haven, my little niche in a crazy, chaotic world.

"Whatever happens next, we're going to figure it out, Audrey. I promise you that."

"I know," I reply, half-smiling as he presses his lips against my temple. His kiss is soft and warm, filling my core with liquid sunlight. The effect that this man has on me is almost immediate, and it pains me deeply because I know I'm at fault here.

One thing is certain, however. With everything that has happened and with everything that is bound to happen next, I have to overcome this hurdle. I have to set my fears and pride aside and grab the bull by the horns. I need to reach out to my brothers and find out who ordered the hit on me. They may be New York-based, but Bratva folks know one other across the United States.

If there's anybody who's able to find out this information, it's Anton and Vitaly.

CHAPTER 14

AUDREY

As crazy as it sounds, the following days are worse than the actual kidnapping attempt.

There is a heavy silence between Jason and me, the kind of silence that seeps into every aspect of our relationship. Even our lovemaking feels cloaked in a shadow of secrets and lies —all of my own doing. I feel awful, yet I can't bring myself to tell him the truth, not about the Bratva or the baby.

I can't live like this for much longer, however. Guilt is like a sickness, quietly eating away at me from the inside. Combined with what I'm guessing are pregnancy hormones, it's giving me major mood swings and making me highly volatile, which means I have trouble regulating my own emotions.

"What are you thinking?" Jason asks, his voice dragging me out of my self-sabotaging thoughts.

I'm not sure how to answer that, but I am in his office, sulking in his guest chair while browsing through real estate ads, looking at comps in the area, and trying to figure out a reasonable selling price for my apartment. I need to sell it, there's no doubt about that. I'll need money to leave at a moment's notice, if necessary.

My brothers have yet to respond to my messages. I have no idea if they will give me the information I seek or if they will assist me in disappearing. And the thought of leaving altogether ... that just breaks me over and over again every time it enters my mind. It's not fair to this child I'm carrying, Jason's child. It's not fair to Jason, and it's not fair to me. None of this is fair.

"Sorry," I mutter and close the laptop, stuffing it back in my bag. "Just going over some emails, nothing special."

"I just heard from Officer McKinley," Jason says.

Sitting behind his desk, he truly resembles a king overlooking his domain. Sometimes, I feel like I'm dealing with a whole different side of him as soon as he takes that seat. It's as if he transforms into a titan of sorts, a person who doesn't take no for an answer, who doesn't tolerate any form of rejection or disrespect. I feel small whenever I'm in here. It's a strange sentiment, but I know it's exacerbated by the guilt that I carry on a daily basis.

"What did he say?" I ask, nervously picking at my thumbnail. It's a habit I'd thought I'd gotten over. One brush with the wrong side of the Bratva, and all of my compulsions have returned as if they were never cured. "Did he find the Russians?"

"No, but he thinks they were with the Abramovic family," Jason replies.

Oh, shit. I know that name. That's an ugly name in my world. A terrible name. My father and brothers taught me to stay as far away as possible from anyone bearing that name.

"Abramovic," I say it out loud. "It doesn't ring a bell."

I hate myself.

"That's odd because your body language tells me otherwise," Jason bluntly replies.

For a moment, I'm frozen in place, sitting stiffly as I look at him, trying to figure out where he's going with this. There's an angle here, and he has tried it before. Each time, I've managed to dash along that thin red line, avoiding tense conversations and arguments about my honesty.

I fear I've run out of free passes, though. Jason almost died that night. One bullet would've been enough to kill him, and I would've had only myself to blame for it.

"I don't understand," I say, already eyeing the door and looking for an excuse to leave.

"Audrey, how many more times are we going to do this ridiculous dance where I pretend to be ignorant and ask you to tell me the truth, and you continue to lie to my face?" His tone is low but still warm. He's trying so hard to be patient, and I'm not helping.

"You're calling me a liar?"

"I'm calling you a bad liar, but I know it's coming from a good place," he says. "I know you well enough to understand when you're being truthful and when you're trying to sell me some Grade-A BS. Here's the thing, Audrey. Whatever it is, you're not telling me; I know you're not doing it to hurt me. You're doing it because you're scared."

I shake my head slowly. "I'm scared, yes, but everything else is ... Jason, please, let's not have this conversation again."

"We are going to have this conversation again and again and again until you tell me the fucking truth," he snaps. "I got shot at, Audrey. Two Russian mobsters tried to take you away by force, and I'm pretty sure they would've killed you and dumped your body across state lines had they succeeded. You're not some stranger I picked up off the streets; you're my woman. I think I deserve to know the whole story."

"You know what?" I blurt out, my blood boiling with a mixture of anger and shame. "I think I'm going to spend the next couple of nights at a hotel. I think we need some time away from each other."

As if suddenly possessed, Jason shoots up from his seat and crosses the room in a split second. Before I can register the movement, he's got me pinned against the wall, his thigh wedged between my legs and pressing upward against my sensitive center. Almost instantly, I feel my breath leaving me as liquid heat drenches my panties, arousal flaring through my veins.

"What are you doing?" I manage, my voice barely a whisper.

"Reminding you who it is you're talking to," he shoots back and captures my mouth in a rapturous yet furious kiss. His lips press hard, his tongue clashing with mine. The effect that this man has over my senses is damn near devastating, and I quickly become putty in his hands. "When are you going to learn, Audrey, that you can't lie to me and get away with it? I've been more than patient, but said patience is running thin. I can't fucking protect you unless I know what's going on. I can't be with you unless you're honest with me, and I hate to have to pull this card, this ultimatum. I hate it."

"It's just—"

He kisses me again, cutting me off. It's as if his very soul is begging me for the truth, and I still can't find the strength or courage to just lay it all out on the table. He deserves it. He needs it. But I need him. I'm in love with him. I'm afraid he won't want anything to do with me if I tell him who I really am and where I come from.

At the same time, I'm painfully aware that I have to get away from him because I don't want him or Lily or Rita, or anyone else, for that matter, getting hurt.

All I can do is make the most of every moment we have left together, and this constant drilling for the truth only causes deeper dents in an already strained relationship. Why can't we just make the most of what we have before I muster the nerve to finally leave everything behind and start fresh somewhere else?

As far away from here as possible.

"The more you prolong this misery, the harder it'll be for us," Jason says, his breath ragged with arousal, his eyes clouded with dark desire. "I can't hold on to you for much longer, not unless you come through on your end, Audrey."

"I can't ..." Tears sting my eyes as I manage to pull away from his ironclad grip. "I can't, Jason. I'm sorry."

Upon reaching the elevator, I press the ground floor button and wait for the doors to slide closed. I see Jason coming out of his office and staring at me with a sullen look on his face. The remaining seconds seem to last forever before I lose sight of him, but as soon as the doors close, I burst into tears.

All the pain and anguish that I've been holding on to for quite some time now breaches the surface, and I start sobbing like a little girl. I hardly register the cab pulling up outside the office building. He was just rolling by, but I managed to hail him and get in the backseat. I barely remember where I asked him to take me.

It's not until I see the hotel up ahead, about three blocks down from Jason's office, that I regain some of my clarity.

Chicago is not my home anymore.

CHAPTER 15

AUDREY

The Landon Hotel is a beautiful place, one of the better establishments on this side of Chicago. It's on a busy street but with plenty of security cameras and a side door for guests who prefer more privacy. I will make good use of it whenever I go in and out of the building.

I check myself in under an assumed name. I'd secured a fake identity when I first moved to Chicago in case I might need it one day, and I intend to stay here until I sell my apartment. In the meantime, I'll have to send for my clothes and belongings.

I know I need to tell Jason the truth. I keep coaxing myself into it, and just when I'm about to reach for the phone and call him, some part of me manages to pull away from doing it, keeping me anchored in fear and uncertainty instead.

Staying silent has become my comfort zone because telling the truth would bring too much *dis*comfort. It's messy enough as it is, and frankly, I lack the courage.

Sighing heavily, I look both ways as I cross the street and dip into the side alley. My heart starts racing as I constantly glance around, worried I might've caught a tail. I was careful, though. As soon as I left the school, I switched cabs twice and used another subway station aside from my usual one in order to get back to the hotel.

Nobody appears to be following me. Just the everyday stream of people making their way up and down the busy street, eager to shop and see the sights that Chicago has to offer. It's a tourist-dense area, which serves me well, seeing as I currently require anonymity.

Once I'm inside, I pass by the ritzy reception desk to check if anyone has left a message for me. I'm not expecting anything, and I still have the same cell number. Jason knows where to reach me, as do my coworkers and Mrs. Ashel. The potential message I'm curious about is to make sure no one else has figured out that I'm here.

"Nothing for you today, Miss Delaware," the receptionist says.

"Thank you, David."

I smile at him and hit the elevator before other guests can beat me to it. I try to keep away from people, in general. While I'm not exactly an introvert, I have found peace in this strategy, especially while I'm trying to hide from Abramovic assassins.

A million thoughts bolt through my head as I listen to the smooth, jazzy elevator music, my mind wandering every which way. I keep going back to Jason, to his demand for the truth, and my inability to give that to him. It's cowardice, that's what it is, and it needs to stop.

By the time I reach my floor, I am practically berating myself, phone in hand. Maybe this time, I'll hit the call button and just spill the beans, including the one about the baby.

I owe him that and so much more. God, I miss him. I hate being away from him. We're still texting, but we can both tell it's not what it used to be. The spark isn't gone— my body cries out for him every damn night. But the tension between us is spoiling everything.

When I approach my hotel room, I see someone standing outside the door.

I freeze in the middle of the hallway, bathed in a golden light from the ceiling-mounted, smoked glass and bronze fixtures, staring at the man. I recognize myself in his cold, blue eyes and curly blonde hair.

Anton is dressed in a tailored navy blue suit, which brings out his best features.

"Little sister," he says, beaming like the sun as soon as he recognizes me. A broad, almost charming grin slits across his handsome, boyish face. "You look wonderful!"

"Anton. What the hell are you doing here? How did you find me?" I manage, my voice trembling. I don't know whether to be impressed or terrified.

"I'm resourceful, remember?" he chuckles softly and takes a step in my direction.

Instinctively, I move back. "Hold on. How did you find me?" I repeat.

"Audrey, when are you going to understand that I will always know where you are?"

"Ah, shit, you tracked my cell signal, didn't you?"

Anton measures me from head to toe. His blue eyes are reduced to inquisitive slits as they shift focus, inch by inch. I feel like I'm stuck inside an X-ray machine, unable to move. "I've always known where you were, little sister," he says. "But don't worry, we didn't tell Papa."

"We?"

"Vitaly and me. You didn't think I'd keep our big brother out of the loop, did you?"

I exhale sharply, pinching the slender bridge of my nose with moderate frustration. "I swear to God, I never understand anything with you two. So, you knew where to find me this whole time?"

"154 Maple Street, Emerald Residence. Apartment 230," he says with a confident cockiness. "Before that, 23 Sudds Drive. Rental. Before that, the Madison Inn, 45 East Street. That one was smart, I'll give you that. Papa would've never thought to look for you at a motel like that."

I stayed at the Madison when I first got to Chicago. I looked for the cheapest motel on the nastier side of town to keep my head down for a while and wait for the Fedorov storm to pass. "How'd you track me to Chicago, though?" I ask, still rather confused. "I switched Greyhounds like five times."

"Audrey. Vitaly and I taught you how to disappear without a trace," Anton replies, almost laughing. "Why would we teach you that if we didn't know how to track you ourselves? I knew you were thinking about running away from New York. I knew it as soon as Papa mentioned Piotr and the arrangement he proposed."

Piotr. That's a name I'd hoped I would never hear again. It causes a feeling of disgust to form in the back of my throat. It's a hard name to swallow, and I shudder as I try to push the image of him out of my head. He still gives me the creeps.

"I've kept my distance this whole time," Anton says, pursing his lips for a moment. "I am only here because you summoned me."

It's too late to un-summon him; that much is obvious. Every statement my slightly sociopathic brother has made up to this point only proves that I will never truly get away from my family.

He has always known where to find me, yet he chose to keep this from our father. I don't know how far I can trust him or Vitaly, for that matter. Our father has a way of sinking his teeth deep into his sons, deep enough to indoctrinate them, to brainwash them into being his perfect little soldiers.

That never worked with me.

I wonder how far in Anton and Vitaly have gotten with the Bratva in the years that I've been away. Do I even wish to find out? I should be feeling relief at this moment. I called for help. Help is here. So why am I so wary?

Because I know who I'm dealing with.

My brothers have always been slightly milder versions of our father, though both can be just as ruthless when the situation demands it. To my relief, they've also always had a major soft spot for me, their little sister. Even when Papa tried to marry me off to Piotr—his business partner, Bratva lieutenant, and a man old enough to be my grandfather—Anton and Vitaly understood that it wasn't what I wanted.

They worked hard to convince our father not to go ahead with the arranged marriage. They failed, and I had no choice but to run away before Piotr could put a ring on my finger. To their credit, they left me alone with my illusion of safety until I reached out to them in desperation.

"You've always known where I was," I mutter as a waiter brings us tea and biscuits.

We are sitting at one of the more private tables of the hotel's tearoom, out of sight and well out of earshot, under a dim, amber light. Anton waits until it's just the two of us again before he answers, casually adding four sugar cubes to his cup. It's a miracle he hasn't developed diabetes.

"Yes," he confirms.

"But you never came after me."

"I must know where you are and to make sure that you are safe and happy. You were safe and happy in Chicago, so I didn't see any reason for me to spoil that," Anton replies, his eyes searching my face. "There's something different about you."

"Oh, you mean the daily terror I now carry after the Abramovic Bratva tried to kidnap me?" I shoot back, my brow furrowed with discontent.

"Audrey, I swear, we had no idea they found you," he sighs deeply. "Had we known, rest assured, they never would've gotten close enough to lay a hand on you."

"Does Papa know I'm here?"

He shakes his head. "I told you. No. Not yet anyway."

"Not yet?"

"That depends on how you behave going forward," Anton chuckles again, and it's the snickering tone that gets to me every damn time. I never know what side of Anton I'm getting. Never. One minute, he's the calm and protective brother, and then the next, he turns into this heartless sociopath who blackmails and manipulates people—Vitaly and me included—until his bidding is done. "We're going to have to figure something out, little sister, because the Abramovic Bratva is not to be messed with."

"Yeah, I know they're not to be messed with," I hiss. "They want to destroy our family. If I remember correctly, they've always had ambitions of moving and taking over New York."

"That's right, and Papa and Grandpapa before him have repeatedly stopped them."

"If they get to me—"

"They won't."

"But if they do, they'll use me to force Papa and the whole operation out of New York, won't they?" I ask.

Anton thinks about it for a moment, quietly stirring his tea while I take a long sip of mine. I welcome the jasmine and honey flowing down my throat and filling my stomach. An assortment of macarons and jam biscuits is beautifully arranged on a porcelain plate between us, and I'm so hungry all of a sudden I could eat the whole table. My brother watches me with subtle amusement while I stuff my face and wash it all down with more tea.

"Or they'll force him to give them a generous cut of his operations," he finally says. "No, there's something else that's different about you. What is it?"

"I don't know what you're talking about," I reply a little too quickly.

"You're a terrible liar."

Yeah, Jason said the same thing.

"Anton, what am I going to do? I can't go back to New York."

"I wouldn't want you back there anyway. Piotr put a price on your head."

"Wait, what?" I gasp, breaking into a sudden cold sweat.

"Ah, I know what it is. You're in love," Anton says, changing the subject quickly enough to throw me off my game. "I have seen that look before. Vitaly used to glow like that when he was shacking up with Serena."

"Hold on, he's not with Serena anymore?"

Anton lets another heavy sigh roll from his chest. "No. They called the wedding off not long after you left."

"Why?"

"Serena wanted a life outside the Bratva. Vitaly is the Bratva. I guess you emboldened her, and since she never had any ties to any of the Russian families, it was easier for her to just return the ring and call the wedding off."

"What did our father say?"

Anton laughs lightly, eyes twinkling as he remembers what I assume was a funny scene, at least funny to him. "Oh, he was pissed off and then some. I told Serena to move out of the city for a while. Her family had properties in Chappaqua, so she took a job there."

"Is she okay?"

"Yes. I think she'll move back to New York at some point. Vitaly keeps better track of her."

"All right, so Piotr put a price on my head," I say, determined to better understand the kind of mess I've unknowingly gotten myself into. My brother nods once. "Why? It's not like we announced an engagement or anything."

"His pride, Audrey."

"And what did Papa think about it?"

Anton lowers his gaze for a moment. "He tried to talk some sense into Piotr. He keeps trying, for that matter. Every month, he takes the old geezer out for a round of golf. He keeps sending him expensive gifts. We believe Piotr will give up on this nonsense sooner or later."

"So, he's fine with it," I scoff, crossing my arms. "The man is actively trying to kill his only daughter, and Papa takes him out golfing."

"It's more complicated than that, Audrey. And you know it."

"Not really, Anton. It's actually pretty simple. Family before everything. Does our father think I put him in a precarious situation with his business partners when I left?"

My brother nods once, a flicker of amusement lingering in his cold, blue eyes.

"But he didn't think Piotr put him in a precarious situation when he put a price on my head. What the fuck?" I say.

"I'll admit, pride can often get the better of Papa. But we both know he will welcome you with open arms should you return."

"And we both know I will never do that. And apparently, I can't."

"I know," he sighs deeply. "Listen, Audrey, I know it's complicated and it's infuriating, but he had plans for you. He still has plans for you. That's why I want you to stay away. But you can't stay here, either, with the Abramovics knowing where you are."

"I am ready to move to another city if I have to. I'd rather stay here with the people I'm genuinely fond of, though. Anton, I didn't call you here so you could rescue me. I called you here so you can help me get rid of the Abramovic people."

Anton runs a hand through his hair, then pours himself another cup of tea, taking a moment to taste one of the pistachio cream cakes while I watch in heavy silence.

"I can't fight the whole clan for you. I can't go to war with them without dragging Papa into it. And if there's one thing we've steered clear of until now, it's precisely this—going into the others' turf. You, on the other hand, should've picked a different city to live in."

"Oh, I'm sorry, Anton. I forgot to check my Russian mob app to see which city in the whole United States of America I could move to without crossing an Ivan or a Sergei," I almost laugh at the ridiculousness of his statement.

"You're a Fedorov, Audrey, whether you like it or not. Whether you use a fake ID or your own identity, you're still a Fedorov. You were born one, and you will die one. That is never going to change, and it's about time you accept that. It doesn't matter that you're not active in the Bratva; you are still a member of the family, and that makes you a valuable asset. That's why Abramovic is after you. He wants to muscle his way back into New York, and you just happened to come into his city. I can't blame him for trying."

"Thanks for the pep talk."

"I'm trying to help you."

I'm baffled. "How exactly? I just need you to reach out to those pricks and ask them to back off. Propose a deal or something. Give them a warehouse area by the pier or some neighborhood in the Bronx. Pay them off. We've got cash to spare."

"The best I can do is give you your own security detail until you figure out where you're going to move next," Anton says, lowering his gaze for a moment. "I'm not all-powerful, Audrey. I'm not even first in line for the throne. If Vitaly finds out I spoke to you, he'll hand my ass back to me, and then our father will do worse. Appreciate that I came all this way in the first place."

I can't help but feel sorry for my brothers. They were born into this, just like me. Except, unlike me, they would've never considered running away because the Bratva gives them a sense of belonging, especially since our mother died. They couldn't leave our father on his own. And someone needed to protect me as well. There's much more responsibility and expected loyalty from the males.

I ran off, and they were left behind to pick up the pieces. And our father can be so mean, cruel, and unforgiving. I'm sure they suffered tremendously in my absence. I'm certain he punished them for not keeping a close enough eye on me.

To this day, I still suspect that Anton and Vitaly chose to look the other way while I made plans and implemented them in order to escape from New York. I doubt they will ever admit it, but the mere fact that Anton is here without the whole family in tow to drag me back with them sort of confirms my suspicion.

"I'm sorry, Anton," I say after a long silence. "I'm sorry I ran away without telling you or Vitaly anything. And I'm sorry that I haven't reached out before now and that I left you behind."

"You did what you felt was best for you. I can't hold that against you, little sister."

"But still, I'm sorry. And I'm sorry for asking you to fix this mess, too. I know it's not fair. I just didn't know who else to call."

"What about Jason Winchester?"

I felt my face drop. "What?"

My blood runs icy cold. I'm paralyzed in my seat, staring at Anton as though he were the devil himself. He knows about Jason. If he's known where I've been this whole time, along with every other place I've lived, of course he would know about Jason, too.

"Are you two serious?" Anton asks, half-smiling.

"I'm in love with him. Please, don't hurt him. Leave him alone, Anton."

"As long as he doesn't hurt you, Audrey, he's safe," he says. "From what I've read, he's quite accomplished. I'll give you credit there; you picked a fine one. Does he know?"

"Know what?"

"About your heritage. About that baby you're carrying. I presume it's his."

A gasp escapes from the back of my throat as I glower at Anton with all the outrage I can muster. "How dare you?" I hiss, leaning forward to make sure no one else hears me. "How dare you violate my privacy like that?"

"If there's one thing you seem to have forgotten about me, it's this: Your safety and well-being will always be my business, mine and Vitaly's, no matter where you go or who you're with," Anton calmly replies. "The minute you sent me that message, warning me about the Abramovic Bratva, I made it my mission to find out everything there is to know regarding your new life because everything can be eventually used against you. Do you have any idea how much worse it's going to get for you if Abramovic finds out you're pregnant?"

"No."

"He will turn the city upside down. He will kill anyone who stands in his way, including your precious Jason Winchester and his cute little daughter," Anton says. "You are already valuable purely on account of your last name. Rumor has it that Abramovic is dead set on conquering New York, and we're standing in his way. Having you under his nose is like a gift. That maniac will stop at nothing until he gets what he wants. And if Papa finds out that you're pregnant—"

"You will keep your mouth shut!"

"Pipe down," Anton hushes me. "I said *if*. I'm not going to be the one to tell him, so relax. But if I was able to find out, he will, too. And when he does figure it out, Audrey, there won't be a fucking pebble left on this earth for you to hide under. You may think he's putting his family second, but that couldn't be further from the truth. He will crush anyone who threatens any of us—"

"What about Piotr?"

Anton waves that concern away with a mere flick of his wrist. "Oh, forget about that old fool. He's just throwing a tantrum. He'll come back around eventually."

"Does our father know about the Abramovic Bratva's attempt to take me?" I ask, my voice trembling slightly.

"Not yet. We don't have that many eyes and ears in Chicago. We will from now on, though, because I'll see to it."

Minutes pass in eerie silence as Anton and I seem to have reached some sort of arrangement. It may be unspoken, but

I find comfort in knowing that he's got my back in the only way that he can, given the circumstances.

Being a Bratva lieutenant and having our father's trust gives him freedom of movement and expenditures without anyone second-guessing him, which is why Anton can afford to give me his security detail.

I wish he could do more, but it was a long shot to begin with. Even so, it's better than nothing. At least I'll have trained professionals who are familiar with the Bratva's tactics to watch my back while I sell my apartment and prepare to start a new life somewhere else.

"Does he know?" Anton asks me the question again.

"Huh?"

"Winchester. Does he know about your pregnancy?"

"He doesn't know, and I would appreciate it if it stayed that way," I sigh. "I have to leave Chicago under these conditions. I can't just drop the bomb and then never be seen again. It would destroy Jason."

"It's not fair to him, either way, but I guess it makes sense."

"What he doesn't know can't hurt him. It only hurts me, Anton."

Anton chuckles softly. "I wish we'd been born into a different family; I really do. I would've liked to have had some Ivy League friends and to have been able to enjoy a nice gin negroni on a Friday night with you and Vitaly, but alas, it wasn't meant to be. We were raised by wolves, and we live as wolves. I hope you understand that now. You're a lone wolf, Audrey. You won't make it far without your pack."

"Don't rub it in."

"But it's the truth. It's your reality, can't you see? You left New York thinking that you'd be able to live a white-picket-fence life with a husband and two kids, that you'd teach kindergarten for the rest of your days, and possibly take up gardening when you retire. Come on, Audrey. That is not what we were made for."

"We decide what we were made for," I insist. "Just because you got comfortable being Daddy's good little soldier like Vitaly doesn't mean I had to fall in line, too. There's more to life than what he planned for us. Hell, our lives were never his to plan in the first place."

"You're going to be a single mother," Anton reminds me.

Oh, God, that sounds awful. I don't want that. I want Jason. I want to be with him, to spend every single day with him. To watch Lily and our own child grow up together and become better people than all of us combined. I want us to gather the sweetest memories so that we'll have quite the story to tell in the sunset of our lives. This is not fair; it's not right. Tears prick my eyes. I try to blink them back, but I fail miserably, so Anton gives me a tissue.

"No matter what you decide, Audrey, I will always have your back," he adds. "It may not always seem like it, but I love you. I can't always protect you from your own choices, though, especially since I still have my own ass to cover."

"I don't want to put you in an impossible situation," I say, shaking my head slowly. "The security detail sounds good until I decide what I'm going to do next."

"Perhaps you could take Jason with you. The girl. The nanny."

I chuckle dryly. "You make it sound so simple."

"It is that simple when you truly love someone."

The way he says it makes me stare at him for a while. His expression shifts from sadness to a kind of longing that feels all too familiar. I think he may have feelings for someone and difficult decisions to make himself. Anton never struck me as the type who would ever fall in love, but then again, when lightning strikes, it burns through everything.

"Jason doesn't even know my true last name," I concede with a heavy, guilty heart. "He thinks my name is Audrey Smith."

"I saw a copy of that fake ID of yours. Excellent work. Did you pay Evgeni for it?"

I can't help but smile. "You can tell?"

"I'd recognize his graphic skills anywhere. Besides, it makes sense that you'd go to the best guy for that sort of job. I would've done the same if I wanted a new, pristine, and ironclad identity." His humor fades as he glances somewhere behind me. "Audrey, I thought you said no one else knows what hotel you're staying at."

"No one else does."

"Then why is your boyfriend walking in and looking at me like he's about to rip my spine out through my mouth?" Anton shoots back and instantly stiffens in his seat.

I get up and turn around just in time to see Jason stalking across the tearoom with a furious look in his eyes.

"Jason," I mumble as he reaches us.

"Would you mind telling me what the fuck is going on here?" Jason says, his voice low and dripping with insurmountable fury. It sends shivers down my spine and an ache soaring through my ribcage as I find myself stuck between a rock and a hard place. "Who's this?" he nods back at Anton.

"Jason, please, calm down. We can discuss this—" I try to reason with him, but my brother speaks up, standing to shake his hand and cutting me off in the process.

"Forgive my sister's manners, Mr. Winchester. I'm Anton, Audrey's brother."

And that's all it takes to bring Jason to a sudden halt. His eyes become blank, devoid of any reaction. His lips press into a thin line while a frown pulls his brows close together. He's stunned. Speechless. Even more confused than when he first walked in. And I've no doubt he's got a lot of questions.

CHAPTER 16

JASON

"Audrey's brother," I mutter, my gaze darting between them. "I didn't know you had a brother."

"Two, actually," Anton says, chuckling. "The Fedorovs are a large family."

"The Fedorovs?"

Audrey gives him a startled look. "What the hell, Anton? One thing, I asked you for one thing!"

"I'm sorry, little sister, but the man deserves the truth, and if you won't tell him, then I will," her brother replies. "It's not fair to Mr. Winchester, and you know it."

"Will you please just shut up, Anton?" she says through clenched teeth.

"Why should he shut up, exactly?" I ask, tempted to let my anger get the better of me. "From where I'm standing, I've got a feeling that Anton here is the only one interested in being honest with me."

"No, it's not that simple; there's more to this than—"

"Audrey," Anton cuts her off, placing a hand on her shoulder. As soon as he touches her, I notice that she instantly shuts down. There's respect there, but there is also a subtle threat in his presence, something that adds just enough tension to her frame, just enough for me to notice. She respects him, but she also fears him. "Jason needs to know who you are. Whatever else you want to tell him, that's on you. But at the very least, he needs to know who you are and why the Abramovic family is after you."

Something tells me the truth is about to hit me hard and right in the gut.

I'm not going to like it.

"I think your brother and I agree," I tell Audrey.

The pain in her blue eyes cuts right through my soul, but I'm certain she also understands how important the truth is at this moment. Now, more than ever. If I can't trust her, if she can't trust me, how will we make it work in the long run? I can't be with another woman who betrays me, who breaks me, and then leaves, only for me to pick up the pieces.

"Here's the deal, Jason. In Audrey's defense, she has been working hard to be true to herself," Anton begins. "She left us; she left New York, the only home she'd ever known, so that she could start fresh somewhere else. To my dismay, for some reason, she chose Chicago. I'll never understand it. She could've picked any other city in the country, but she chose the land of deep-dish pizza—"

"I suppose you're going somewhere with this," I exhale sharply.

"Yes. My point is, do not blame my sister for not telling you the truth. Honestly, I wouldn't have told you, either. You probably could've gone your whole life together without ever having to deal with this. But the problem is, somebody in Chicago recognized Audrey somewhere, at some point. Likely a rat from New York, here on business, or hiding out from my family."

"Your family."

"I'm Anton Fedorov. She is Audrey Fedorova. We have an older brother, Vitaly, who will inherit the family business. I'll be working alongside him, but Audrey chose a different path. My brother and I will never hold it against her. Our father, however, is not so pleased with her."

I shake my head slowly. "I'm still waiting for the conclusion."

"You've never heard of the Fedorovs?" Anton frowns, albeit slightly amused by my ignorance. I offer a shrug in return. "Well then, let's just say we rule New York from the shadows. How about that?"

The puzzle pieces click into place. "You're the mob."

"No, we're Bratva, Jason. The kind of people you want to be friends with, but not too friendly. You definitely don't want us as your enemies. You'd be better off if we don't know anything about you, in all honesty."

"And the Abramovic family … they're what, Chicago's rulers from the so-called shadows?"

"Also Bratva, yes," Anton says. "There used to be two families running business in New York in the early 1900s, but the Abramovic clan moved their operations to Chicago as soon as the Italians started their gang wars. They took advantage of the chaos and deregulation, the Abramovic becoming the Chicago Bratva, while we solidified our reign over New York."

"Why are they coming after Audrey, then?" I ask. "To get to you?"

She lowers her gaze, unable to look me in the eyes. I don't know whether it's fear or shame or both, but it's tearing me apart to see her like this. It also makes me furious, learning about all of this only now. She could've told me. She *should've* told me, dammit.

"Yes. Because she is still a Fedorov, fake ID notwithstanding, like I said, somebody probably recognized her, then ran straight to the Abramovics to tell them that she's in Chicago. They've probably had her under surveillance for a while, watching where she was going, who she was meeting with, what she was doing, that kind of thing," Anton says.

My blood starts to simmer until it reaches its boiling point as I glower at Audrey. "You knew, then? You knew that they were specifically after you, and you knew why, as well?"

"Yes. They snuck a note under my door," Audrey sighs heavily. "It's why I wanted to get away from The Emerald."

"So, you lied to me."

"I was scared, okay? I was ashamed. I'd already kept so much from you, and I couldn't risk your and Lily's safety," she says, her voice trembling with raw emotion. "Jason, I'm sorry."

"But do you realize that you put us in danger by *not* telling me the truth?" I ask, my throat tightening with unbridled fury. I know I need to get a grip on myself, but I'm struggling to do so. I draw the line where Lily's safety is concerned, especially after all the crap I went through with her mother, Ramona. "For fuck's sake, Audrey! You should've told me so I would've been better prepared. I would've been able to better protect you. They never would've gotten close enough to almost kidnap you or worse!"

"I'm sorry," Audrey sobs, blinking back tears as Anton puts his arm around her shoulders. "I'm so sorry, Jason. I panicked, okay? You have been so good to me, so kind and patient. We were doing so well that I almost believed I had a shot at a normal life. I just ... I froze; I didn't know what to do. I wasn't sure what was worse—the fact that I was lying to you or that simply being in my presence was dangerous."

"It wasn't your decision to make. And it's not yours to make now either," I snap. "You lied to me. You kept secrets. I repeatedly asked you for the truth, and you repeatedly rebuffed me. Hell, you walked out in a fury the other day just because I pressed you further on the matter."

"I know."

"I'm sure Audrey had the best intentions," Anton tries to pitch in, but I'm too angry to make decent use of my reasoning capabilities, so I raise a hand to silence him.

"I can't have you anywhere near Lily anymore, you do understand that, right?"

She nods slowly, barely able to speak. It's killing me, but my instincts have taken over. I have to protect my daughter. I have to keep my baby safe, no matter what. Everything else fades into the darkness, simmering away into a dim background because my mind can't fathom anything except Lily's safety.

"I can't do this anymore," I say as I get up and walk away.

I hear Audrey's whimper as she watches me leave, held back by her brother while I keep my focus on the exit. A few more steps and I will be out in the street again, away from her and the Bratva. The farther away I get from her, the better it will be for Lily and Rita. I can't risk their lives. Had I been on my own, the conversation would've been completely different.

But I am not on my own.

I am a father first. And while my heart is bleeding, I can't go back.

CHAPTER 17

AUDREY

I was so ashamed when Anton told Jason the truth, but I was also relieved. The cat was finally out of the bag, and there was nowhere left to hide. Jason had the truth—most of it, anyway—and he made his decision.

I am Audrey Fedorova, the daughter of a powerful Russian mobster. There's a price on my head, and no one around me will ever be safe unless I'm out of the picture. That's a hard pill to swallow, even now. It's what I didn't want Jason to know: how nuclear I am. How nuclear I've always been, even though it was never my choice.

My brother is right. There are some things we can leave behind, some things we can say no to. But there are also things we cannot escape, no matter how far we run. Things we just have to learn to live with.

Given that a baby is growing in my womb who will likely never meet their father, I have to figure things out fast. I have to pull myself together and find a way to live with my last name and the dangers that come with it. The last thing I want is for my child to grow up in fear.

"You're not going to tell Jason about the pregnancy, are you?" Anton concedes as he escorts me back to my hotel room. He's been so patient, so kind, and comforting while I've been crying my heart out and miserable.

I shake my head slowly. "If I tell him, he will have to choose between this child and his daughter. I don't know what that would do to him."

"You're so grown-up," my brother states.

Anton looks both ways, content to see two big fellas in black suits walking toward us from the fire escape door on the east end of the hallway. "Ah, here they are. Yuri and Andrei will be looking out for you while you're living here. You have my number on speed dial, as well."

"Thank you, Anton."

"Don't thank me yet. I don't know how any of this is going to work out, but I'm hoping to sit down soon with the eldest Abramovic to see if I can get him and his goons off your back somehow. Once all of this is cleared up, Papa will want you to come back home. You know that, right?"

"I do, but I won't go back, Anton. I can't."

Anton gives me a dry smile. "I know. Worst-case scenario, you get the hell out of Dodge and let someone else handle the sale of your apartment. I'll wire you some cash to keep you covered in the meantime."

"You've already done enough," I sigh deeply, unable to shake off the ache that has taken such a firm hold of my heart.

"We're family, Audrey. Whether you like it or not."

I roll my eyes at him, well aware of how it irritates him. "It's not you I have a problem with, Anton. It's Papa."

"And Vitaly, just a little bit. Admit it," he laughs.

"This is all because of Papa," I groan harshly. "If only he'd given me some space to figure things out for myself, to *be* myself, my own person, and not some possession that he's looking to sell to the highest bidder. We're in the twenty-first century, Anton."

He pauses and gives me a sad look, tucking a lock of hair behind my ear. "I'm sorry to see you suffer like this. You and Jason had something good going on. Something that wiped that worried crease from between your brows. For a long time, I thought that was just your face," he says, and I jokingly slap him on the shoulder. "Seriously, I am sorry. For a moment, I actually thought you would be happy out here on your own."

"For a moment, I actually *was* happy," I tell him. "I was an idiot to think it might work out."

"It could've," Anton says. "Maybe another time, another place. Until then, however, let's see if there's anything I can do to help you stay in Chicago. Perhaps once the clouds clear, Jason will see things differently and give it another go."

"Thank you, Anton."

He pauses to shake Yuri and Andrei's brick-sized hands. "Fellas, you know the drill. Nobody comes anywhere near this door. Not even the service staff unless Audrey tells you beforehand that she's expecting someone."

"Da, Boss. We've got her," Yuri replies with a thick Russian accent.

He and Andrei seem pretty young, most likely Moscow imports. The Fedorovs continue to support Russian immigrants coming to New York, often giving them jobs within our circles to help them get on their feet.

Occasionally, my brothers pick out the biggest and the strongest among them, training them so they can serve as a private security detail. If I'm to leave my personal issues aside, I have to admit that my family has given out more jobs across New York than the mayor himself.

"I'll be in touch," Anton says, then plants a kiss on my temple and leaves.

"I'll be going to bed early," I tell Yuri and Andrei. "I'm not expecting any company."

"Yes, Miss Fedorova," Andrei replies.

I leave them both outside my door and lock myself in my room. Taking deep, measured breaths, I get out of my clothes and jump into a hot shower. Letting the water stream down my body, I take my time to scrub the day's events out of my skin.

Once I'm squeaky clean and my muscles feel mildly relaxed, I pat myself dry and slip on a pair of silk pajamas. The minibar is loaded, so I help myself to some salty and sweet treats, washing everything down with orange juice while I turn the TV on.

A distraction is exactly what I need. Something to keep my mind off Jason.

And Lily. I'm going to miss that sweet girl. She's so smart and surprisingly mature for her age; then again, so was I, growing up without a mother. Life is rarely fair, but we learn to adapt, we learn to push through. I think Lily is going to be all right in that sense. With a father like Jason guiding her, I believe she will become a powerful and dangerous woman in the best way possible.

I would've liked to have been able to say a proper goodbye to both Lily and Rita. But it's all in the past now. Something else that I must leave behind.

My thoughts soon pull me away from the waking world, and I fall asleep with the TV on and a few empty treat bags discarded on the nightstand. My dreams are a greyish haze, familiar faces popping in and out of my frame as I try to find my way back to them. I keep running toward Jason, calling out to him, but I can't hear my own voice, even as I scream.

A loud thud has me sitting up, briefly wondering if I'm still asleep.

The darkness of my hotel room, its impersonal designs flaring out wherever the moonlight strikes through the window, reminds me of where I am and what I'm doing here. Did I dream the thud, or did the thud wake me? I'm not sure, but I am compelled to get out of bed and check. The room itself seems clear of danger.

Footsteps echo somewhere nearby. They sound rushed.

"Get him!" I hear Yuri shout.

My heart jumps. Immediately, I grab my phone and try to call Anton while simultaneously looking through the peep-hole. I can't see anyone, but the hallway is generously lit. There's no answer, but my instincts are ignited and exceptionally sharp.

I poke my head out through the door just in time to spot Yuri and Andrei drawing their weapons at the end of the hallway, close to the elevators.

The sound of muffled gunshots makes the blood rush through my body as Andrei is the first to fall, taking two rounds to the chest. Yuri tries to hold them off—whoever they are—but there are so many bullets flying out of guns fitted with silencers that my feet start doing my thinking for me.

I run out of the room and in the opposite direction, slipping through the fire escape door. I'm barefoot and still in my pajamas, phone in hand and my heart in my throat as I glide down the stairs. The same door I left through opens and shuts again. They're coming after me. I can hear their boots thudding, each step bringing them closer.

All I can do is run as fast as my feet can carry me.

I slip through the hotel's service entrance, damn near tack-ling an incoming concierge on my way out. "Sorry!" I mumble and keep running.

"Hey, watch it!" the guy shouts back.

I take a left turn at the end of the alley. I need to steer clear of the main streets. It's late at night, it's cold and damp, and I need to get somewhere safe until I figure out what

I'm going to do next, until I can get a hold of Anton, at least.

My mind is rushing every which way until I reach a corner store. I'm panting, the cool air making my tired lungs burn, but I'm still not safe. I'm off the boulevard, however, and whoever is after me hasn't caught up just yet.

I remember that I've got a ride sharing app installed on my phone. With trembling fingers, I use it to call a car to my location, grateful I had the wherewithal to grab my phone when I ran out of my room. I keep looking around, ignoring all the curious looks from the late-night passersby.

Two minutes later, a grey Prius pulls up, its plates matching the ones in my app.

I get in the backseat and give the driver the first address that pops into my head. As the car drives off, I see them coming up to the corner, not that far behind on my trail. Four men dressed in black. I recognize one from his temple scar, but the others are unfamiliar.

They don't see me in the back of the Prius, and I slide down into my seat for good measure, worried that my heart might explode from what just happened. They came into the hotel with loaded weapons and silencers; they more than likely killed both Andrei and Yuri.

Even after two years of being away, my survival instincts are still sharp as a razor's edge. It's one of the few times when I'm actually proud to be a Fedorov because I know how to react when someone is literally gunning for me.

They're still out there, scattering across the street, angrily searching for me.

Jason's apartment building seems eerily calm, clad in darkness, with only the streetlights casting an amber tint across the brick façade. For safety reasons, however, I instruct the driver to drop me off around the corner but only after we circle the block once so I can make sure there's no one watching Jason's place. The driver likely has questions, but he keeps them to himself, not minding the extra mile since it means a pricier charge at the end of the trip.

I get out of the car half a block down and choose to walk the rest of the way. Once again, I look over my shoulder and thank the stars that this is a residential neighborhood and that the street is practically empty at this late hour.

I go around the back of the building and punch in the access code, thankful—yet surprised—that Jason hasn't changed it.

Once I'm inside the building, I linger in the darkness of the stairwell for a while, struggling to catch my breath. My heart can barely handle all of this fear and anxiety. I try calling Anton again. Still, no answer. I'm starting to get worried, wondering if they were able to get to me because they got to my brother first.

I convince myself that isn't the case. Anton isn't stupid. He's better at hiding than I ever was, especially in hostile territory. I shake the terrifying thoughts away and run up the stairs. God, I hope Jason doesn't hate me for this. I guess I'm going to find out soon enough.

A couple of minutes later, I stand in front of his penthouse door, listening to the silence. I'm alone in the hallway, a stark white light coming down from the ceiling fixture just above my head. I am cold. I am scared and exhausted. I feel exposed. Yet, I somehow find the courage to knock.

It takes a while, but not as long as I'd expected, for Jason to open the door.

"Hey," I whisper, shaking like a leaf as the adrenaline leaves my body. I'm cold. So cold.

He looks exhausted and grim. "Audrey ..." His gaze softens when he recognizes me. His eyes are tired and bloodshot. He wasn't sleeping. "What are you doing here?"

"I'm so sorry; I didn't know where else to go ..."

Tears begin to stream down my cheeks, and I let it all out. I can't keep anything in me anymore. Tonight has been a fucking nightmare. Instinctively, Jason pulls me into his apartment and his arms, holding me tight as he shuts the door behind me.

I bawl like a little girl, my face hidden in his grey t-shirt, as he keeps me locked in his embrace. His heart thuds against my ear, and I listen to that drum beat, allowing it to soothe me. He doesn't say a word; he simply holds me and hears me out. I tell him about Yuri and Andrei, about what happened, and how I made it here.

"They didn't follow me, I swear," I whimper softly. "And I circled the block to make sure nobody saw me come in, either. I'm so sorry, Jason. I just ... I had nowhere else to go."

"It's okay," he says, his voice low and warm. "I've got top-notch security on this building and armed bouncers on the ground floor. All of them are ex-Army buddies of mine. No one's going to make it up here without my say-so."

"My God, Jason, I brought the Bratva into your life. I didn't mean for this to happen."

"I know," he replies, gently cupping my cheek with his hand. "I've been thinking a lot. I couldn't sleep, Audrey. I felt bad about how I reacted earlier."

"You had every right to walk away."

He shakes his head. "No, baby. A man doesn't abandon the woman he loves." He pauses, waiting for the words to hit me. The gong bell rings in the back of my head, my gaze locked on his, my whole body softening in his embrace. "That's a fact, Audrey. I love you. And while I don't yet know how we're going to handle all of this, one thing is for certain—you showing up here in the middle of the night is my sign from God. I'm not letting you leave ever again, and I'm never turning my back on you, either. Forgive me."

"There's nothing to forgive," I mumble, and he kisses me. Deeply, lovingly, pouring all of his soul into the joining of our lips, tongues meeting. "I love you, too."

"We'll figure it out," Jason says. "But until then, we need to get you warmed up."

Careful not to wake Lily or Rita, we cross the penthouse and go into his ensuite bathroom. He helps me out of my pajamas and turns on the hot water. I reach for the brush to handle my messy hair, but Jason takes it away. "I'll do it. Get in the shower," he commands me.

Half-smiling, blushing like a peony, I take a couple of steps forward until the hot water stream covers my body. I welcome the heat and steam relaxing every muscle, my bones almost melting in the process. Jason patiently combs my hair until it's smooth and shiny again, then takes his clothes off and joins me in the shower.

"I'm going to take care of you tonight, baby," he says. "And tomorrow, we'll have breakfast and discuss our options. Okay?"

"Okay. I'm so sorry."

"Stop apologizing. I get it. It may not have seemed that way earlier in the tearoom, but I get it, Audrey. We all have skeletons in our closet. Some are worse than others. For a long time, I thought my past with Ramona was a heavy burden, but realizing where you come from, after having learned more about Grigori Fedorov and the New York Bratva, I have to say ... I'm amazed you managed to get out and live for yourself at all. I'm in awe of you."

I stare at him, liquid sunshine flowing through my veins as I listen to his voice as I let him cover me with lavender-scented lather, gently cleansing me from top to bottom. His hands linger on my breasts for a while, but I don't mind, even though they're full and tender. He gently squeezes them, pinching the nipples between his fingers until they're hard and plump, naughtily perking up at his touch.

"Jason," I whisper, tilting my head back as he nudges me back under the hot water.

"Hold on, I'm not done yet," he replies, his gaze darkened with desire as his hand slips down and slides between my legs, fingers eagerly teasing my wet folds. "Oh, honey, you're already wet and ready for me."

"I'm always wet and ready for you," I moan as his finger circles my swollen clit, sending electrifying sensations through my limbs and up my spine. "Don't stop."

"I had no intention of stopping."

I hold on to his broad, muscular shoulders, watching the water droplets roll down his smooth skin as he works my pussy into an aching frenzy. We stand close together, my gaze wandering downward to find his cock hard and twitching to be buried inside me. Quietly, I let my hand do the same as his and gently stroke my man, slowly and steadily at first, to match his rhythm.

But he soon has me close to the edge, two fingers testing my entrance while the bottom of his palm is pressed against my clit. I move my hand up and down, squeezing at the base and softening my grip at the top, then reversing the movement as a droplet of precum gathers on his tip. I lick my lips, eager to taste it, but a crumbling orgasm rushes through, interrupting my plan.

"Oh, Jason!" I cry out as he finger-fucks me off the edge of the world, my pussy rippling under the shower's hot stream. I hold on for dear life, my nerves flaring, my hips grinding in a rocking motion as he squeezes every drop out of me. "I need you inside me right now."

"Right now?" he mutters in my ear, nibbling on the lobe.

"Right now."

"You're giving me orders?"

I pause and look up at him, biting my lower lip. "No, sir. I'm just stating my utmost desire. Will you please take me? All of me?"

He stares at me for what feels like a very long time. "I suppose so. Since you're asking so nicely. Turn around."

"Yes, sir," I giggle.

Somehow, the events of tonight have drifted away like side-walk chalk under a heavy rain. The world outside has vanished altogether. I do as I'm told, turning around, eager to move as far away from reality as possible.

Gently, Jason guides my hands onto the marble-paneled wall in front of me. "Don't take your hands off unless I tell you," he says.

"Yes, sir."

"Such a good girl," Jason growls, then slaps my ass.

The sting burns through my buttock, quickly melting into raw pleasure, and I moan harshly, eagerly spreading my legs for him. Jason watches me for a moment, I can see his reflection in the polished marble.

"I love how the water runs down your body. I've missed your curves," he says, sliding the tip of his cock between my buttocks before moving downward to my glazed entrance. "Fucking hell, it's like coming home."

He fills and stretches me and I gasp, suddenly remembering precisely how big, how thick, how perfect he is. This monstrous erection of his was made for my throbbing pussy, like pieces of the same puzzle. My blood simmers as he takes his sweet time, getting reaccustomed to being inside me.

But then he slowly pulls back before thrusting himself hard and deep.

"Ah!" I manage, tempted to take my hand off the wall so I can touch myself. I'm in desperate need of another orgasm, especially now that he's fucking me from behind. It's my favorite position. But Jason won't let me.

"Hands on the marble, Audrey. Tell me what you want."

"Make me come, my love. Please."

"Why the rush?" he grunts and smacks my ass again.

I bite the inside of my cheek as the sensation swirls through me, making me slicker and slicker as he pounds into me, deeper and deeper. A rhythm grows between us, my breasts bouncing with every thrust.

Jason goes harder, one hand firmly holding me by the hip while the other slips around and cups my tender pussy. "Yes, sir!" I cry out when his fingers start flicking and rubbing my overly sensitive clit.

Instantly, a surge of volcanic heat shoots through me.

I clench myself tightly around his cock while he drives deeper, fucking me so hard that I can barely breathe. I can only listen to the sound of skin slapping skin under the running water, to his ragged breath and my moans of pure, unadulterated pleasure. I can only watch his reflection as he claims me, yet again, as I am close to unraveling.

"Come for me, Audrey. Right now!" he commands me.

I let go in an instant. I explode like a burning star, begging him to fuck me harder and harder, barely able to stand as he takes me, as he transforms into a mindless beast and devours me, as he dismantles me completely. Breaking me down and building me back up. I feel him come inside me, his cock pulsating in the throes of pure ecstasy. I welcome him wholly, tightening myself around him and squeezing every drop out of my man.

He bites into my shoulder, his low growl sending shivers down my spine.

I am his, and he is mine. Every damned inch.

I have no idea what will happen after tonight. I don't know where it ends. But being here, right now, in this precious moment, I understand one thing:

I couldn't walk away from him if I wanted to.

CHAPTER 18

JASON

Morning finds me in an odd state.

I'm at peace. That's what is strange about this whole situation. I am actually at peace. Content with being here, in my bed, with Audrey. It's a fleeting moment, and I know that. Danger lurks in every corner, even with my high-level security and precautions. We will never be able to be together and be completely safe until we resolve this Abramovic issue, one way or another.

I had hoped that my heart would find a woman with less baggage than mine, but the universe saw fit to laugh in my face. I wouldn't want any other woman except this blonde-haired, blue-eyed Russian goddess currently sleeping in my arms, warm and soft and naked under the covers.

Her heart beats against my ribcage, head resting on my shoulder.

Her breathing is nice and even. She's in a deep sleep, and I hate to wake her. But I have to. Judging by the sheer amount of sunlight pouring through the window, it's late in the morning, and her phone has been buzzing nonstop.

"Audrey," I say softly at first. She doesn't hear me, so I gently caress her bare shoulder and say her name again. "Audrey."

She stirs awake, head popping up first to briefly check her surroundings. It's a trauma response, and it breaks me to see her this way. Yet as soon as she remembers where she is, as soon as she feels my body next to hers and her hazy eyes find mine, Audrey relaxes, allowing herself a lazy smile. "Good morning," she says, then moves in for a kiss.

I welcome her lips on mine, giving us both a few minutes of slow and tender making out before we get out of bed.

"I'm going to make some coffee," I say as we come out of the shower. "I think you should eat something, too."

"Where are Lily and Rita?" Audrey asks. Slipping into one of the t-shirts and yoga tights she left in a dresser drawer the last time she was here, she looks more at ease in this space than ever before. It's as if she is truly home for the first time. "I didn't hear them at all this morning."

"You didn't hear anything this morning," I chuckle as I put on a pair of pants and let Audrey follow me into the kitchen. "Lily's in school, and Rita is running some errands, so we've got the penthouse to ourselves for a few hours."

She settles by the counter island while I get busy on the espresso machine. "Oh, can you make mine a decaf, please? All this stress ... I really don't need to add caffeine to it."

"Are you sure?" I ask, giving her a curious look.

"Yup," Audrey replies with a flat smile. Maybe I'm paranoid, but I still feel like there's something else she's not telling me. Whatever it is, it won't beat the Bratva princess tale, that's for sure. But I oblige and brew her a decaf, letting her choose her favorite syrup for some extra flavor before she adds steamed milk into the mug. "My gosh, it tastes delicious."

"I made a friend at the coffee shop downstairs and got him to order me a few bottles of what they use in their menu. It has definitely changed my coffee-drinking experience." I pause as I get my espresso brewing as well.

The silence that follows isn't uncomfortable, but it is filled with things unspoken. It's calm enough to fool us into a slight sense of security yet tense enough to make the hairs on the back of my neck prick up with every deep breath that I take.

"I miss my students," Audrey says with a heavy sigh as she gazes out the window. "I can't go back there anytime soon. I'm glad they were able to find a long-term sub to take my class for the rest of the year."

"I am truly sorry, Audrey," I reply, joining her by the counter. "Have you spoken to your brother yet?"

"No," she says. "I saw plenty of missed calls from him, but I was so miffed that he didn't pick up when I actually needed him that I just texted back, telling him I was safe and not to worry about me. He's got enough on his plate."

"You shouldn't push your allies away, especially after what happened last night."

"I don't know, Jason. Sometimes, I wish I could just disappear. Maybe then they would all leave me alone."

"That's not going to happen, either. Whether we like it or not, there's an obstacle standing in our path to peace and happiness. We need to remove it together," I say and kiss her lips gently. "You're not going to be dealing with the Bratva, or anything else for that matter, on your own. I hope you understand that by now."

Audrey gives me a worried look. "You have your daughter to look out for, Jason. I appreciate the gesture, I do, but Lily comes first. You're definitely right about that."

"She and Rita can take an extended holiday to visit Rita's family in Nebraska for a couple of weeks," I declare, texting my secretary and asking her to handle the arrangements. The entire trip itself, including flights and anything else that might need booking, permissions from the school principal, and so on. "They'll be far enough away and out of harm's way. I'll arrange for Lily to do her schoolwork virtually due to a family emergency. If the Chicago Bratva wants to come for me, they're more than welcome to try."

"Jason, they're heavily trained and ruthless bastards. But so were Andrei and Yuri. What happened at the hotel last night, oh, God ..."

The horror imprinted on her face only serves to charge me up even more. "You seem to forget who you're speaking to."

"I'm not forgetting anything. I know your military history. But they're—"

"Baby, I am not going to war with the Chicago Bratva. That's not what I'm saying at all. But we can't cower in fear, either. There needs to be a conversation, first and foremost. I suggest we speak to your brother again. The two of us, together."

Audrey raises a skeptical eyebrow. "I wouldn't bet on Anton to untangle this situation for us. The Fedorov's credibility was partially shot to crap when Grigori's princess of a daughter—that would be me—ran off into the night. Anton told me about the issues they've been having after you left yesterday. The rumors, the unrest. And now, with the Abramovic Bratva looking to muscle their way back into New York, well, the sharks caught the scent of blood in the water."

"We should talk to him, nonetheless. The more support you have from your brothers, the better."

"How do you think we should handle this, then?" Audrey asks. "Because I have no idea. I either go back to New York and let my family protect me, or I leave Chicago and start fresh somewhere else. Those are the only two options I see. And neither one feels right. I don't want to leave you."

She's about to cry, so I pull her in for another kiss, eager to reassure her. I taste the coffee on her lips, the subtle hint of hazelnut lingering between us. "Audrey, you're not going anywhere. We're going to deal with this together."

"How, Jason? You don't know these people; you don't know what they're capable of."

"Oh, I've got a clue, considering what happened the first time they tried to take you," I say, trying not to let my anger get the better of me. "Believe it or not, Audrey, even the Bratva has its weaknesses. We just need to find them. Keep in mind, they will never be above law enforcement or the military."

"There are hidden interests here," she grumbles and lowers her gaze. "The local authorities let them run their shady businesses because a lot of money goes into a lot of political pockets."

"We need to find the Abramovic family's limits. They have to draw the line somewhere, and I bet your brother Anton can help us with the details."

"Okay, I'll call him back," she says and reaches for her phone.

A heavy knock on the front door has us both still as statues for the longest second. Audrey looks at me with fear in her eyes.

"Are you expecting anybody?" she whispers.

I shake my head. "No. Go in the bedroom and lock the door."

"Jason—"

"Do it."

A moment later, Audrey dashes out of the kitchen and runs into the bedroom to hide. As soon as I hear the lock clicking, I head to the front door and look through the peephole. It's Anton. I breathe a sigh of relief and open the door, only to realize that he's not alone. And the look on his face tells me this isn't going to go well.

Standing next to Anton is an older man with similar features. He's in his early sixties with close-cropped white hair and a flurry of fine lines surrounding his cool, blue eyes.

I can see where Audrey and Anton get their icy aesthetic from. The man is well-dressed in a dark grey suit custom-tailored to fit his tall, muscular frame. By comparison, he seems like a titan next to his mortal son.

But it's the four goons they've brought along with them that make my blood run cold.

"What is this?" I ask, keeping my voice down.

Every muscle in my body feels tense, and my senses tingle in the presence of undeniable danger. No matter what happens next, I have to protect Audrey from both Bratvas. No matter what. The elder man puts a hand on Anton's shoulder, prompting Audrey's brother to give me a nervous half-smile.

"Pardon the intrusion," the elder man says in a thick Russian accent. "But I believe you have something of ours."

Anton smiles apologetically. "I tried to keep the old man out of it, Jason, but—"

"But nothing," his father cuts him off with a sharp tone, then looks at me with smiling eyes. "I'm Grigori Fedorov. You must be Jason Winchester."

"I am. And I don't recall inviting any of you over."

"Like I said, you have something of ours, and I'd like it back now," Grigori replies.

"By 'it,' you mean your living, breathing daughter? I'm sorry, she's not in right now," I shoot back.

Grigori scoffs while his goons come closer. Only now do I see the holstered guns on their leather belts and the cold, deadly glares they're wearing, especially for me. I could try and take them on, but I'd be outnumbered. My guns are in the living room safe. Even if I do try to get to them, I won't make it in time. One of these fuckers will shoot me first.

The inability to do anything in order to protect Audrey becomes painfully, stingingly clear. However, I can't bring myself to accept it. My honor demands that I try something. Anything.

"Mr. Winchester, I understand that you have genuine affection toward my daughter, and I respect that," Grigori says. "But Chicago clearly is no longer a safe place for her. I've come to take Audrey home, where she belongs."

"Mr. Fedorov, Audrey left New York for a reason," I insist. "You should respect your daughter's wishes."

"And you should stay out of family business," Grigori warns, his tone sharp and definite.

His goons inch closer as if placing an underline under what Grigori just said for special emphasis. I look at Anton with genuine confusion—the man I see now is not the man I met yesterday—but then I realize that he's no longer in charge when Grigori is around. Anton is cold and calculating, confident and charming, but when his father steps into the picture, he's clearly second in command. With his power diminished, he can't do a thing without Grigori's permission.

"I thought you were going to help your sister," I remind Anton.

"I am helping her. She'll be safe in New York while we negotiate with Arkady Abramovic," he replies.

"Arkady Abramovic?" I ask.

"The firstborn and de facto leader of the Chicago Bratva," Grigori cuts in. "I'm told his father has taken ill. For the past couple of years, Arkady has been pulling the strings in this city, and he's the one who has his sights set on my daughter. I will handle the negotiations while Anton and Vitaly will make sure their sister is protected."

"From what I understand, this Arkady prick is only coming after Audrey because he wants to take a bite out of your turf," I say, raising my chin in defiance.

"It's none of your business," Grigori snaps.

"Anything pertaining to Audrey is my fucking business."

Anton sighs deeply. "Give it up, Jason. He's going to take Audrey away. There's no stopping that."

"Wanna bet?" I hiss as the four mooks barge into the apartment, slamming into me like linebackers.

I try to fight them off, but I'm met with ironclad blocks and an elbow shot that damn near tears my jaw off. I curse under my breath and try again, but Anton is compelled to intervene, shoving me against the wall. He whips out a gun and presses the muzzle against my temple. "Don't move a fucking inch, or I swear to God I'll shoot you," he whispers. "Don't make it worse."

"Fuck you!" I growl.

The four goons go through the living room and kitchen first, then wander through the hallway until they find the master bedroom at the far end. Grigori stays back, hands casually resting in his pockets as he looks at me. "Mr. Winchester, I suggest you calm down. No one can protect Audrey better than me," he says.

"Why are you doing this, Anton?"

"It's not like I had a choice. I tried to go under the radar, but there was always the risk of Papa finding out," he says in a low voice. "Don't move, Jason, I'm serious. Stop fighting this. Audrey's safety is paramount."

"How in the hell is she going to be safe with the very people she ran away from?"

The men burst through the bedroom door, and Audrey screams. I'm compelled to struggle and help her, but Anton's gun reminds me that I can't move. Not without getting my brains blown out, anyway. I don't know these people, but Audrey did warn me that they are ruthless fuckers, especially when Grigori is present.

The man is a fucking menace, and I can see that clearly now. He's a psychopath, a man who thrives when everyone around him is deathly afraid yet still reveres him like a god.

"LET ME GO!" Audrey screams as she struggles, but she is no match against four massive bodyguards.

They quickly slap a pair of cable ties around her wrists and drag her out of the bedroom. Fury takes over, the fury of a helpless man, as I have no choice but to watch as they take my woman away. Audrey tries to reach out to me, but they hold her back and gag her, apparently for good measure. I'm roaring on the inside, burning up as the blood flashes hot through my veins.

The horror in her eyes stabs my heart.

"I'm sorry," I manage as I watch Audrey get carried out of my home, the one place where she thought she'd be safe, the one place I promised her *would* be safe. "I'm so sorry."

"Hello, sweetheart," Grigori briefly salutes his daughter as they take her away, then pauses at the door. "I'd advise you to keep your distance, Mr. Winchester. I have plenty of bullets to spare if you try to intervene. I implore you to think about your own daughter."

I freeze, suddenly reminded of precisely how fucking dangerous this man is. It's an impossible situation.

My survival is everything if I'm to do anything to help Audrey in the future, and my daughter needs a father. I'm torn and inwardly raging, yet all I can do is try to measure my breaths and try not to lose control.

"I don't care who you are. If you threaten my family again, I will show you who *I* am, Mr. Fedorov, and trust me when I say you have no idea who you're dealing with."

"Nor do I wish to find out. So why don't we just go our separate ways?" Grigori replies although I can tell from the look in his eyes that he is quickly starting to realize that he may have underestimated me. "It's better for everyone."

"Not for Audrey, it isn't."

"Audrey is no longer your concern," Anton tells me. "Protect yourself and your daughter. My sister is with her family now."

Grigori leads the way out, and Anton lets go of me with one final warning glare—I need to keep my distance. That's what he's telling me in the absence of words. I give him a slight nod, but I'm sure he can tell I have no intention of letting them take Audrey back to New York by force.

Anton leaves and closes the door behind him.

CHAPTER 19

I'm taken to a hotel in the heart of the city. It's a five-star residential palace with the kind of security that could give the White House a run for its money. Granted, my father came here with what I assume is half of his Fedorov fleet, so the whole place looks extra tight.

Anton says they've occupied a third of the hotel's rooms with their people. They're stationed on every floor of the building, and they've got armed guards working alongside the hotel's own security. The managers couldn't object if they wanted to.

They know who my father is. Fedorov money holds considerable sway in any city.

I am scared out of my mind and virtually helpless, but I've stopped fighting them. The more I object, the tighter my leash is going to be. My blood boils as my father has me escorted all the way up to the presidential suite.

Once we're inside, he stations four men outside my door while Anton double-checks the entire room for any wires or listening devices.

Sitting in a chair by the window, I watch my father as he stands in the middle of the lounge area, his cold eyes scanning me from head to toe. "You're looking good," he says. "The Chicago air seems to suit you."

"Then why take me away?" I shoot back.

"My lovely zaika, you belong with your family until you are married. I'm simply fixing the broken timeline here."

"I belong where I decide I belong."

Anton sighs as he joins us. "Sister, for once in your life, just shut up and listen to the old man. He's trying to talk some sense into you."

He's back under our father's boot; that much is obvious. Anton has always had a slight rebellious streak to him, though he never stepped out of line. I bet his coming to Chicago on his own really riled up the old man.

I can tell from the look on my brother's face that he's in hot water and trying his hardest to make amends. He's in an impossible situation, and it's difficult for me to hold it against him since I know our father just as well. I understand what the old man is capable of doing to get his way.

"So, what? You're just going to drag me back to New York?" I scoff and cross my arms in a rebellious fashion.

"If I have to, yes," my father says. "Though I'm hoping you'll come of your own volition."

"Never. Chicago is my home. It's been my home for two years now. It's not my fault that you can't beat back the Abramovics on your own," I reply bluntly.

Anton shakes his head. "I swear, Audrey, you sure love digging your own grave."

"It's the truth. If they were really fearful of our father, they never would've come after me the way they did."

"Unfortunately, my little zaika, he does have a point. Fortunately, I have a way of fixing that," Papa says.

The past couple of years have not been kind to him. Whether he's hiding some illness or simply aging at an alarmingly faster rate, Grigori Fedorov doesn't look as spry as he used to.

He's still tall and broad-shouldered, impeccably dressed, not a hair out of place, but his face is thinner, the shadows under his eyes have gotten darker, and he seems to have lost some weight.

"What are you talking about?" Anton asks him, somewhat confused. "I thought you only came here to take Audrey home."

"Oh, no," Papa chuckles lightly. "I need to do my rounds while I'm here. Chicago needs to be reminded of their place."

"You can't start a war with the Abramovic Bratva," my brother mumbles.

Papa gives him a sour look. "Do I look foolish to you?"

"He wants a show," I cut in. "He wants as many Bratva lieutenants as possible to see him parading around Chicago without a care in the world, flaunting his wealth and confidence, proving that he is still the top guy in New York like a peacock trying to impress the peahens."

"More like a lion displaying his mane," my father chuckles dryly.

"You're very pleased with yourself, aren't you?" I ask.

"Of course. I've got my family back together, and I'm about to remind those Abramovic monkeys that I'm not to be trifled with," he says. "And once you're back in New York, and enough time has passed, you will understand, my little zaika, that everything I ever did was for the sake of this family."

Oddly, he refers to himself as a lion while he calls me his "little rabbit." It kind of goes against everything he says about protecting our family when I'm the prey or, even better, the bait he's using to prove a point. "So, you're going to marry me off to Piotr like nothing happened," I reply. "Anton told me the old geezer put a price on my head."

"Oh, that was just a tantrum. As soon as he sees you, he'll be over it and will welcome you back with open arms."

"And then you'll go back to business as usual, right? For the family, of course," I shoot back, keeping my tone as flat as possible in order to get my message across.

Papa narrows his eyes at me for a long, uncomfortable second. I think every fiber in his body is screaming at this point, his ego demanding that my attitude be checked. He wants to make me pay for going against his guidelines, but he can't because I'm his daughter.

SEXTING THE SILVERFOX | 179

In the olden days, he would've simply smacked me around a couple of times to put me in my place, but that doesn't work anymore.

He can, however, still control my destiny if I go back with him to New York.

He can hold me hostage until I'm forcibly married to Piotr. I could live the rest of my life as a prisoner in my own home, a shrinking canary in a gilded cage, while he gets what he wants.

"Audrey, this is the life you were born into," my father says, almost echoing my own thoughts. "Just like I was born into it before you. No one gave me a choice, but I made the most of what I had. You should've done the same. You don't belong here in Chicago. It may be different from everything you know, but this is not your home, and that Winchester man is not your family."

"Keep his name out of your mouth," I nearly spit.

What will happen when he learns about my pregnancy? How will he spin that, I wonder? What will Piotr say? I'll be spoiled goods in their eyes. I could tell him now, but that could lead to potentially horrific consequences. He might take it out on Jason or worse. I think I should keep my mouth shut and figure out a way to get out of this.

I can disappear again. I have some money in my savings account to hold me over, at least until I sell the apartment.

"I suppose you're aware of last night's attack," I say, looking at my father and brother. "Anton, I tried calling you several times."

"He was busy explaining certain things to me," Papa replies. "But yes, we are aware."

"What happened to Andrei and Yuri?" I ask.

Anton lowers his gaze. "They didn't make it."

"He lost two good men because he thought he could handle the Abramovic goons on his own," Papa scoffs. "Which is why I'm here. To clean up his mess and yours. Everyone would've been better off if you'd just stayed put like you were told."

"I don't want the life you have planned for me, Papa. And sooner or later, you will need to understand that."

"I don't care what you want, Audrey. I care about what is good for the family."

I raise an eyebrow at Anton, deliberately ignoring our father. "And what does Vitaly think about all of this?"

"As my successor, Vitaly is on board with every decision I make," Papa says.

But Anton lowers his gaze again, and I can tell there's more to this particular story. I'm guessing that Vitaly is not, in fact, on board with every decision that our father makes. But as long as the old man is running the show, he can't say anything about it.

I could play along and wait for Vitaly to take over, but that could take years. And once the marriage contract is signed, it will be damn near impossible for me to get away from Piotr. Oh, God, I can't even fathom a wedding night with that lizard. Hell, no, I need to get out of here.

"Anton will stick around for a little while, but there are armed guards outside your door," Papa adds, but I cut him off.

"Yeah, good, 'cause armed guards worked like a charm the last time," I say, rolling my eyes.

"Nobody will come for you again," Papa insists. "The word is out. They know I'm here. They won't dare to be that stupid. I'll be taking this whole conversation back to them, anyway. Starting now," he adds, briefly checking his watch. He gives Anton a slight nod. "You know what you have to do."

"Yes, Papa."

"And you," he says to me. "For once in your life, set your stubbornness aside and listen to your father. It's for your own good."

He walks out then, and the heaviest silence falls between my brother and me. Anton's demeanor undergoes such a dramatic change whenever our father is in the picture, and I'm left dealing with two completely different versions of my brother.

"At least you didn't tell him that I'm pregnant," I mutter.

"I'm sorry, Audrey," Anton lets a heavy sigh leave his chest. "We both knew this might happen. I only hoped I'd have another day or two to try things my way before he caught up with us."

"They tried to kill me last night."

"I know. We didn't hear about it until the hotel called the police. Andrei and Yuri were supposed to check in with me on the hour, so there was a forty-five-minute window where I actually thought you were okay. But then they didn't check in, and Papa was busy chewing my ass six ways from Sunday. That's why I couldn't pick up."

"I'm sorry, Anton," I say. "I'm sorry he broke you beyond repair."

"Don't talk down to me," he replies. "I'm a Fedorov, and I'm proud of it. Just because you want a life outside this family doesn't mean that Vitaly and I want that for ourselves, too."

"I never said that. But I'm sure the three of us can agree that there are certain Russian traditions that really need to be left behind."

"Not while the old man is still alive."

"Which leaves me screwed, either way," I reply. "Anton, I can't go back to New York. You know that, right?"

He nods slowly. "I can't help you, Audrey. Not now. Not anymore."

"Anton—"

"Don't push it," he snaps and walks out as well.

I'm all alone in this massive suite. On any other day, I would've appreciated the fine design and the opulent luxury a lot more.

But I'm a prisoner here.

I cannot let them take me back to New York. There, I will be truly powerless. I will be radioactive, and nobody will wish to even get close to me, let alone try and help me. New York is deathly afraid of Grigori Fedorov.

Even the mayor owes him a couple of favors, not to mention the state senators who have been living in his pockets for the past few election cycles. The Bratva influence runs deep, and there isn't a single corner in the Big Apple where I will be truly safe on my own.

I need to figure out a way to leave this room and run as far away as possible, at least until all this drama dies down. I need to warn Jason, as well, because if I do somehow manage to escape again, his is the first place that Papa will hit. Nobody wins in this story, that much I know. No matter what path I choose, someone will get hurt.

I can't let myself fall back down the rabbit hole again. My father calls me his little zaika, but I am not his little zaika anymore. I'm a grown woman, and I will fight him with everything I've got until I'm free again. I will live the life of my choosing. I will sacrifice my brother's and my safety if I must. But I will find my way out of this hotel room and out of the Fedorov shackles.

CHAPTER 20

JASON

A day has passed since Audrey was taken from me.

I've been making plenty of calls in the meantime. While I'm not connected or knowledgeable about the Russian mob, I did serve with a wide variety of people in the Army. We spent countless nights in the trenches together, not caring where we hailed from. We were all the same in the heart of war.

"Paddy, you son of a bitch. You're getting younger while the rest of us are getting older," I declare as I meet with one of my former staff sergeants, Patrick Maguire, in his family-owned pub, the Golden Shamrock.

The cops know this place well. The Irish mob owns it. It's where they run some of their business, even though the judicial system was rarely able to pin anything on them. Patrick is the youngest of the Maguire clan, heavy hitters in the aforementioned Irish mob. He's the only one who can give me some intel about the Bratva.

Ironically, we never talked about his family or their dealings while we were in the service, nor after we came back. Today, however, is different. Today is the day I cross every boundary I swore I'd never cross in order to get my woman back and save her from whatever nasty fate awaits her in my absence.

"That's a crock of shit," Paddy replies and traps me in a bear hug as he steps out from behind the bar to greet me. "You look ten years younger, my brother!"

"I just dress better," I chuckle.

"How've you been, Jace? It's been ages!"

I nod at one of the corner booths. "I need a word in private."

As soon as the words come out of my mouth and he registers the tension in my voice, Paddy's body language changes. He's not the warm and friendly, red-haired and green-eyed, freckled pub owner who's nice to everybody anymore. Now he's downright menacing.

"What's wrong, Jace?" he asks, his tone low.

"I need your help."

Immediately, he barks a few orders at his bartenders, letting them know that he's going to be busy for the next hour or so, then makes sure we get some of today's specials brought to our table straight from the kitchen, along with a couple of draft beers.

"I haven't seen you look this serious in a long time. Tell me what's going on?"

The music is loud, so I carefully look around and then lean across the table. "I've got some Russian mob issues, Paddy. You're the only one I can trust to help me."

"Holy shit," he mutters, his eyes wide with shock. "They've been dropping a lot of bodies since yesterday. You have anything to do with that?"

"No."

Indeed, the news outlets have been flooded with reports of suspicious deaths sprinkled all over the city. Various Russian-mob-related individuals keep popping up dead, either poisoned or hanged, each of them tied back to the Abramovic family. There have also been a couple of Fedorov-linked deaths, as well.

"There's a silent war happening between the Fedorov and the Abramovic Bratvas," I tell Paddy. "And it all tracks back to Audrey, Fedorov's daughter."

"How are you connected, though? I thought you were a straight arrow, man."

"I still am. But Audrey and I—"

"Oh, no," Paddy instantly puts two and two together and starts shaking his head. "No, man, that's the worst thing you could become involved in. And your daughter ... oh, man, no, get as far away from them as possible."

"Not an option, Paddy," I insist. "I love her, and she loves me. She ran away from her family. Moved out here a couple of years ago. She wants nothing to do with the Bratva but somebody in Chicago recognized her. They told Arkady Abramovic about her and that maniac has tried to kill her—

twice. And now, her father has come to Chicago and taken her away."

Paddy pinches the bridge of his nose. "And he's letting Arkady know that he won't tolerate any attacks on his family."

"From what I'm told, Arkady is trying to muscle his way back into New York. He wanted to use Audrey as leverage," I say.

"Dumb move. Grigori is a weathered wolf, Jace. He will burn this whole city down before he lets a single Abramovic set foot in New York."

"Either way, the gauntlet has already been thrown," I sigh. "And Audrey and I got caught in the middle." I go on to tell him about how we met, about the secrets and lies that nearly tore us apart, about the attempts on her life, and Grigori's visit to my apartment.

Paddy listens quietly while the waitress brings our food and drinks over, but I can't eat or drink anything. I'm too wired, too anxious, too eager to resolve this before it's too late. "I need to know everything there is to know about the Bratva, Paddy."

He thinks about it for a moment, then takes a long sip of his beer, quietly looking around. Contemplating. Likely wondering whether he should play the neutral part or help me. I get it—the Maguires don't want to deal with the Russians. The Irish and the Russians steer clear of each other, in general. It's the same in New York, from what Audrey told me. Sort of an unspoken pact dating back decades.

"Here's the thing, Jace," Paddy finally says. "I can't do anything to help your girl out. Lord knows I'd send some guys over to the Aspinall in a second."

"The Aspinall?"

"That's where the Fedorovs are staying. The whole underbelly of Chicago knows about it," he says.

"You've already told me something new," I mutter. "I've been trying to find her since yesterday."

Paddy chuckles dryly. "I can imagine. But if Grigori doesn't want you to find her, you won't. Listen to me, Jace, and listen carefully; I can't get involved."

"I'm not asking you to—"

"As soon as you leave this table, I won't know you anymore, you hear me?"

I give him a confused look. "What do you mean?"

"Whatever it is you're going to do with the information I provide, I can't be linked to it in any way. So, for safety's sake, let's consider ourselves strangers once this conversation is over. It's the price you got to pay for what I'm about to tell you."

It pains me to hear him say such things, but I get it. He's next in line to take over the Maguire empire. That's a lot of men, plenty of businesses, and billions of dollars. Dark money that ultimately feeds into the city. He cannot be perceived as a rat or a snitch. The old-school mob game is still on, and snitches still get stitches. They still put cement shoes on people in Chicago, and I don't want Paddy to take the fall for anything pertaining to my mission.

I nod slowly. "I understand. Okay."

He takes a deep breath before he begins. "Back in the early 1900s, the Fedorovs and the Abramovics ran New York together. There were the occasional skirmishes, but they got along for the most part. The cops couldn't do anything about them, so they just let the Russkys do their thing, provided they paid a little tax under the table if you catch my drift."

I nod again. "I see. What happened?"

"Prohibition. That brought out the worst in everybody, including the Bratva. They didn't get along anymore. The Fedorovs wanted to try different avenues, but the Abramovics were keen on smuggling booze. The latter declared war, and the former gave it to them a little too hard. What was left of the Abramovic family took off and sought refuge in Chicago," Paddy says. "Not long afterward, Hitler rose to power. The war left the city ripe for plucking, and the Abramovic Bratva were there to fill in for the Irish and the Italians. By the end of the 1950s, they were just as big and as influential."

"As were the Fedorovs in New York, right?"

"Right. The 1980s, however, started to get even more interesting. Cocaine was the game, and everybody got into it. Igor Abramovic, Arkady's father, played that game, and he played it hard. When Grigori took over the Fedorov Bratva, he focused more on the guns and other illicit substances, even banning cocaine deals on his turf."

"They were still at it, then, even from afar."

"Of course. The war never ended between the two families. And the Abramovic fellas have been keen on going back to New York since before they left," Paddy says. "I'm telling you this so you'll understand precisely how stubborn Arkady Abramovic is about New York. That man carries the grudge of entire generations, while Grigori carries his. Audrey is but a pawn."

"I need to get her out of there."

"In order to do that, you need to know where each of the Bratva bosses are headed, what they're doing, who they're talking to, who they're in business with. You need intel, Jace, and I can give that to you. But like I said, it'll cost you."

"Our friendship. I get it. I'm sorry."

He smiles gently. "I know love when I see it, brother. I can't blame you."

"So where do we start?"

"Grigori Fedorov. This isn't his first visit to Chicago, but it's the first *official* one. He's come around before if only to personally monitor certain spies he's had living here since the early eighties."

I feel my eyebrows arching upward with surprise. "He's invested, then."

"More of a micromanager. He's the same with his sons, mind you. Long after Vitaly takes over the Fedorov Bratva, Grigori will still be pulling the strings from behind the curtains. The old man won't stop running the show until he takes his last breath," Paddy scoffs. "But that's a good thing because he's also a creature of habit. Very particular about where he sleeps, what he eats, who cooks his food, who brews his coffee … I mean, the man has taken every page out of a Russian dictator's playbook and made it his own."

"I can track him based on these habits."

"Yes, and I'll send you a text after you leave here with a list of his known aliases. I know you're still in touch with Ronnie."

"He's in the Bureau's Chicago field office," I confirm.

"Ronnie can help you with those aliases. Use him. The kid worships you. He'll do anything for you."

"He caught a bullet for me," I sigh, briefly remembering the incident in Fallujah that cost Ronnie his kidney but saved my life when we were ambushed. "I'll run it by him. Thank you, Paddy."

"I'm not done," my friend says. "You need to know a few things about Arkady, too."

And so, I sit quietly while I listen to his tales about Arkady Abramovic, about his business dealings and operations across the city. It's enough information to paint a clear picture of the monsters that I'm about to go up against.

It also gives me spectacular insight into a world that, up until a few days ago, seemed surreal, like something out of a Hollywood movie. Ever since I got out of the Army, I steered clear of asking for favors from the men whom I served with. The situation I've found myself in now, however, demands that I make a few more calls—one to Ronnie, in particular. I need the help of my brothers in arms if I'm to do this right.

"You might have to get your hands dirty," Paddy warns me.

"Yeah, I'm aware."

"Do you still have your sniper rifle?"

"Yeah."

I keep it in a locked cabinet in my home office. It's been years since I even opened the case, let alone fired a single shot. Paddy nods slowly. "You're going to need it. You won't be able to get close enough—"

"Long range, huh? I can't just hand the intel over to the Feds?"

"Not without burying me," Paddy says, his brow deeply furrowed.

"I'd never do that."

"It's the cost of doing business with the mob, Jace. If you want Audrey, if you really want her, you have to be ready to do for her what you did for this magnificent country of ours."

The thought hits me like a hammer to the gut. I've considered the possibility already. It didn't sit well then, and it doesn't sit well now. But if push comes to shove, I'll do it. I'll tap into my darkest side and let the monster out to play again. I just need to make sure I don't forget who I am in the process. Otherwise, I will never be able to look my daughter in the eyes again.

"I will never be able to repay you, Paddy," I say to my friend.

"Just don't call me if shit hits the fan, Jace. The Irish boys can't help you."

CHAPTER 21

JASON

The next morning finds me outside the Gordon Office
Building, owned by Lisa Abramovic, a front for the
Chicago Bratva. It's supposed to be neutral territory,
housing some big financial companies and a couple of
restaurants, but Ronnie warned me that it is rife with
Abramovic goons. All it takes is one wrong move, and I
might find myself dismembered by one of Arkady's
bodyguards.

His office is on the top floor; that much I know for sure.

Wearing my best suit and a pistol strapped to my ankle
discreetly hidden under my pants, I walk into the main
lobby and stop by the reception desk.

The receptionist looks up from the computer while I briefly
scan the lounge area, immediately spotting the on-duty
Abramovic guards sitting sipping coffee and pretending to
read the newspaper while they keep stealing glances at me.

"Hi there, Melinda," I say to the receptionist, her name tag
pinned to the pale blue lapel of her jacket.

She gives me a pleasant nod and a smile. "Good morning. Welcome to Gordon. How may I help you?"

"My name is Jason Winchester from Winchester Holdings. I'm here to speak to Arkady Abramovic."

"I'm sorry, there's no one here by that name," Melinda says a little too fast.

One glance over my shoulder tells me I'm definitely in the right place. The goons, albeit impeccably dressed in black suits, have already stood up and are confidently walking toward me, so I shift my focus back to Melinda, looking calm and unbothered.

"I think we both know that's a lie. He's expecting me, I assure you."

"Mr. Winchester, I'm truly sorry, but we don't have—"

I give her a wry smile. "Melinda, just call him up," I say, cutting her off.

A split second later, I see dread in her eyes as I find myself flanked by the two massive and likely heavily armed gentlemen. I take deep, measured breaths and keep my cool when I feel the muzzle of a gun pressed into my ribs.

"I suggest you leave," one of them says in a thick Russian accent.

"And I suggest you tell Arkady he'll want to speak to me. I may not be one of you fellas, but I've got enough useful people on speed dial to make sure your boss never opens another fucking taco joint in this city going forward," I bluntly reply as I stand my ground.

To my relief, Melinda is already on the phone, muttering something into it while looking at me with a mixture of fear and concern. Once she hangs up, she nods at the two men. "Mr. Abramovic says he'll speak to Mr. Winchester," she says.

Instantly, the gun disappears from my side, and I turn to the guy who held it against me. "You really need to work on your manners."

"Search him first," Melinda says.

Fuck. Well, I should've seen this coming.

I exhale sharply. "Before you so eagerly start fondling me, let me be honest. I did come packing," I say, prompting the two men to instinctively reach for their weapons again. "No need for violence. I'm just letting you know. And now, I will slowly reach down and take the piece out for you to hold on to until I leave, okay? I want it back when I'm done. It's a family heirloom."

The second bodyguard nods once, and I stay true to my word. Slowly, I crouch down and remove the gun from my ankle holster, holding it up with two fingers. He takes it and then motions me toward the elevator. "Come on. He doesn't like to be kept waiting."

"After you, fellas."

Once we're on the top floor, the entire atmosphere changes. If downstairs is intended to be warm and welcoming, up here is supposed to be as intimidating and threatening as possible.

The walls are a dull grey. The floor is sleek black, and shiny enough to display my reflection. The lighting is minimalistic and brutal, and the temperature is uncomfortably cold, part of the psychological warfare that Arkady Abramovic wages against anyone who dares to come into his lair.

I find it interesting that he chooses to keep his office here, hidden among the mortals, camouflaged by finance bros and corporate heads.

I would imagine it's hard for the Feds to waltz into this place as often as they'd like. They would require warrants, and Arkady knew that when he designed it. He's more exposed to rival mobsters here than he is to the cops.

"Nice digs," I say as I'm unceremoniously shoved into Arkady's office.

The door slams shut behind me.

I stand in the middle of the room, quiet for a second while my eyes scan the space. Everything is black, an annoyingly clean black. The desk and chairs are stainless steel and thick glass. It wreaks of toxic masculinity.

He sits behind his desk, an evil emperor overlooking his domain.

Sitting on the guest sofa are two large wearing dark grey suits that are a little too small for them and black ties. They look at me with murder in their eyes. I'm guessing these are the guys who taste Arkady's food and drinks for him, just in case someone thinks about spiking his dinner with polonium.

"Jason Winchester," Arkady says, half-smiling as he looks at me with ice-cold eyes. A scar on his temple catches my eye. His hair is close-cropped, military style. His skin is pale.

He's bulky enough to intimidate but still looks good in an Armani suit. "I never imagined I'd see you here."

"Honestly, I never planned on coming here," I reply with a casual shrug. "But you kind of forced my hand. And it's time for you and me to have a little chat."

Arkady gives his men an amused glance, but I don't bother to pay them any attention. The key here is to exude confidence without appearing as a threat.

"So, what is it you wish to talk about?" Arkady asks me.

"It's private," I say, nodding toward his bouncers. "They need to leave."

He laughs. "You're audacious, I'll give you that."

"I was already searched downstairs. I'm not here to cause trouble, but the information I have is far too sensitive. It's for your ears only."

"Entice me," he says.

"I believe we both share a common enemy. A certain old wolf named Grigori. I know how to take him down."

And there it is on his face. The sparkle of curiosity. The hunger. The greed that takes over and clouds his otherwise calculated judgment. I've struck gold, just like Paddy said I would. Arkady thinks about it for a moment, then gives his men a brief order in Russian. They clearly aren't happy about it, but still, they oblige and leave the room.

I take a step forward.

"All right, you have my attention, Mr. Winchester."

"I'm here to help you."

"Help me, then. Just get on with it already; I have other meetings scheduled for the rest of the day."

"Very well," I say as I take out the secondary gun I have in the back of my pants. The guys downstairs were too distracted by the weapon I mentioned and offered to them— they didn't search for another. The second piece of brilliant advice that Paddy gave me. "So, here's the deal. I need you to leave Audrey Fedorova alone."

Arkady's good humor fades as he stares down the barrel of my 9mm.

"I was wrong. You are not audacious. You are downright stupid," he mutters.

"Relax, Arkady. I'm not here to kill you, though that would certainly take care of one issue. I really am here to talk, but not just about Grigori."

"The daughter."

"That's right. Stop coming after her. Fight her father and brothers all you want. Kill one another and be done with it, as far as I'm concerned. But leave her out of this. She's not with them, she will never be with them, and she deserves freedom from what has already been a difficult life as a Fedorov."

He gives me a wry, overly confident smile. "You love the little rabbit, don't you?"

I ignore his question. "I'm more than happy to negotiate potentially fruitful business transactions between Winchester Holdings and whatever front you've got running in this building. I'm sure my money would be put to good use."

"You want to buy Audrey's safety," Arkady says.

"Either that or I will blow your brains out right here, right now. It's your choice."

"Not really a choice, though, is it?"

"You've pushed me past my limits not once but twice."

He shrugs and lets out a sigh. "I do not care for you. Frankly, I do not care for Audrey, either. And I don't know what you're talking about."

"See, this is insulting. It's making my trigger finger itchy," I say.

"Mr. Winchester, have you ever considered the possibility that maybe the Fedorovs are the ones who tried to take her? I've heard about the incidents, and frankly, if I really wanted to hurt Grigori, I'd simply find Anton or Vitaly in any of their New York brothels and send their heads over on a silver platter."

I find myself somewhat confused by his words. "What the hell are you talking about?"

"I'm an efficient businessman, Mr. Winchester. If I wanted to kill Audrey, I would've killed her. I can see why someone might want to grab her, perhaps thinking that they'd be doing me a favor. An action I certainly do not condone, I might add. But I heard about what happened at the hotel the other night, and I assure you, that wasn't us."

"Who was it, then?"

"Isn't it a coincidence that as soon as the little pup Anton set foot in Chicago, there was an attempt on Audrey's life?"

"You're telling me the Fedorovs tried to kill one of their own?"

Arkady shrugs in an almost dramatic fashion. "Meh, I wouldn't say kill her, per se. More like scare her enough for her to go running back into her daddy's arms."

My blood runs cold and my stomach drops as I begin to understand the implication behind his words. And now, it's starting to make sense. Grigori Fedorov is a cold, ruthless man. His sons are either his accomplices or his pawns. Either way, that whole shootout at the hotel could very well have been staged.

How do I prove it, though?

"Would you be able to point me in the right direction? I've got a bone to pick with the people who shot at Audrey," I say. "If you are innocent, Arkady now's your chance to send this hunting dog as far away from your scent as possible."

"I can tell you where they're staying, but I would advise against going in there half-cocked like this," he replies, somewhat amused. "Grigori is in town on business, and he never travels light."

"He's in town on business with you."

He chuckles lightly. "You could say that. I got his message loud and clear. He's a fool to think he can make me kneel before him."

"How many people does he have with him?"

"Expect at least thirty, and all of them excellent marksmen," Arkady replies. "But I should warn you—tonight's not a good time to try anything. Morning is your golden hour, during the guard's shift change."

"You seem to know quite a lot about their movements," I say.

"Of course. A good general learns everything they need to know about the enemy."

That's unsettling but logically correct. I know I'm not going to get much more out of him. Something tells me Arkady is doing me quite the courtesy already. He probably has a panic button under his desk, and if he wanted me out of here sooner rather than later, he would've pressed it by now.

He didn't, which further proves that Arkady was not responsible for the hotel attack. Therefore, it strengthens his theory. Grigori and Anton—either one of them or both—orchestrated it, then swooped in to grab Audrey from my place.

I have to get her away from them and fast, one way or another.

CHAPTER 22

I've yet to figure out a way to escape. Security is too tight. Along with the two guards constantly outside my door, the entire floor has been strategically occupied, and they've got armed men on every level handling the staircases and elevators, making sure no one suspicious slips past them.

Anton comes in every other hour, bringing me food and drinks. He's careful not to say anything about our father's movements, each time trying to strike up a more casual conversation instead, but I tell him off every time. I'm too angry with him to do anything else.

"Vitaly is here," he says as he brings me a fruit salad from the hotel's restaurant. "He would like you to join us for dinner downstairs this evening."

"What's he doing in Chicago? Who's manning the mother-ship back in New York, then?" I frown as Anton sits across the table from me, watching as I scarf the salad down, one juicy chunk at a time. "And I'm pretty sure I'm not allowed to leave this room, so how am I supposed to join you for dinner?"

"Our father is due to meet with Arkady in about an hour," Anton replies, "to put an end to this whole skirmish and negotiate a ceasefire. We've done enough damage to get the bastard interested in peace talks, so that's a good thing."

"I asked you something else entirely."

"Papa called Vitaly in to talk some sense into you while he handles the business side of things," my brother says and sighs deeply.

I scoff. "He couldn't trust you to get me to come along nicely, huh?"

"Can you blame him?"

"No, and I can't blame you, either. You can bring Vitaly in to try, but the outcome will always be the same—sooner or later, I'll get away from you again. You'll find me in another couple of years, drag me back, and then I'll run off once more. Over and over, until you all understand that I do not belong in New York, I do not belong with the Bratva, nor do I want to be there."

Anton's eyes search my face as if he's trying to figure me out. Oddly enough, he is one of the very few people in this world who actually knows me. I don't know what's left for him to learn. "You've grown stronger," he says.

"What do you mean?"

"You weren't so determined to piss off Papa before," he says. "You'd just say yes to whatever he demanded, but then

204 | K.C. CROWNE

you'd go and do things your way anyway. You've gotten bolder. You have courage."

"Where did that get me, huh? I'm still a prisoner."

"I can't help you, Audrey. I wish I could. Honest to God, I did try."

I shake my head slowly. "Well, technically, you could. But I get why you won't."

"As for who's manning the ship, it's Derek."

My brow furrows with brief confusion until I remember who he's talking about. "Ah, Vitaly's right-hand man. Is he still alive?"

"And kicking," Anton chuckles. "The guy's a hard-ass. He may not be a Fedorov or even Russian, for that matter, but he is made of steel, and he is beyond trustworthy. Papa allowed him to take Vitaly's seat in our brother's brief absence. Of course, you know Papa also has eyes on Derek."

"Yeah, he probably knows what time Derek takes his morning dump, too," I mutter.

My brother cannot disagree. It's the truth. Our father will continue to run the New York Bratva for as long as he can draw breath. Whoever is put in charge, whether it's Vitaly, Anton, or any one of their trusted lieutenants, our father will always have one hand on the wheel and his foot on the gas. The man takes micromanagement to a whole new level. He's a control freak. No wonder he's so adamant about bringing me back into the family and forcing me to do his bidding.

But I'm not giving in this time around.

I've seen what life is like outside our family. I want my freedom now more than ever.

A couple of hours later, I join Anton and Vitaly in the restaurant downstairs. To my surprise, the whole place has been reserved for us. There are no other customers, just the three of us, while six men stand outside the glass doors to steer anyone else away. I can tell the staff isn't comfortable with this arrangement, but they are courteous and hospitable, nonetheless.

"Please, tell me you paid handsomely for this dinner," I tell my brothers.

Anton was nice enough to shop for some dresses and shoes earlier in the afternoon, so at least I'm looking the part.

Vitaly can't take his eyes off me. I notice he's gathering a few fine lines under his grey eyes. He looks more like our mother. Not a day goes by that I don't imagine what our lives might've been like if she were still alive.

"What is it, Vitaly?" I ask, my tone clipped as I refuse the waiter's offer to pour wine into my glass. "I don't want to drink. Is that a problem?"

"Not at all. I'm just admiring you, little sister," he says, half-smiling. "You've grown."

"I was done growing way before I left New York"

He gives Anton an amused glance. "You were right. She's meaner."

"No, I'm just tired of having to deal with you people after I specifically made it clear that I didn't want anything to do with you," I shoot back, prompting the two of them to give me their signature puppy dog eyes. "Oh, don't give me those looks. You know damn well that I don't want to be here."

Vitaly leans forward while the waiter carefully backs away from our table.

"Audrey, for what it's worth, we've kept our distance and we've kept our father in the dark regarding your whereabouts," Vitaly says.

"But you still don't have your spines fully developed," I grumble.

"You tried; I'll give you all the credit in the world for that," he says. "But it's time for you to admit it, little sister. There is no life outside the Bratva for a Fedorov. There never was."

"It's no use," Anton chimes in. "She'll scram the first chance she gets."

"Until then, however, we need to try to convince her to accept reality. Because even if she does run off again, our father will keep hunting her."

"And I'll keep running until he dies. He's not going to live forever," I reply.

"Audrey, let me put it this way. For Jason's sake, you'd do well to obey and return to New York with us," Vitaly says. "You know Papa will do whatever it takes to make sure you never think of running away ever again."

"And he expects me to just smile and wave as he marries me off to some old, impotent fart who, up until yesterday, still had a bounty on my head," I scoff.

"We're still trying to talk him out of the whole arrangement with Piotr," Vitaly sighs. "I need a bit more time for that. But I promise we'll find something agreeable for everyone involved."

"The only scenario that is agreeable for me is if you let me go right now," I say. "Nothing else matters. I've built a life here, Vitaly. I'm happy. For the first time in my miserable existence, nobody cares who my father or brothers are. Nobody knows me."

"Well, the Chicago Bratva knows," Anton reminds me.

Bitterness lingers on the back of my tongue but I don't have a snappy comeback for that particular remark. I notice a frown pulling Vitaly's eyebrows tightly together as he swirls the red wine in his glass.

"Something is bugging me," my oldest brother says.

"What's that?" Anton asks.

"I get the kidnapping part, but why'd they try to kill her the other night?" Vitaly replies. "It doesn't make sense. Audrey would be more useful to Arkady Abramovic alive, not dead. Her death would only lead to an all-out war that not even the Feds could stop. The streets of Chicago would run red with blood. Our father may be the way he is, but I know for a fact that he would burn the whole city down if Audrey were to ever—"

"Don't even say it," Anton cuts him off, genuinely startled. "I don't want to think about it."

"Vitaly's right, though," I say. "What was the point of them trying to kill me?"

It's a good question. Unfortunately, none of us have the answer. Only the certainty that the feud between the Fedorov and the Abramovic families must be resolved sooner rather than later before it gets worse.

"There is one thing I can guarantee, Audrey, when all this is over," Vitaly says.

"Amaze me," I grumble.

"Jason and his daughter will be safe. I spoke to our father, and he gave me his word. The Abramovic Bratva will know to never go anywhere near them," he replies.

"Does that come with some kind of condition? Come on, spit it out. Papa would never do me a solid where Jason is concerned. There has to be a catch."

Vitaly smiles. "Assuming you stay put and stop embarrassing him."

"So let me get this straight. If I'm a good girl and do as I'm told, Papa will make sure that the Abramovic Bratva never touches a hair on Jason or Lily's heads. But if I run away again, he will no longer be responsible for whatever might happen to them, am I right?" I ask, my blood running hot and cold at the same time.

"Basically, yes," Vitaly says, his gaze softening slightly. "I'm truly sorry, Audrey. You don't deserve any of this, but it is the hand that you were dealt. You have to play it. You can't leave the table."

The conversation isn't going anywhere, and they cannot help me. Our father's grip on them is simply too tight. Unshakeable. They were conditioned into their roles and responsibilities, and while they may have averted their eyes from choices I made for myself, our father wouldn't allow it.

Therefore, they must enforce his will, whether they like it or not.

As long as Grigori Fedorov is alive, I will never truly be free, nor will I be able to fully rely on my brothers for support.

I must fend for myself.

As the hours pass, my brothers switch from wine to vodka. After the last of the dessert plates are cleared from the table, we linger, talking about our childhood—happy memories, of which there are few; not-so-happy memories, of which there are some; and terrible memories, of which there are plenty. We wouldn't be the people we are today without them, but I dare imagine a version of myself that didn't require all that suffering to become precisely that.

I'm stone sober, and I watch in mild amusement as my brothers ramble on in a mixture of English and Russian, reminiscing with glassy eyes about what it was like when Mom was still alive.

"She was beautiful, wasn't she?" Anton asks Vitaly.

"You barely remember her," Vitaly sighs. "You were so little when she passed. Audrey even more so."

"I still see her in my mind's eye," I tell them. "It's a vague picture without an actual photograph for reference."

"Time tends to do that to people. It makes us forget," Anton says. "Eventually, you'll forget all of this, too. Someday, you'll need a photograph for reference when you try to remember what Jason Winchester looks like."

"Wow, you went straight for the heart with that one, huh?" I mutter, crossing my arms.

Anton smiles wryly. "Just telling it like it is, little sister. In my defense, I really did try to help you out."

"I know."

It's past midnight, and most of the restaurant staff has gone home, except for one waiter.

I should try to get some sleep, too, but my current situation has me constantly frustrated and restless. My gilded cage is closing in around me, and there are moments when I feel like I simply can't even breathe.

Glancing past the glass doors, I see our family's private security detail. Six men, each of them tall, dark, and menacing. There's a subtle yet nagging feeling pecking at the back of my neck. Something doesn't feel right. The men stir, and a long shadow stretches into the hallway.

Vitaly's phone buzzes. He briefly checks the screen before he answers. "Yes, let him in," he says and hangs up, giving me a troubled look. "Arkady Abramovic is here."

"Wait, what?" Anton mutters. "Isn't he supposed to be in a meeting with Papa right now?"

"I thought so, too, but the guys at the door checked him for weapons. He's clean. Says he's just here to talk," Vitaly replies.

As soon as the restaurant doors open, my heart stops. I freeze in my seat while my brothers get up to cautiously greet the man. I've seen him before. *The scar on his temple.* He was the one watching my apartment. He's the one who tried to kidnap me. He had his arm around my waist. My blood runs cold as ice, and sweat blooms along my temples as I watch him casually approach our table.

"My apologies for interrupting your dinner," Arkady says, then gives me a warm smile that makes my skin crawl. "Forgive me, Miss Fedorova."

"For what? For stalking and trying to kidnap me? For trying to kill me the other night?" I spit out, my tone harsh as anger takes over.

"What are you doing here, Arkady?" Vitaly asks with a furrowed brow. "Where is our father?"

"Oh, he's fine. Probably still at the Stadium, waiting for me to show up," Arkady chuckles dryly. "It's not him I wish to speak to. It's you, Vitaly."

My eldest brother seems confused. "I don't understand."

"Grigori is old. One foot is already in the grave. But you and I, we can do some great business together," Arkady says. "I just want that bastard out of the way first. He's got his boot so far up your asses; you don't even realize what a privileged position you find yourselves in."

"This isn't right," Vitaly says. "Our father should be here."

"Hello, did anybody hear me?" I snap. "This prick tried to kidnap me!"

Anton nods once. "We're well aware, and I'm hoping it's one of the reasons why he is here tonight. Perhaps to apologize?"

"Are you seriously trying to be nice to him?" I croak. "Our father would never—"

"Your father isn't here, though, is he?" Arkady hisses, giving me a hard, ill-tempered look. "For what it's worth, I do apologize. It was never my intention to hurt you, Miss Fedorova. Only to make good use of your presence in Chicago."

Vitaly shakes his head and proceeds to call our father. "No. Papa needs to be here."

"Ah, I now see why the old hound still runs the family business. You two are positively spineless," Arkady declares.

My skin tingles all over. Something wicked this way comes, and I can't pinpoint it. I'm paralyzed, staring at Arkady as he carelessly debases my brothers while he callously smiles at me.

"If this is your way of addressing peace talks between our families, you're off to a really bad start," Vitaly says. "I've reached out with an olive branch before, and you ignored my messages. Yet when our father came into town, you went all-in, guns blazing, and now you want peace talks? What gives?"

Arkady tips his head. "I may have overplayed my hand. I've rarely had to deal with Grigori but my father did warn me about him before I took over, and based on the recent events, I can certainly see why I should've stayed in my lane."

"That you should have," Anton scoffs. "What did you think was going to happen once you had Audrey?"

"Anton," Vitaly tries to shut him up, but Arkady waves his concerns away with the flick of his hand, smiling in a most unsettling way.

"Now, now, he's entitled to his opinion," he says. "I haven't exactly abandoned my original plan. A man's weakness can be found in his children. And I figured I'd make the best out of a bad situation when Audrey slipped through my fingers. It was only a matter of time before I'd get all three of you in the same room."

"What are you talking about?" Vitaly asks, understandably confused.

The words leave my lips before I can process them. "It's a ruse," I whisper.

"A what?" Anton asks.

"I just needed the old fucker out of the house, so to speak," Arkady replies and takes out a small gun from his jacket pocket.

I scream.

He shoots Vitaly first.

My scream pierces the restaurant's heavy silence, echoing across the room.

Anton reaches for his gun, but Arkady fires his next shot. My brothers are both down, each injured and bleeding on the floor, their eyes wide with shock as Arkady points the gun at me. I cannot move. I cannot breathe. Fear grips my senses, and my survival instincts tell me that I need to be still.

214 | K.C. CROWNE

"The trouble with Grigori is that his men don't respect him as much as they used to, and since his sons are still under his thumb, they haven't made themselves worthy of such respect, either," Arkady casually remarks. "Do you have any idea how little it cost me to bring twenty of your men into my fold, Audrey?"

"What?"

I follow his amused gaze somewhere beyond the glass doors and realize that our security detail are all still there, quiet and unmoving, watching as Arkady commands the room.

They betrayed us.

Arkady bought them off, and they let him walk in here with a gun. I don't know if the people we have upstairs are also on his side, but it doesn't really matter anymore. He's got me.

"It was a matter of when, not if," he says.

I glance down at my brothers. "Vitaly," I cry out and try to reach him, but Arkady pulls me away, squeezing my arm so tightly it hurts. "Anton!"

"They'll be fine. I didn't nick any arteries; relax," Arkady replies.

"You son of a bitch!" I scream.

He smacks me hard with the back of his hand. "I won't tolerate disrespect," he says, suddenly transforming into a cold, ruthless bastard. He raises his hand to hit me again.

"No! I'm pregnant!" I blurt out, wincing as half of my face is stinging from the smack.

"Oh," Arkady stills, hand still in the air, eyebrows arched with genuine surprise. "Oh, that's interesting. It doubles your value, sweetheart."

The pain spreads through my jaw as I struggle to keep a clear vision. Arkady grabs me by the back of the neck as I steal one last glance at my brothers. They're alive but severely injured, and if they don't get medical help soon, they could die. Oh, God, this can't be happening.

"Come on, we've got places to be," Arkady snarls as he drags me out of the restaurant.

"Do something!" I scream at the treacherous bodyguards who stay behind, watching us leave with sour looks on their faces. "Call for help!"

Anton reaches out for me. I can see him, albeit briefly, on the restaurant floor just before I'm dragged out into the lobby. I cannot help him. I cannot even help myself. The one thing I feared has come to pass—Arkady will use me against my father.

CHAPTER 23

I'm in a dark room with shuttered windows. Through the cracks, I can hear the occasional traffic outside. I'm guessing it's early morning. I believe I'm somewhere on an upper floor, but I don't know much else since I was too scared and in shock to pay attention to the details. I'm still in the city; that much seems clear, though I'm not sure where exactly.

Judging by the grime on the walls, the dank smell hanging heavily in the air, and the layers of dust meeting my fingers whenever I touch a table or a windowsill, it's an abandoned building, probably an old, condemned apartment building.

I hear footsteps outside, most likely Arkady's men watching my door. They exchange words in muffled Russian.

The floor creaks under my feet, so I move as little as possible. I don't want to draw anyone's attention, not even for a second. I struggle to wrap my head around what just happened, wondering what's coming next.

I don't know much about Arkady's plans. He wasn't that talkative after we left the hotel. I've been on my own for the past couple of hours, sitting here in tomblike silence, shaking like a leaf, and praying to all the gods to keep my baby and me safe. This unborn child of mine deserves better.

I keep thinking of Jason. I wonder where he is and what he's doing. Is he safe? Are Lily and Rita safe? Is he looking for me? I hope he sent them away like he said he would. They need to be as far away from Chicago as possible until this storm passes.

I'm not sure when that will be, however. The game that Arkady and my father are playing is a dangerous one, and I doubt it will end cleanly. Someone has to lose, and when the victor is announced, the streets of Chicago will be bloody either way.

Whether it's Arkady's or my father's blood remains to be seen.

I just want to get as far away from this hot mess as possible. I miss my kids, my job, my life before it all went tits up. I had a semblance of peace and a promise of love and happiness dangled in front of me like a carrot on a stick.

My mind is plagued with horrible scenarios and grim possibilities. I keep trying to find something better to think about, something good to hold on to. Every time I'm tempted to curl up in a ball and cry myself into a never-ending sleep, I remind myself of the life that is growing in my belly, this innocent soul who deserves a brighter start than anything I or my brothers had.

Suddenly, I'm startled by the sound of approaching footsteps. They are heavy and determined. The door is unlocked and swings open and a river of light suddenly pours into the room from the hallway.

"Arkady," my lips move in a timid whisper. "What do you want?"

The smell of freshly brewed coffee hits my nose, and I start to think my thoughts have turned into hallucinations. I was just thinking about coffee, wasn't I?

"It's decaf," Arkady holds the paper cup up for me to see. "I wouldn't want to hurt your baby just yet."

"Just yet?" I mutter.

"Ideally never, but your father can be a stubborn, ill-tempered mule. I'm not a fan of violence against women, Audrey," he says. "If push comes to shove, however ..."

"That's very reassuring," I try to add sarcasm to my voice to mask the fear.

He chuckles as he walks across the room, leaving the cup on the table next to me. "Sorry for the absence of lighting," Arkady says. "The wiring in this place is a mess. This whole building is scheduled to come down sometime next month, so everything has been cut off. Lighting, running water, gas, all of it."

"I hope I'm out of here long before that happens."

"Believe me, Audrey, I don't want you to be here for that, either."

"Then what exactly do you want?"

Arkady takes a deep breath, then pulls up a chair so he can sit in front of me, leaving about five feet of space between us.

"It's all about power, Audrey. Power and influence," he says. "My forefathers were fools to leave New York in the first place. I'm just taking back what was always ours."

"So, all of this is about territory?"

"The minute you disappeared from the family, I knew something was off. My men in New York told me about the rumors, about Piotr's bounty on your head, about how your brothers were scrambling to find you before Grigori could," Arkady says. "That told me plenty about your daddy dearest, Audrey. A man who cannot control his own family can hardly control an entire Bratva. I'm like a shark in the water, and I caught the scent of blood."

"How did you track me down?"

"I didn't," he laughs. "That's the beauty of this entire moment. I didn't track you down. A former Fedorov enforcer saw you and followed you back to The Emerald Residence. Then he came running to my office, hoping he'd earned himself a favor with me. He wouldn't tell me why he'd moved to Chicago in the first place but putting two and two together was a no-brainer for me. So, I put a bullet in his head instead, then planned my operation carefully around you."

"Why kill him if he gave you my whereabouts?"

Arkady stares at me for a long, uncomfortable moment. "I don't condone treachery, Audrey, even if it serves me in the end. That man was quick to sell you out after having sworn to your brothers and father that he would forever be loyal to the Fedorov Bratva. Yet he walked into my office and sang like a fucking canary. I can't trust someone like that."

I shiver but deep down, I understand his way of thinking.

"I don't know how well you planned that operation of yours, though," I add, glancing over his shoulder. I see two men flanking the doorway, and I'm guessing there are more stationed all over the building. "You didn't exactly catch me the first time. You didn't kill me the second time, either."

"I never planned on killing you," Arkady says. "But I'll tell you what I told your boyfriend—that hotel ruckus, that wasn't me."

For a second, I'm lost. My mind feels blank, unable to process any of the words coming out of Arkady's mouth. "What are you talking about?"

"Jason Winchester popped by to see me. He's been looking everywhere for you, trying so desperately to save you. That's a good man right there, Audrey. It's a shame I beat him to you," he adds with a mirthless laugh.

My head is spinning as he takes out his phone and snaps a quick photo of me. The flash from the camera temporarily blinds me, and I hear the clicking sound of his onscreen keyboard.

A split second later, his phone rings. "Ah, he's quick," Arkady laughs and answers, tapping the speaker icon in the process. "Hello, Grigori."

"What the fuck are you playing at?" my father's voice growls through the phone and echoes across the room. I can feel his fury reverberating and burning through my veins.

"Dad?" I call out with a whimper.

"Audrey!" my father gasps. "Are you okay?"

"Dad, don't—"

"Hush, hush," Arkady cuts in. "I'm only letting you hear her voice so you know I'm serious. It took a while, but hard work pays off." He motions for me to shut up.

"What do you want?" my father asks.

"What I've always wanted, but I'll go easy on you. Give me East Harlem first," Arkady replies. "East Harlem, and I'll make my way into the South Bronx by New Year's Eve."

"Or else, what?"

"Or else you get Audrey back in itty-bitty pieces. I went easy on your sons because I figured they might still be useful, Grigori. Don't forget that. I got to them once; I will get to them again, so imagine what I'll do to your precious little angel here and her unborn baby if you don't submit to my demands."

My father curses heavily in Russian, prompting an amused chuckle out of Arkady.

"Dad, where are Anton and Vitaly? Are they okay?" I ask, tears stinging my eyes.

"They're both in surgery," he says. "Those deceitful fuckers at least called an ambulance before they ran off."

"Dad—"

"What did I just say?" Arkady hisses, giving me a deadly glare before clearing his throat. "It's time for the Fedorov and the Abramovic clans to learn how to share the same playground again. We're coming back to New York, whether you like it or not. But I'd rather do it nicely."

"You call shooting my sons and kidnapping my daughter nice?"

"It's better than shooting my way through your entire organization and hanging all four of you by your entrails from the top of the Empire State Building, isn't it?"

My father scoffs. "I'm willing to have a conversation about this as long as you don't lay a finger on Audrey."

"That's the spirit. Tonight, eight o'clock sharp. I'll text you the address. Just you, Grigori. No security. No cops. Nothing. Just you, or the next time you hear from me, is when the courier delivers the first pieces of Audrey to your doorstep. Tread carefully, old man."

"If your father were alive, he'd—"

"He'd pat me on the shoulder and congratulate me for having the balls to do what he and my grandfather have always wanted. Your glory days are over, Grigori. You might as well come to terms with that before you lose what's left of your family."

He hangs up.

The silence that follows as he stares at me and I stare back at him is so heavy that I can barely breathe. He is a cold, calculating man, and I believe him. He will absolutely chop me into bits and pieces to prove his point. Arkady Abramovic doesn't care about anyone or anything except himself and his desires.

Right now, his greatest ambition is to bring his family and his operations back to New York.

Even if my father does give him what he wants, how long before he takes more and more and tries to get rid of my family for good?

CHAPTER 24

JASON

There are so many cops outside the hotel. Blue and red flashing lights are everywhere. Neighbors and passersby have gathered around the yellow tape as the crime scene investigators buzz in and out of the building, constantly liaising with detectives and a few suits—my guess, federal agents.

Whatever happened in there was serious enough to close off the entire street. Reporters are moving closer and closer to the scene, only to be dispersed by carefully positioned beat cops. Everybody has a job to do, and each one revolves around keeping the ground floor of the hotel clear of any interference.

I'm in the driver's seat of my car, parked a safe distance away but close enough to see everything that's going on. My contacts in the police department aren't picking up; I'm guessing there's probably a lid on the whole thing, and our friendship doesn't supersede their duties. I get that, and I can't blame them. I am, however, frustrated and angry because I can't see Audrey anywhere.

Cautiously, I get out of the car and make my way across the street, my gaze constantly scanning every person in sight. I catch bits and pieces of conversation from people surmising what happened even though they weren't around when the incident in question occurred. I try not to pay them any mind, but the buzzwords coming out of their mouths still get to me.

"Mob hit," a lady tells her friend.

"Russian," another guy says. "Somebody got shot. They took a girl."

I stop in my tracks and give the man a startled look. "Where did you hear that?"

"Officer Friendly over there," he says, pointing out a rookie cop with big eyes and not enough meat on his bones to keep everybody at bay. His partner keeps giving him dirty looks, but he's busy getting a statement from one of the waiters, so I have a window of opportunity, albeit a small one.

Arkady told me where to find Audrey. But I shouldn't have heeded his advice on timing. Clearly, that was a massive mistake. I should've been here last night. Whatever has happened—I pause and take a deep breath, not yet ready to berate myself for trusting the wrong Russian—I am ready to accept that none of those Bratva fuckers are to be trusted. Ever.

I reach the rookie cop and give him a slight nod. "Hey, officer. Sorry to bother you. I'm supposed to be meeting someone in there. What happened?"

"Who were you meeting, sir?" the rookie replies.

"My girlfriend." That is not exactly a lie.

"You'll have to meet elsewhere. We've sealed off the entire ground floor, and guests have been advised to use the service entrance."

"I suppose you have officers stationed there, as well," I say.

"Yes."

"What happened?" I insist.

The rookie glances over his shoulder, briefly content to see his partner is still busy. "A shooting," he tells me.

"I heard somebody was taken?"

He looks around again, growing increasingly nervous. "I can't give out any more information."

"Who was taken?" I ask, my tone clipped as my patience wears thin.

"A woman," he finally says. "I didn't catch her name, but the detective said they're putting a BOLO out on her."

As if summoned, I hear engines roaring as a slew of black SUVs come rolling past the roadblocks. Camera phones are snapping. Murmurs rise from the swelling crowd behind me. The detectives in charge are agitated and start barking orders. This is it. My window is closing, and I need to get more information, one way or another.

Somebody took Audrey right out from beneath the Fedorovs' noses. It makes me sick to my stomach, knowing I am back to square one or worse. I feel like a complete fool as I keep replaying my conversation with Arkady Abramovic in the back of my mind.

Urgency blows through me, yet I need to keep my wits sharp and my temper in check as I analyze the situation and take a few steps back.

I can't speak to anybody among the investigators, but I can still watch the scene unfold and pick up a few more details before I leave. I have no idea where to go from here, though. I can't go back to Arkady. They won't even let me back inside the building after I threatened to kill him. I bet they'd shoot me on sight.

The cops are definitely out of the question. They're here cleaning up what looks like a mess of amplifying proportions. I have friends in the Bureau, and if my instincts are correct, this has the potential to grow into a massive RICO bust.

I have information they might be interested in. I'm sure they have plenty of data already gathered on the Fedorov and the Abramovic Bratvas over the years. I might as well try that avenue.

I spot a couple of detectives coming out of the hotel with a Fedorov bouncer in tow. The man is scared out of his mind, pale-faced and covered in sweat, his black suit soiled with dust and cobwebs. Where the hell was he hiding? Some closet, probably. Slowly, I slip past the yellow tape line and slide between crime scene investigators, casual in my approach as I try to get closer.

"Where'd you find him?" an agent asks as he gets out of one of the black SUVs. His windbreaker says he's ATF.

"Broom closet," one of the detectives chuckles.

They cuff the guy and keep him standing outside the SUV while the ATF agent asks him questions. I can't hear everything on account of all the commotion unfolding around me, but I do get enough bits and pieces to figure out what happened.

"Abramovic bought them off," the disheveled bouncer says. "The guys discussed it and decided to take his money. They offered me money, but I didn't want it."

"But you had to take it," the agent replies, playing the sympathy card. "Otherwise, they would've killed you. They couldn't risk a rat, right?"

"Da," the guy says. "I had to take it. But I wanted no part in what they were planning."

"I need a gurney," a paramedic shouts from the crowd.

Tape tears somewhere to my left.

Reporters are clamoring closer, the beat cops no longer able to effectively hold them back, but ATF backup comes in— broad-shouldered gentlemen with the authority and the ability to push the media farther away from the front of the hotel.

"Old man Grigori will kill me," the bouncer squirms as they shove him in the back of a van.

"You'll be fine," the ATF agent tells him.

He'll go into protective custody, most likely. They'll cut the guy a deal if he talks, which means a shit show is about to hit Grigori's doorstep. But if Audrey was taken, I doubt the bastard even cares about what's happening at the hotel right now. I need to find him.

My phone rings. It's Rita. A perfectly efficient distraction. "What's up, Rita?" I ask as I make my way back behind the yellow tape and lose myself in the crowd.

"You need to come home now."

"I thought you and Lily left this morning," I reply, a knot quick to form in the back of my throat. "What's wrong?"

"Now." She hangs up.

My senses expand as fear grips me tightly, its claws digging deep into my flesh.

CHAPTER 25

JASON

I manage to drive home in record time, practically jumping out of the car and flying up the stairs until I reach my apartment. The door is unlocked, and the silence is deafening. I stop in the hallway and look around, waiting, listening. Subtle clicking sounds drizzle in from the living room. Lily's laughter.

"What the hell?" I whisper and storm in, only to freeze at the sight before me.

Rita sits in one of the armchairs, framed by two men the size of bulldozers, both clad in black suits and sporting guns on their leather belts. Russians. No doubt about it because Grigori fucking Fedorov is playing checkers with my daughter at the ivory game table.

She has no idea who this man is or what he's doing here, my innocent angel. She's just glad someone took the time to play with her.

"Grigori," I manage, my voice weak, my legs threatening to give way.

He sits comfortably in his chair, a warm smile stretching across his face whenever he looks at Lily. I don't see cruelty in his eyes this time. I see something else, something profoundly human, fatherly, an emotion I can definitely relate to—pain wrapped in thick layers of fear.

"Mr. Winchester, I do apologize for the intrusion," Grigori says, his tone even and calm.

"Hah! I beat you! Again!" Lily quips, delivering the final move across the game board.

Grigori laughs wholeheartedly. "That you did, little zaika; that you most certainly did. Congratulations on a game well played!" he pauses and gives me a long, hard look before his gaze softens back to my daughter. "I'm afraid your daddy and I have some business to discuss now. Would you please excuse us?"

"Lily, honey, why don't you and Rita go back to your room and wait for me there?" I suggest, keeping a strained smile on my face. It's hard to keep my composure with armed mobsters so close to my daughter.

Rita cautiously gets up and motions for Lily to follow her, but my daughter wants to hug me first. "Daddy!" she says. "Can we play checkers when you're done? Mr. Greg taught me how to play."

"Of course, baby," I reply, gently stroking her pink, warm cheek. "Go with Rita now."

"Okay!"

"I'm so sorry, Jason," Rita tries to tell me, but I wave her apology away.

"It's fine, please. Just get her out of here," I reply quietly so Lily doesn't hear.

Once my daughter and Rita are out of the room, I feel as though I can breathe a bit better. Though I'll be able to take a full inhale when Grigori and his goons are on the other side of the fucking continent.

"What in the ever-living fuck are you doing here?" I hiss, working twice as hard not to charge at him, not to break every bone in his body. "Where's Audrey?"

"That is why I'm here," Grigori replies, then points at a chair across the table. "Please, have a seat. We need to talk."

I'd rather beat him to a pulp, but his security detail won't let me. Besides, I've clearly reached a point where all options are nothing more than possibilities. Working with the Feds, working with the Bratva, working with anyone who might help me get Audrey out of this mess before it's too late. Whomever, whatever it is, I'll take it.

Grigori stares at me for a long, torturous minute, his eyes searching my face.

I stare back; my jaw clenched as I take my seat, the checker-board between us, pieces left strewn across. He is torn and tired, that much I can tell. There are smudges of dried blood on his white shirt, partially hidden by the teal jacket he's wearing.

"What happened at the hotel?" I ask.

"Arkady Abramovic happened. He played the game well; I'll give him that," Grigori replies.

"Details, Mr. Fedorov."

"He arranged a meeting last night, only he never showed. He had his secretary and a few other so-called associates keep me busy at one of his restaurants while he went back to the hotel, shot my sons, and kidnapped my daughter."

My stomach drops. In hindsight, I was a fool to trust Arkady.

"Your whole security team turned against you," I say, trying so hard not to kill the bastard with my bare hands.

Grigori nods. "He bought them off. Gave them enough money to secure new lives for themselves. I was a fool to think loyalty was still a thing, but I listened to Vitaly's advice and went soft on my people. Played for honor instead of fear. And now, Vitaly is in surgery, fighting for his life. Anton should make a full recovery. And Arkady has Audrey."

"He played us both," I mutter. "This must've been his plan all along."

Grigori frowns. "He played everyone from the very beginning. I know you are former military."

"That I am."

"I cannot go to the police. They will want to make a deal. They don't care about Audrey."

"And you do?" I scoff.

"I am here, aren't I?" Grigori snaps. "I cannot trust my own people, clearly. I only have you, Mr. Winchester, the only man still standing who is willing and able to assist me."

"What the hell do you want me to do, Mr. Fedorov? If Arkady Abramovic has Audrey, he's calling the shots," I reply.

Grigori shakes his head slowly. "He wants to meet. Just me, him, and Audrey. He wants to negotiate. But I don't trust him, and I know it won't be just the three of us. I'd like you to be there. I will provide you with whatever you need, but I want my daughter safe and sound and as far away from that bastard as possible."

"There's a catch here, right?"

"Yes."

I take another deep breath, my skin getting tighter with every exhale. My body temperature rises, the blood rushing to my head as I try to think of a way to follow through with this. It requires tapping into my dark side again. I did it before to save Audrey; I will do it as many times as I have to. But I don't like the hard look on Grigori's face.

There are strings attached, the kind I might end up hanging myself with if I'm not careful.

"What's your deal, Grigori?" I ask.

"I need you to kill Arkady Abramovic and anyone who comes near Audrey and me during that meeting. I have the location, and I can provide you with blueprints and any other technical details that you might need. You were a sniper in the Army, right?"

"Right."

"I will require that skill tonight, Mr. Winchester. And then, I will take Audrey back to New York with her brothers. She will return to her family safe and sound. In return, I will forget that you ever existed, and you and your daughter will always be safe from the Bratva, provided you don't try something stupid. It is the only deal that I can offer."

"You cold bastard," I growl. "You know I'll take it because I love Audrey, and I want her safe."

"Precisely. All is fair in love and war, is it not?"

Nausea unfurls in my throat, a bitter taste glazing my tongue as I look at this man and wonder how a marvelous creature like Audrey came to be with half of his genetic profile.

"You disgust me," I say, peculiarly calmly.

Grigori flashes a smile. "I am well aware. But we need each other, at least for tonight. After it's done, you have my word. No one will touch you or your family. No one."

"You don't deserve your children," I reply. "Even Vitaly and Anton are too good for you. Loyal men, capable men. I know enough about them from Audrey to actually understand why they are still in your service. They love you, but you don't deserve their love."

"I don't deserve much of anything, Mr. Winchester, which is why I always take what I want. It's how I was raised, and it's how I intend to leave this world. Until then, however, it is my solemn duty to uphold the Fedorov values against any and all who try to make a move against us. And right now, Arkady Abramovic has my daughter, the woman you love, in his clutches. Surely, you want to get her away from him."

"I want to get her away from anything pertaining to the Bratva."

"I'm afraid that's nothing more than wishful thinking."

I can see why he says such things. I wonder if he's aware that there is already a plan hatching in the back of my head. Ideas forming. Ways to take advantage of this complex web of lies and treachery.

Grigori doesn't know that I know about his involvement in the kidnapping attempt on his daughter. Audrey doesn't know he had a hand in it. Arkady doesn't know I'm here, negotiating with Grigori. He probably thinks I'm the ultimate stooge after his little game of so-called cooperation. I'll be only too happy to prove them all wrong.

"Fine, Grigori. I'll help you. I'll handle Arkady if that's what it takes to save Audrey."

"I'm glad we're able to reach an agreement," he says, offering his hand.

I shake it. Firmly. Briefly. But it's enough to give him that smidge of confidence that he clearly so desperately needs.

CHAPTER 26

AUDREY

As night falls over Chicago, I am taken out of the stinky apartment and loaded into the back of a black sedan. I'm getting flashbacks of the first time that Arkady tried to take me, and I can't help but wonder about him, watching him join me in the backseat. He is looking downright giddy and excited. It's as if he's going to the county fair with his prized cow. It irks me.

"How come you do so much of the dirty work yourself?" I ask.

The driver pulls out into the main road while I fiddle with the end of my zip tie. I don't think I can loosen the damn thing. Its edge is eating into my skin.

"What do you mean?" Arkady replies, casually looking through his phone and texting.

"You were there; I saw you," I tell him. "Watching The Emerald, watching *me*. You were there with your men when you tried to take me the first time."

"With a precious asset such as yourself, Audrey, I had to make sure. First, I needed to confirm your identity. You know how rats can be—they chatter but there's no substance. Second, I needed to be present in case things went sideways."

"They did go sideways," I shoot back with a smirk.

He shrugs. "Yes, well, I didn't take the ex-military boyfriend into account. Lesson learned. But then your daddy dearest came to town, and everything changed."

"Is that why you tried to have me killed back at the hotel?"

"I'll say it again because you clearly missed it the first time. That wasn't me."

"I don't believe you."

Arkady shrugs while I gaze out the car window. It's tinted, but I still have a decent view of Chicago's crummier streets as we're taken across the south side to what I presume is our rendezvous point.

My chest tightens along with my throat with each turn. I struggle to breathe as I try to figure out my future. It's all so uncertain now that I am not in control, and the odds are stacked against me. I cannot escape, nor can I fight these monsters.

I don't want to go back under my father's rule, either. That will be a different kind of death for me. The death of my soul. But what Arkady just said has my interest piqued. "If that wasn't you, who was it then?"

"Maybe you should ask your father," he says.

I nearly laugh. "You're trying to insinuate that my own father tried to have me killed?"

Arkady lets a smile curl the corners of his mouth for a long, lazy second as he stares at his phone. "Here's the thing, Audrey. This world is made up of two kinds of people—predators and prey. Sorry, make that three. I forgot about the bottom feeders. Three kinds of people. The predators, well, you're sitting next to one right now, and you should consider it an honor."

"Your over-confidence will be your undoing."

"Just stating the facts. I took down both of the Fedorov heirs and grabbed the daughter on my way out. It didn't even take that much of an effort, just enough cash to get the bottom feeders interested. That's what bottom feeders do, Audrey, which is why I choose my people carefully, while your father picks them out of any Russian-speaking crowd. Did you know, by the way, that over half of my employees are, in fact, genetically eons away from Russian bloodlines?"

"No, I did not know that."

"Russians can be fiercely loyal, yes, but in Russia. In America, the game is played differently. There's a reason why the Bratva here is so unstable and the families relatively easy to dismantle. The old heads come in with the old-school values, but the turf is new. It's fresh. The grass is green, and capitalism thrives here; it moves everything. In Russia, you rule with an iron fist and just enough polonium in your cupboard to get the message across. In America, it's all about the Benjamins."

"So basically, you're telling me that you can buy anybody, including my father's supposedly most loyal servants."

"Precisely, which is why you're in this predicament now, and why Grigori will have no choice but to abide by my demands, and why I will return to New York on behalf of my forefathers, stronger than ever and victorious, and why Grigori will eventually lose more territory in less than a decade. If his sons survive, they will have little left by the time he's dead and buried."

This man is either delusional, or his plans have been so carefully and intricately hatched that there is no room left for any kind of error. It may sound like madness to most, but I am his prisoner, my brothers are in the hospital as we speak, and Arkady is about to meet with my father so they can negotiate the terms of my rescue.

It makes me sick to my stomach to admit it, but I'm starting to think that Arkady may, in fact, do everything that he set out to achieve for himself and for the Abramovic Bratva.

"Ah, we're here. Come, now, little rabbit, put on a warm smile for your papa," Arkady quips. "He's going to be so relieved to see that you're still alive."

Ahead is a massive warehouse with rusty, corrugated iron panels covering the walls, a crumbling roof, broken windows, and flickering white lights burning inside. We're in the rougher side of Chicago, one of the former industrial sectors that used to thrive in the first half of the twentieth century.

All around us are similar derelict buildings—former storage facilities and factories, mostly. Old, box-shaped structures with aging facades and dusty courtyards filled with equipment left to rust and gather mold and grime. This whole block is perfect for mob and drug deals. There are no security cameras, half of the streetlights are broken, and it's far enough away from any residences that anyone could get murdered without anyone bearing witness.

"Come on, little rabbit," Arkady says, motioning for me to step out of the car.

"Stop calling me that," I snap.

He laughs. "Sensitive, aren't we? Those daddy issues run deep." But then, his good humor fades, the mask slipping from his face. "Now, get the fuck out of my car, Audrey."

I bite the inside of my cheek and do as I'm told, my eyes carefully surveying the area. I spot his goons quickly— there's about a dozen of them standing next to their slick, black SUVs—but I see a few more scattered across the property as well. They move in pairs, circling the building and communicating via radio, while another car waits outside by the gates, the lights off.

A few minutes pass while Arkady speaks to one of his lieutenants. I keep quiet and listen, my ears picking up noise in the background.

"He's coming," Arkady's lieutenant says. "Robbie just confirmed. One minute out."

"Is he alone?"

"Yes. Dark green Volvo, Illinois plates. Busted taillight."

"Good. Anyone following him?"

The lieutenant shakes his head. "No one except our guys."

"Grigori finally understood the assignment," Arkady mutters, a broad smile cutting across his pale face as he looks at me.

"There he is," Arkady says, watching as a dark green Volvo pulls into the courtyard.

I see my father behind the wheel, his cold blue eyes already scanning us. There's a glint of relief when he notices me, and all I can do is nod in acknowledgment.

He stops the car and carefully gets out while Arkady's security guards pat him down.

"He's clean," the lieutenant says.

"Welcome, Grigori," Arkady states, smiling disingenuously. He stays close to me, making me feel increasingly uneasy. I am his shield, whether I like it or not, because we can both sense the silent rage oozing from my father.

"Arkady, you piece of trash," Papa says, then gives me a short but comprehensive glance. "Are you okay, Audrey?"

I shrug in return. "So far, so good. Thanks for asking." My tone is deader than the Dead Sea. None of these men deserves any respect or sympathy from me. I'm just a fucking bargaining chip.

"Let's hear it, Arkady. Lay out your terms," my father says, sighing deeply, hands at his sides.

I take a moment to really observe him. His body language and choice of clothing say more than he ever will. The jeans and black boots tell me he's ready for trouble if push comes to shove. It's been a while since he's been directly involved in violence of any kind, but Grigori Fedorov is a former heavyweight boxing champ, revered and reviled in the Bronx.

His black shirt and smart grey Armani jacket tell me he's come to talk business. He wouldn't want to get any blood on it. But he will if he has to.

"I thought I already stated my terms," Arkady tells my father, then takes out a folded contract from his jacket's inner pocket. "I even drafted them on paper. All I need is your signature."

"And who is going to verify this? Who's going to sanction it? You speak as if there's some higher Bratva court that's going to legalize this thing," my father scoffs, unable to hide his contempt.

"It's for my peace of mind. It's what I will hold up for you to read while I peel the meat from your daughter's bones, should you ever think of double-crossing me," Arkady bluntly replies. "I consider myself a fair man, Grigori. I'd like to make a fashionable return to New York, not a bloody one. Securing your signature on this piece of paper will get the other families on board, and things can be official. So, if ever you decide to fight me, I'll have the paperwork handy for them to know they need to keep their fucking distance while I kill you all. Does that make sense?"

The Fedorovs may be leaders of the New York Bratva, but they're not the only ones. There are others, smaller families and clusters, gangs and organizations. At this point in time, they have sworn their allegiance to my father, paying protection taxes to the Fedorovs in exchange for being able to do business in New York. If someone like Arkady comes in from the outside, these people will fight alongside the Fedorovs.

But they are also annoyingly strict. If Arkady dangles a paper with my father's signature on it, then the same families and clusters are honor-bound to stand back because if a man like Grigori Fedorov goes back on his word, then he is not a man, nor is he someone worthy of following into the fire. He will lose all credibility.

And the Fedorovs alone are not enough to stand against Arkady and his men. That much even I know.

I look at my father and wait for his reaction as he reads through the contract, one page at a time.

"You've done your homework; I applaud you," he finally says.

"I had to," Arkady replies, "out of respect for the Bratva."

"However, you will never get what you want."

My jaw drops. *What?*

Arkady's bravado falters, and he gives my father a confused frown. "You do realize what's at stake here, right?"

"I do," Papa says. "And I'm telling you what is going to happen, even if I do give you what you want. I'll give you a chunk of my territory as per your request, but you will never get the support you desire. New Yorkers are a different breed, Arkady. You don't know them like I do. You will never get them in line."

"That's my problem to deal with, not yours."

"It will become my problem because your inadequacy will lead to unnecessary violence," my father says calmly. "It will spill out into the streets, and the NYPD is remarkably well-staffed. You'll inevitably bring more cops to our doorsteps. And that's when the others in the Bratva will demand that I take action. They will look to me for guidance and protection."

Arkady cannot believe what he's hearing. I bet he's never been told no before.

"I will take what is mine, whether anyone in New York likes it or not," he says. "But I really don't want to do it by beheading your daughter. Think about it, old man. You're not cut out for this game anymore."

"Your youthful spunk is just that," my father replies. "You're a flash in the pan. I have years on you, Arkady, and I know your father was just as reckless, just as foolish. But at least he knew his place in Chicago. He stuck to his lane, while I stuck to mine because he understood the New York spirit. You cannot handle us."

"Funny you say that because I believe I handled your kind pretty well back at the hotel. How are your sons, by the way?"

The jab is meant to deliver a gut punch to my father, but the Fedorov wolf is not easily rattled. There are moments when I despise him, yet this is one of those rare instances where I find myself admiring him for his self-control and composure.

I see it now. The reason why New York is ultimately behind the Fedorovs. My father may be a cruel and ruthless man, but he is also poised and unshakeable.

"Vitaly and Anton will both make a full recovery," Papa says, and it does take some of the edge off for me. "And I would like my daughter back now, Arkady. I'll give you what you want, but you will not be able to keep it."

"Sign this, then," Arkady says, nodding at the contract. "Prove you're a man of your word."

"Prove you're a man of yours first. Release Audrey."

"That's not how this works."

"Then how am I to trust you?" my father asks. "What stops you from killing us both once I sign this paper of yours, Arkady? Do I look like I was born yesterday? Don't insult this old wolf."

To my surprise, this gets on Arkady's nerves. He takes out his gun and waves it around, having lost most of his patience. "Listen to me carefully, Grigori. I don't have the time or the patience for your bullshit. Sign the fucking contract and take your daughter away. I have no intention of killing you or her. How will the other Bratva families of New York respect me if I'm the one breaking his own bond?"

"You did say you buy people's loyalty," I mutter, quick to pick up on my father's game. He wants Arkady to get mad, to lose control, to let his ego take the lead. "It's how you got me out of the hotel, isn't it? You paid our people off."

Arkady gives me a sour look. "like I said, I am a man of my word. I need this contract signed, and as much as I hate to admit it, I need you alive in order for those New Yorkers you praise to take me seriously. You said it yourself: I'll have a hard time with them. I'll have an even harder time if I off both of you right here right now."

"You sound like you mean it, but you have a tell," my father says with a chuckle. "Did anyone ever tell you that?"

"What the fuck are you talking about, old man?" Arkady snaps.

"Your voice gets just a little bit higher when you lie," he says. "It's almost indistinguishable, but I've heard it enough to pick up on it. See, that's the difference between you and me. Yes, I am old; yes, I am a traditionalist, and yes, I'm a dying breed. However, I have experience. I'm a couple of decades ahead of you, which means I've met my fair share of liars and charlatans, many of them better dressed and decidedly smarter than you."

Arkady stares at him for a few seconds, and it's as if the whole world has stopped spinning on its axis. Even his men are quiet, motionless, as they look at us. My breath is stuck in my throat, the air thickening in the room. I can almost feel the electricity crackling in the atmosphere, lightning licking at my skin, and pricking the hairs on the back of my neck.

Unpredictable people like Arkady are exceptionally dangerous when they're thrown for a loop. They get reckless, and I can tell from the tone of his voice that he is extremely close to losing it.

"Grigori, you're a piece of work," Arkady says with a forced laugh, a strained cackle that speaks volumes. "Here I am, offering to give your daughter and your unborn grandchild back in exchange for a signature, and here you are, making everything way more difficult than it's supposed to be. Just take the offer, man. I'll make sure to tell the New York families that you fought hard to keep your empire intact, I promise. Just don't make me do something I've never done until now. I don't kill pregnant women, Grigori. Don't push me."

My stomach sinks.

My father's eyes dart around us, then somewhere farther up. They linger there for a brief second, and I'm tempted to follow his gaze, but he smiles and looks at me next. "Everything will be okay, my little zaika, I promise," he says.

"That's funny, coming from the man who sent hitmen after his daughter so he could swoop in and save her," Arkady cuts in, gun still waving around.

"What are you talking about, Arkady?" I ask him, my mind suddenly blocked, unable to process anything. But as I look at my father, as I see the color drain from his cheeks, I manage to put two and two together, and nausea rushes up to my throat. "Oh, no .... You .... sent those hitmen to come after me. Anton's bodyguards, you ... killed them ..."

"He didn't, actually. Andrei and Yuri are currently watching over your brothers' hospital rooms," Arkady replies with a contemptuous smirk. "Anton will be pissed off when he wakes up, of course. I'm told he had absolutely no idea."

"Oh my God," I shudder to my core. "Papa, what the fuck did you do?"

"I needed to bring you back into the fold. You had to see precisely how dangerous Chicago could be for you," my father calmly replies.

"So, you sent people with guns to shoot at me after the Abramovic goons had already tried to kidnap me? That's a whole new level of deceit and depravity, even for you."

I think I'm going to be sick.

I'm lightheaded, wobbling sideways as I put a bit of distance between Arkady and me. He shakes his head in sour amusement while my father folds the contract back. "I did what I had to do to put my family back together, and I will never apologize for that," he says.

"Dad, seriously," I gasp, unable to believe what I am hearing. Yet, to my own astonishment, I am not as shocked as I could be. I know the man too well. It's not that preposterous when I consider how far I know he would go to make his point and get what he wants.

"Audrey let's talk about it another time," my father says.

For the first time in ages, I note a tinge of nervousness in his voice. He keeps looking around, and I'm starting to think there's something else going on here, something no one has any clue about except my father.

"What's happening?" I ask him, but he doesn't answer. He just keeps looking around.

Arkady frowns and glances over his shoulder, following my father's lead.

CHAPTER 27

JASON

A udrey is carrying my child.

Grigori clearly knew about it, yet he chose to push through with his evil plan. Did he know she was pregnant when he orchestrated his so-called assassination attempt? Did he knowingly put Audrey in harm's way just to manipulate her? My blood has reached its boiling point, and a muted rage takes over.

I don't feel like shouting or snarling or breaking everything in sight. I'm all too familiar with this strange calmness. I have felt it before, and it was a prelude to horrible things, things of my own doing. Grigori Fedorov tried to play me against Arkady Abramovic, while Arkady did the same.

Smack in the middle, Audrey was left to fend for herself— scared, defenseless, pregnant, and vulnerable.

The rage I am experiencing is otherworldly and so intense that I need deep and measured breaths to keep my eyesight focused. I picked the highest spot across the yard atop a neighboring warehouse. The night sky, the absence of functioning streetlights, and my position next to a massive air conditioning unit are all excellent tactical advantages.

None of Arkady's goons have seen me, not even his long-range spotters. I can see all of them, however, and from this vantage point, I can easily take as many of them down as necessary. My sniper rifle is an M110 SASS, perfect for this target-rich environment.

I honed my skills on this baby, and one shot can reach hundreds of yards. I've done that before successfully.

When Grigori proposed I use my sniper skills tonight, I had my doubts as to where it might end. My heart was heavy, knowing that I might have to let him take Audrey away, despite already knowing the depraved lengths he went to in order to keep her under his control. But knowing that she's pregnant changes everything, including my own mindset. I love her. Deeply. I love her too much to let her go. My instincts are calling, demanding I do the right thing, no matter how wrong it might seem.

That's my woman they're using as a bargaining chip.

My woman. My child.

I cannot allow this farce to continue. As Grigori and Arkady quarrel, I can hear them through my earpiece. I can hear Audrey's furious gasps.

"Grigori, this is the only chance you're going to have," Arkady warns him. "Stop stalling and get that pen out. I've got places to be, people to see, hands to shake. And your daughter deserves the finest prenatal care available."

"Your pride will take you to your grave," Grigori says.

252 | K.C. CROWNE

That's supposed to be the code word. *Grave.*

All right, Mr. Fedorov. Let me show you what I'm capable of when you cross me and when you take me for a brawny fool. My rifle is loaded, and my scope has a precise angle.

The wind is blowing from the east slowly enough to warrant a clear shot at this range.

My finger squeezes the trigger while I hold my breath to stay motionless in my position.

FLIT.

The silencer works wonders.

The bullet pierces Arkady's back and exits through the front, exploding his heart in the process. Blood gushes outward as he falls to the ground, suddenly lifeless.

Audrey screams and jumps back.

Grigori moves to grab her, but I'm not done yet. While Arkady's men scramble in shock, trying to take cover before I empty the whole magazine in their asses, I shift my crosshairs onto Audrey's father. "You're not taking her away from me ever again," I whisper.

For a split second, I'm torn.

He's still her father. If I kill him, will she ever forgive me? Will she understand? I'd be trading one pain for another. But if I don't, he'll simply walk out of there with Audrey. Arkady's goons are useless without their boss. None of them possesses the ambition nor the foresight to take over and continue his mission to conquer New York. They'll let Grigori and Audrey leave. They know better than to kill the head of the Fedorov Bratva in retaliation for what I just did.

They'll show no loyalty to a dead man.

But I can't let him walk away.

I fire a second shot, hitting Grigori in the leg, and fracturing his femur.

Audrey jumps back a second time and hides behind the nearest car while Arkady's men are still scattering like terrified geese. A couple of them shoot randomly into the night, unable to guess where my shots are coming from.

I didn't want things to go this far or get this ugly. I had hoped for a better conclusion. But they pushed me. They all pushed me to this dark conclusion.

But the darkness is where I'm most comfortable. I know every corner of it. I spent years exploring the darkness, living in it, thriving in it. I guess I never really left it behind. I see that now. I'm just sorry that Audrey had to bear witness to it.

I fire a couple more bullets into the thinning crowd of Abramovic bodyguards, giving them a minute or so to jump into their cars and get as far away as possible. Now, Arkady's words come back to me. Their loyalty was short-lived. Money-based. They left his body on the ground, not caring if the rats ate him. No last rites. Nothing.

The irony is glaring, to say the least.

By the time I get to them, they are alone.

Grigori groans in sheer agony, barely able to look at the bloody mess of his leg while Audrey kneels beside him.

"It'll take one hell of a doctor to fix that," I say as I cautiously approach them.

As soon as she sees me, Audrey jumps to her feet. "Jason, thank God."

"It's going to be okay," I calmly tell her and put the rifle over my shoulder. "But we need to get you out of here, now."

"I don't understand." She pauses upon noticing my weapon. The color drains from her face. "Oh. Jason. You're the one who—"

"Killed Arkady? Yes."

"And shot my father ..."

"An ambulance is already on the way," I tell her. "He'll live, trust me."

She gives her father a brief but accusatory glance. "You used him! You deserve way worse than a fucking bullet for everything you've done."

Grigori reaches a hand out, blood dripping from his fingertips. "Audrey don't do something you'll regret. Everything I did, I did for—"

"Yourself," I cut him off. "You did for yourself. Cut the horse shit already, Grigori; nobody's buying the stern but loving father shtick anymore. You allowed all of this to happen the minute you decided that your Fedorov pride was more important than your daughter's well-being."

"You need to—"

"I need to what?" I talk over him, forcing him back into his aching silence. "You manipulative piece of shit. You came to me, you asked for my help, you had terms and conditions, yet you somehow failed to tell me that Audrey's pregnant. I see you clearly now. You have no business being anywhere near her or my family." I pause and take Audrey's hand, pulling her close. "You saw how good my aim is, Grigori. Don't even think about coming after us because if you do, I won't go for the leg again. I'll go straight for your head."

"Jason ..." Audrey gasps.

Everything is happening too fast, sirens wailing, louder and louder with each passing minute. Red and blue lights flash in the corner of my eyes. "Come on, we need to get you out of here," I say and pull her away from Grigori.

"This isn't over!" he growls, but he's too weak to get up.

"Yes, it is," I reply.

With an arm around Audrey's shoulders, I take her out of the courtyard and down the road. I parked my car a couple of blocks east, having left it between two delivery vans. We're both quiet as we walk, but it's not a heavy silence.

The look she gives me speaks of relief, of contentment, of peace.

I needed to see that twinkle in her eyes again, that fear withering away.

Our battle is far from over, but at least I've got her back, at least she's safe.

CHAPTER 28

For the better part of an hour, Jason and I barely speak, but there have been plenty of fleeting glances. I can breathe again. I sink into the passenger seat of his SUV, traffic lights dashing past us as we leave the city behind. Chicago glimmers in the rearview mirror while I quietly pray for my father's recovery.

Part of me feels guilty because his demise would put an end to all of my problems. It's a terrible thought to muster, but given everything that has happened, I can't exactly blame myself for thinking this way. Jason was right. We don't get to choose the family we're born into.

Once the guilt subsides and the adrenaline wears off, I go over tonight's events, the steps that ultimately led to Arkady's death, and I reach the same conclusion as Jason did earlier—all of it could have been avoided if only my father had left me alone.

"Where are we going?" I ask after a while, noting the indifference on his face as he drives us farther away from Chicago.

"A friend of mine has a house up in Crystal Lake. We're going to stay there for a while," he says, one hand on the steering wheel while the other searches for mine.

I welcome his touch, letting his fingers mingle with mine. It fills me with a familiar warmth that envelops my entire body. Nothing much has changed except that the Abramovic Bratva isn't really my problem anymore. From what I understand so far, Arkady was the only one who had his sights set on New York. The rest of the family and most of his associates had repeatedly expressed concerns about such a risky move. I doubt they'll come after me in his place.

That leaves my father. He's still a problem. He won't give up until he has me back. I know it, and Jason knows it. For now, however, I welcome the brief feeling of peace.

"He'll be all right," Jason says, as if able to read my mind. "That leg is shattered, and he'll need a cane for the rest of his life, but it'll slow him down a bit. Perhaps it'll give your brothers the opportunity they need to actually take over the family business and push him out. Who knows? I didn't think that far ahead."

"What *were* you thinking?"

"I wanted to kill him, too," he replies without hesitation, giving me a sideways glance. His eyes search my face, and I muster a soft, timid smile. "I honestly considered it, and I'm sorry."

258 | K.C. CROWNE

"No, I get it. I would've been tempted as well under the circumstances," I say, my voice trembling slightly. "But then he would've won. Those who fight monsters should be careful not to turn into monsters themselves, right?"

"Nietzsche said that if I remember correctly. Yeah, I agree. I just needed him down and momentarily disabled so I could get you out of there."

"He's going to pay for everything he did to us," I say.

"We'll check up on your brothers once we reach Crystal Lake," Jason says. "I've got a friend at Grand Memorial, where Anton and Vitaly are hospitalized. He'll update us on their condition. Your father's, too. I imagine they'll take him there, as well."

"You were incredible," I say. "Back at the meeting."

"I wish it didn't have to get to that point."

Me, too. But it did. And we survived it. It's all that matters to me tonight.

His friend's place is a townhouse right on the edge of Crystal Lake. At this late hour, there's not much to see, with the exception of a few twinkling lights on the other side of the lake.

Once the door is locked and the lights are on, I take it all in.

For a moment, I feel as though I've stepped into a corner of paradise. I love every inch of this place. Mostly, I love that it has nothing to do with any aspect of my life.

"I knew you'd like it," Jason chuckles softly upon seeing my awe.

"God, yes."

He takes me into the kitchen, where to my delight, there is a generous variety of tea in the cupboard. "Here, let me show you something cool," Jason says, smiling as he takes out a gorgeous glass teapot with a gold-brushed rim.

"I'll help," I reply and put the electric kettle on, then rummage through the available tea bags. I settle on jasmine and ginger, my tongue already tingling with the anticipation of the wonderful combination.

"Saul showed this to me when he first bought it. Honestly, I was never much in favor of tea before, but ever since I got to play with it a bit, I swear it's a game-changer."

"It's so pretty," I mumble as I look at the unique teapot.

We sit down at the kitchen table for a while, sipping in silence while gazing at one another. It's so nice to be able to talk about trivial things such as fancy teapots and beach houses with Jason—particularly after everything we've dealt with over the past few weeks. It's nice to be able to feel normal for once.

"I've missed you so much," I tell him. "I didn't think I'd ever see you again."

"Audrey, I was lost without you," he admits, his gaze softening. "But we do need to address the elephant in the room."

"We have a whole herd of them," I can't help but giggle, prompting a smile from him. "I mean, there's my family, there's the whole Bratva thing, all the secrets I kept from you. Where do I begin?"

"You're pregnant."

My face burns, and my heart starts racing. I look down, wondering if it's fear or shame I'm feeling.

"Jason, I'm sorry. I didn't plan for this to happen," I say.

"I know that. It's okay. We didn't consider this as a consequence when we got together," Jason replies, the shadow of a smile dancing across his handsome, tired face. "We were too busy screwing each other's brains out, falling irreversibly in love with one another."

"How do you feel about it?"

Jason takes a second to respond, and it feels like the longest second of my existence until he laughs lightly. "Are you kidding? I'm over the moon!" He gets up and comes around the counter but then stops and gives me a worried look. "Hold on, how do *you* feel about it?"

"Scared but excited and happy," I say, tearing up. " I don't know how it's supposed to feel. It happened in the middle of such a stressful time. I've got my twisted family, and you have such a good and peaceful life and you have Lily ... I don't want to add pressure, and I don't want to be a problem. I need you to be happy—"

"Audrey," he cuts me off and comes closer and I catch a whiff of his cologne. He cups my face in his hands and pulls me in for the sweetest, tenderest kiss. "I want this child and I want you. Can't you see? I picked up a sniper rifle for you for the first time in years. I killed someone for you." His eyes darken to a sullen grey as I lose myself in them, realizing the meaning behind his words. "I love you."

"I love you, Jason, more than I thought was possible."

"Then we're on the same page," he says and kisses me again.

This time, it's deeper, more profound and loaded with emotions that we've both been fighting for so long. We've been so close, yet somehow so far apart. But tonight, for the first time since we met, Jason and I are truly bound, truly open and honest with one another. There are no secrets left between us. No lies. Nothing left unspoken. It's just the two of us, though there are still murky waters ahead.

"My father will seek revenge," I warn him.

Jason's response is to wrap his arms around me and hold me close against his broad chest. I feel his heart beating with mine in a steady rhythm. "I don't give a shit about your father right now. He got my message, loud and clear."

"I really want to believe that."

"You've always thought of him as the most powerful man in the world, right?" he asks, planting a kiss on my forehead. I nod slowly, closing my eyes for a moment. The sound of his voice alone is enough to calm my frayed nerves, to chase away any worst-case scenario that threatens to ruin what's left of tonight. I started the day as the prisoner of a psychopath, and I would like to end it in the arms of my beloved, knowing there's a brighter future ahead. "Grigori may be a powerful man; he may have convinced you that there is no escaping his clutches, but that couldn't be farther from the truth."

"He's not as powerful as he used to be. He's getting older."

"Nah, it's not about that. It's about your perception of him, Audrey. He is powerful. He's got money, influence, and the whole New York Bratva behind him. But he is still just a man, just one player on a big ass board. I'm not as powerful as he is, but if I make the right calls, I could bring him to his knees."

I can't help but quiver in his embrace. "Technically speaking, you already brought him to his knees tonight."

"That I most certainly did," he chuckles dryly. "Will you think I'm a monster if I say I kind of enjoyed making him suffer?"

"Then that would make the both of us monsters."

We share a smile, then drink the rest of our tea before hitting the shower. As the hot water pours over our naked bodies, we make love like there is no tomorrow.

The sun slowly rises in the morning, its golden light gleaming across the lake. I wake up to the trills of birds singing in the garden. Jason left one of the bedroom windows cracked open, giving us a lovely cool breeze that causes us to want to snuggle under the covers. My body is soft and warm against his, my fingers tracing the sharp contours of his face as I try to memorize every fine line, every speck of silver in his hair, every inch of this man who has transformed my entire world.

He sleeps soundly, his breath slow and even while I gaze at him, wondering where fate will take us next. The uncertainty is killing me.

"It's going to be okay," Jason mutters.

"You're awake."

"Have been for a while now. I enjoy listening to your heart beating," he smiles, his eyes peeling open to find mine. There is so much love emanating from this man, and it's enough to make the rest of the world disappear.

By noon, we're downstairs in the kitchen, enjoying a late breakfast. Jason had groceries delivered to our door since it's best for us to stay out of sight and out of the public eye while we figure out the next steps.

"Have you heard from Anton and Vitaly?" Jason asks, adding more bacon and scrambled eggs to my plate straight from the pan. The smell alone is enough to make my mouth water. "My friend told me they are out of the ICU and that they got their phones back. I'm thinking they might've reached out to you by now."

"They have," I say, and show him the text messages.

He laughs lightly. "I see Anton is loving those painkillers. I can barely understand what he's trying to tell you."

"Oh, let me translate," I shoot back and go over his last message. "Papa is pissed and you're screwed." I can't help but laugh despite the possible danger.

"And Vitaly?"

"He's the heir to the Fedorov empire. He's not allowed to be under the influence of painkillers," I sigh deeply. I can tell from the eloquence of his text messages that he is definitely alive and aching all over. "His shoulder will be troublesome for a long while, but with enough physical therapy, he should make a full recovery in less than a year."

"So, Grigori made it to the hospital." That half-smile of his is downright contagious.

"You know, the two of us have a penthouse reserved in hell for this. We're enjoying Papa's misery a little too much."

Jason scoffs and pours himself another coffee, making sure to refill my mug with green tea. I follow his every move, admiring the confidence and the blazing fire within him. This man is determined to go to the end of the world in order to keep me and our baby safe. Our family, for that matter. Because that's what we have become in such a short but incredible time. A family.

"Where's Lily?" I ask. "Are she and Rita safe?"

"Yes, an Army buddy of mine has eyes on them. They're in Nebraska, safe and far enough away until I give them the green light to come back."

"And what about your business, your projects? You had so much on your plate already."

Jason gives me a warm smile before he devours his food. "Baby, everything is okay. I've got executive boards overseeing these things. None of it matters to me unless you are out of the danger zone for good."

"Which brings me to my next question. How will I get out of the danger zone for good? My father is relentless, Jason. He'll come after me, your death threats notwithstanding."

The mere thought of going back to New York with my father fills me with the kind of dread I'd hoped to never feel again. Yet there's a constant nagging feeling in the back of my mind, a sensation that refuses to go away, that it will somehow get worse.

I know my father well. I know my brothers are powerless before him. Jason may have the juice to take him on, but I'm not sure how such a war will unfold and how many people will die in the process. The Bratva is not to be taken lightly, particularly when it comes to family affairs.

"I've made every phone call that I could think of to every contact that might be useful: the DoD, the DoJ, the Army, the Navy, former servicemembers, and a few folks I know in intelligence. I've pointed every single light onto New York to make sure your father keeps busy for as long as possible," he says, but even I can sense the doubt in his voice.

"Will it be enough?"

"I'm not sure. I hope so. But I can't promise a swift conclusion. Maybe we'll wear him out. Add that leg injury and his bruised ego into the mix, and, hopefully, that will be plenty to keep him at bay for long enough."

"We can't hide here forever," I exhale sharply.

But Jason has no intention of letting me succumb to my own despair again. He reaches across the counter and gently caresses my cheek. "Audrey, no one will come between us. I am done letting other people tell us what to do with our lives, with our love. Do you hear me?"

"Loud and clear."

"I know this isn't the ideal scenario, but we do need to lay low until they conclude their investigation. Someone needs to be held accountable for Arkady's death. I covered my tracks and got rid of the weapon and the bullets, too. I was careful, and I've got enough backup in the Chicago PD to never deal with this issue going forward. Let's give it a few days and see how the pieces land on the game board," he says. "The cops might go so hard after your dad that he will simply have no resources left to hunt you down again. Let's not forget that he and your brothers dropped quite a few Abramovic bodies before Arkady took you. They have to deal with that, too."

I'm not the wishful-thinking type, but I am tempted to believe that the legal repercussions of my father's and my brothers' actions will be enough to get me out of their crosshairs. Maybe this was it for them. Maybe the law will catch up, I don't know. The prospect of knowing my family is in prison isn't the prettiest scenario, but it beats having my ass dragged back to New York. It beats being forced into a marriage I don't want.

Besides, I've got a baby on the way, a future with Jason and Lily. I'm beyond determined to keep them in my life, to experience true love and happiness by their side. I deserve a real family, a good family. They are it for me.

As the days go by, the media coverage of the Abramovic Bratva dwindles more and more. My brothers have also gone radio silent, though I'm not sure that's such a good thing. The last time we spoke, they were still in the hospital, and our father was awake and seething. The investigation is underway, and according to Jason's cop buddies, they're definitely looking at the Fedorovs for Arkady's death.

There aren't many witnesses willing to come forward, though, mainly because there's an internal struggle unfolding within the Abramovic family. Arkady's demise left a vacuum of power, and all of his cousins and money-loving lieutenants have been killing each other so they can get that top seat for themselves.

One thing is certain, however. No one in the Abramovic Bratva is interested in Arkady's plans for New York. His death has caused such an imbalance across Chicago alone that they simply do not have the manpower nor the bandwidth to continue his insane project. That puts me in the clear, as far as they're concerned.

Sitting in the living room one afternoon, I browse through the news channels on the wall-mounted TV, hoping to learn more about any new developments in the investigation. The police haven't issued a statement to the press, just a memo stating that they had mounted a joint task force. The FBI, the ATF, the DEA, and the local PD. It's all hands on deck, apparently.

Jason comes in and joins me on the sofa, having just finished another round of phone calls. I give him a curious look while simultaneously making myself comfortable in his arms. This man soothes me with his very presence, but the genuine care he shows for my and the baby's well-being only makes me love him more. Gently, he rests a hand on my belly. "How's the little guy doing?" he asks.

"What if it's a little girl?"

"Good grief. Then it'll be me against three women. Make that four if you count Rita. I'm screwed," he sighs in a hilariously dramatic fashion. I like this playful side of him. "I'll be happy either way. If it's another girl, I will need to prepare for their teenage years. Going to have a lot of boys to scare off."

"I think you'll do just fine there," I giggle. "How is Lily?"

Jason takes a deep breath and kisses my temple. "She's good. I just spoke to her, in fact. She wants to come back to Chicago, obviously. She misses us, but Rita keeps her busy with her schoolwork and activities."

"Lily's way too young to understand."

"Even if she were older, I wouldn't tell her everything. It's too much for her. She's innocent. She doesn't need to know the extreme ugliness of this world. Not yet anyway."

"You can't protect her forever," I say, though I wish I'd been as sheltered as Lily ultimately is. She has no idea of how cruel and unforgiving people can be. Family included.

"I know. But I can still try," Jason chuckles.

A knock on the door has us both standing up so fast that I get dizzy for a second. Jason immediately goes into his protective mode. "Don't move," he whispers. "If I say run, you bolt through the back door, you hear me?"

"Yeah."

I hold my breath as I watch him carefully approach the front door. A second knock has my heart thudding like crazy, the blood rushing through my body and turning the heat up by a thousand degrees. I can see him opening the door, but it's as if he's moving in slow motion.

As soon as I see my brother Vitaly's face, I'm tempted to relax, but then I spot the gun coming up, and I want to scream. I am paralyzed, my voice stuck in my throat, frozen in place as I watch the entire scene unfold in fragments of time that I cannot keep up with.

"Hands up," Vitaly says.

Jason doesn't fight him on it. He puts his hands up and takes a couple of steps back. "Don't do anything stupid, Vitaly; that's all I ask," he calmly replies.

"Shut it," my brother snaps.

I can see the anguish on his face. His good arm is holding the gun, the other wrapped tightly in a white brace up through his shoulder. He appears to have literally tumbled out of his hospital bed to come here and do what, exactly? "Vitaly," I breathe, shaken to the core. "How'd you find us?"

"You continue to underestimate us, little sister," Vitaly retorts with a heavy sigh. "You should've obeyed our father. You should've done as you were told. And you," he adds, careful to keep the gun pointed at Jason. "You shouldn't have done what you did."

"It's not your place to berate him," my father's voice echoes from somewhere behind Vitaly. I gasp as my brother steps to the side, allowing our father to come in. He isn't walking, though. He's in a wheelchair, and he looks miserable. His eyes are sunken in, his face pale, and he looks as if he's lost a few more pounds since I last saw him. If he loses any more, he might just wither away like a dying flower. "Audrey, my little zaika, so glad to see you're alive and well."

I instinctively move away from my father and brother. "What the hell are you doing out of the hospital in your condition?"

"Give the man credit," Jason says, watching Vitaly like a hawk. He must be waiting for an opportunity to disarm him. But outside, standing close to the doorway, I spot one too many Fedorov men in black suits and sunglasses, each of them likely carrying a weapon and ready to use it. "You were right, Audrey, my love. Your father is relentless. Like a cockroach."

"What more do you want from me?" I shout, despair tightening my throat. I'm on the verge of tears, and the last thing I want is for my father to see me crying.

"We need to talk," my father says.

"Vitaly, how are you still condoning this?" I try to plead with my brother, hoping I might get through to him somehow.

But the pained look on his face tells me any effort on my part is useless. "I'm sorry, little sister. This is family. And you know how we handle family affairs."

"It's going to be okay, Audrey, I promise," Jason says, his tone strangely calm under the circumstances.

Minutes pass in heavy silence as my father comes into the living room, the electric wheelchair humming along the way. Vitaly keeps his gun pointed at Jason, and it's making me all the more nervous while I'm unable to actually move. I doubt I'd be able to escape, anyway. They have the house surrounded.

"Where's Anton?" I ask.

"He's still recovering," Vitaly says. "His injuries were a tad more severe. The doctors said he might make it worse if he insists on checking himself out."

"And you didn't make it worse on yourself?" I reply.

"I didn't have a choice."

"That's where you're wrong," I shoot back. "You always have a choice, Vitaly, no matter what our father tells you."

"Little zaika, enough," our father cuts in with a wry smile. "Come, now, it's time to go home. We'll take good care of you and your baby."

Jason scoffs, shaking his head slowly. "I take it you didn't hear a single word I said back at that meeting with Arkady. I made you a promise, Grigori, and I intend to keep it."

"For ridding me of Arkady, I will be forever grateful, which is why I have instructed my son not to kill you, even though you deserve it," my father says. "You should've killed me, Mr. Winchester. Because a surviving Fedorov is ten times worse than an angry one."

"You're not taking Audrey away from me," Jason replies.

"Oh, but I am. And you won't do anything about it. You do not scare me, Mr. Winchester. I'll give you credit; you are ruthless. A man like you would get far in the Bratva. Should you wish to join your business with ours, I'm more than happy to have a chat about it at some point in the future. But Audrey is my daughter. She is a Fedorov. I almost lost her to this wretched city, but now, I am taking her home, where she belongs."

"I belong with Jason," I shout, finding my voice. "Stop fucking talking about me like I'm not even here. I'm pregnant with Jason's child. We're in love. We want to live together, to build something together, to have a family. Do you remember what that is, Papa? Family? Real family, I mean, not this Bratva bullshit you keep trying to shove down our throats." I pause and look at Vitaly. "Do you remember Mom, big brother? Do you remember how happy we were when she was alive? How you and Anton and I would run out of our rooms and almost tumble downstairs whenever she came home?"

For a moment, I spot a glimpse of hesitation in his blue eyes. But then the pain returns and his grip on the gun gets even tighter. "That's all in the past, Audrey."

"I am going to have a baby. I cannot and will not raise my child to become like you or Anton. Or worse, like our father," I say. "How can you be so cruel, so spineless?"

"Enough!" my father snarls, his shout booming across the room. "Family is family, Audrey. Blood comes before everything else. But like I said, once this whole Abramovic nonsense dies down, once we're all cleared and back in business, once you're settled back in New York, I am more than happy to hear a business proposal from your friend here. Consider it a gesture of goodwill. I won't force you to marry Piotr or anyone else. How does that sound?"

"Like you've lost your fucking mind," I reply. "That's how that sounds."

"Grigori, I would never join the Bratva," Jason says, half-smiling. "I have nothing to gain from that, only headaches and legal complications."

"You're not helping," I blurt out.

But Jason gives me a soft nod. "Audrey, I promised you that everything is going to be okay. I intend to keep that promise," he says. "Yet I cannot lie to your father. It would be an insult to the man and the Fedorov name. So, allow me to put things in perspective," he adds and shifts his focus back on

Vitaly. "You're her big brother. You're supposed to protect her from all those who would do her harm, right?"

"Of course," Vitaly replies.

"But here you are, pointing a gun at the man she loves, the man who loves her, the father of her child. Are you protecting Audrey now, or are you just satisfying yet another one of your father's sadistic whims? We all know there is no benefit from keeping Audrey tethered to him like this, aside from asserting his dominance."

"She's family," my brother insists. "Family stays with family."

"Family by blood is a fucking coincidence. You're related by accident," Jason coldly says. "True family is the family you choose to love. Every day, every good day, and every bad day alike. I choose Audrey, Vitaly. I killed Arkady to keep her safe. I was ready to kill your father, as well, to ensure her happiness because I know that if I let her go back with you to New York, it would mean a slow and painful death for her. Is this what you want for your sister, Vitaly? A slow and painful death while your father picks his teeth with your fucking spine?"

There it is the raw anger in my brother's eyes. If Anton were here, maybe we could get through to him. But even so, without Vitaly's support, it's useless. My father curses under his breath and bangs his fist onto the wheelchair's padded armrest. "Enough with this nonsense!" the old man barks. "We have to go."

"Is this how you let him push you around?" Jason asks Vitaly, mockery dripping from every word. "I thought you're the de facto head of the Fedorov Bratva now. The almighty heir. The guy is calling all the shots. All I see is a scared little lapdog still jumping when his daddy says so."

"You should really mind your words, Jason," Vitaly hisses.

Fear courses through my veins, as cold as the blue in my brother's eyes. If there is an unseen force that the universe might employ to stop a bullet from leaving the chamber of his gun, I am now praying for it, summoning it, begging the gods to spare Jason from what's about to hit him.

"The truth will always bother those who have become accustomed to lies," Jason says.

The smirk on my father's lips repulses me. Bile gathers in the back of my throat as I am now guilty of an unconscionable thought. Guilty of the most terrible of sins, wishing Jason had, in fact, killed my father that night. Maybe then I would've been free and no longer the prisoner of a man who wants to control me simply to satisfy his own power-hungry whims.

But then Vitaly turns the gun on our father.

And everything changes.

CHAPTER 29

AUDREY

"I hate to admit it, but Jason does have a point," Vitaly says.

"What is the meaning of this?" our father gasps. "Point that somewhere else, or I will shove it down your throat!"

Vitaly glances back at the men waiting by the open door. I follow his gaze and realize that they're not moving. They're simply standing back, hands in their pockets, watching my brother as he makes his decision. To my astonishment, they're not jumping in to protect my father. Something is different. Something that might very well change the way the Fedorov Bratva will operate from now on.

My brother has finally asserted himself as the leader. And the men have chosen to follow him. It's quite the blow to our father, I can see the shock in his eyes.

"I am the heir," Vitaly says. "You already had me sign all those papers, granting me legal ownership and the administrative authority over our businesses. You had me sitting down with our partners and associates, introducing me as the new head of the Bratva. They acknowledged me. And yet, I'm still taking orders from you. It doesn't make sense."

"Vitaly put the fucking gun down," our father says. "You will regret it."

"Oh, no, the only thing I regret is not doing this sooner. Maybe things would've worked out better for everyone. Maybe Anton and I wouldn't have gotten shot. We could've handled Arkady's attempt to force his way back into New York ourselves. We could've negotiated something to keep Audrey out of his reach, too. If only you'd listened to me in the first place. But you didn't listen. You never listen. Why put me in charge if you're still calling the shots?"

I can tell he's having a hard time holding up that gun, given his recent shoulder injury. Beads of sweat drip along his pale temples, but he refuses to yield. I've never been prouder of my brother. Never. I'm seeing a side of him that I haven't caught a glimpse of since we were children—since the first time that he stood up to our father and ended up in the basement. To this day, I remember the moment he came out of there, merely a boy and the spark was gone from his eyes, never to return.

I'm seeing that spark again, and it fills me with a whole new kind of energy.

"Papa, you've gone too far," I chime in. "Even Vitaly has had enough."

"You need to shut up and remember your place, Audrey," he says.

"Actually, Papa, you're the one who needs to shut up and know your place," Vitaly replies. "What is stopping me from killing you right now? Think about it. You taught Anton and me to shut ourselves down when it comes to pulling the trigger. No matter who it is on the receiving end of the bullet, if it must be done, then I must do it. What if I shut myself down because I have to do this? Because there will be no peace, no real progress, not even a glint of happiness for anyone in this fucking family unless you're six feet under. Killing you would solve all of our problems."

"Vitaly, you don't mean that."

"I do mean it. We'd patch things up with the Abramovic clan. I kill you, and I basically kill the man who ordered Arkady's assassination," my brother says. "I kill you, and there's no one left in New York to question me or my legitimacy. You're the only one still questioning it, frankly. I kill you, and both Anton and I are free to carry on with the family name and the family business. We've got better and fresher ideas for the future, projects you'd never let us do because..." he pauses to mock our father's condescending tone. "It's not our style."

I can't help but chuckle, drawing a sour look from our father. "Don't look at me. He's got a point," I snap. "You've become an inconvenience, Papa."

"And if I kill you, Audrey will be free to live her life as she chooses," Vitaly adds. "It's what our mother would've wanted, and it's what Anton and I want. You're so stuck on the Bratva traditions, on retaining control over the people you're supposed to love and protect, that you don't even care about Audrey's happiness. If she wants a normal life, who the fuck are you to tell her otherwise? You lived yours. Let her live hers. She's not hurting anybody."

"There will always be another Bratva looking to use her against us. Arkady did that with impunity, after all," Papa says.

"She's got Jason," Vitaly replies. "And you've seen what Jason can do. You've experienced it yourself."

Our father scoffs, but even that simple gesture is enough to cause him pain. He winces in his wheelchair and gives Vitaly a cold, harsh glare. "You've betrayed me."

"I think it's time for the two of us to have a chat," Jason politely interjects, his hands still up in a defensive stance. "You and I, Grigori. Man to man. I'm sure we can work something out so that your own son doesn't have to kill you."

My father thinks about it for a moment, biting the inside of his cheek. I can see his mind spinning with the possibilities ahead. He may be stubborn and quite the control freak, but even he has to concede that he no longer holds absolute power over any of us. All it took was for Vitaly to come to his senses and realize that he is, in fact, the true leader of our family. For so long, he was used to taking orders from our father. It's a hard thing to do, getting out from under Grigori Fedorov's heavy boot.

"What are you suggesting?" he asks Jason.

"A sit-down. Just you and me," Jason replies.

I give him a worried look, but he offers a subtle nod in return. His way of reassuring me that it's going to be okay, one way or another. I'm inclined to believe that. Vitaly has crossed one hell of a line just now. Unless Jason convinces our father to back down and let my brother do his thing,

Vitaly will have no choice but to end him—because the old man will never forgive this transgression.

Wolves kill their own pups sometimes. And our old man is the worst kind of wolf.

I sit on the back porch with Vitaly while Jason and our father discuss terms and conditions inside. The townhouse is surrounded by Fedorov men, but I am no longer afraid nor wary of them. They answer to my brother now. Therefore, their prime directive is to protect me, as well. They seem to understand that our father has become problematic.

It's beautiful and sunny out here. The sun dances across the surface of the lake, and the crystalline water gently laps at the mossy shore. I could stay here forever, away from the crowds and the chaos of being a Fedorov in a world that is already so difficult and dismaying. But there is peace in this sliver of tranquility, a peace that my body and my soul desperately need.

"You really stepped in it this time, didn't you?" I giggle, staring at the swaying willow branches that dangle just above the water.

"It's not like I had any other choice," Vitaly says and shrugs. The gun rests in his lap, ready to be used if our father doesn't reach an amicable agreement with Jason. "What else could I have done?"

"Sit back and let the old man push us around some more."

He shakes his head. "I'm tired, Audrey. The men will never take me seriously if I don't stand up to him. Anton said it more than once. You said it, too. Even though it stung to hear the words, it's the truth. I couldn't let him pull the strings anymore."

"Besides, it's detrimental to the family," I reply. "I'm of no use to anyone."

"I wholeheartedly agree," Vitaly sighs deeply. "I'm just sorry I didn't do this sooner."

"You did the best you could, big brother. You've been a loyal son, first and foremost. That was always your duty, and I swear I have nothing but respect for you in that sense. You just needed to come out of your shell I guess. You needed to push yourself out of your comfort zone."

"Yeah, well, killing Papa wasn't on my list until he dragged my ass out of the hospital today to come looking for you," he says. "Anton is lucky that he's still in and out of his drug-induced sleep. Otherwise, we would've had to carry him around with us, too. The man has lost his fucking marbles, Audrey."

A bitter smile tests my lips. "He is losing control, and he's not used to it. He doesn't know how to handle it. All he's ever known is now being taken away from him, year after year. I left. Anton is all grown up. You are now expected to lead the charge. What does that leave him with?"

"Retirement. Few Bratva men actually live to see it. I thought he'd look forward to it."

"Look forward to what exactly? Sitting on a porch like this and looking back at his life? Seeing the faces of all the people he killed? The people whose lives he destroyed?" I look at my brother and notice the consternation on his face. "It's what you and Anton signed up for as well. You may not see it now, but you will as time goes by. Everything you do as a Fedorov will ultimately come back to haunt you. Every life you take, every life you shatter, you'll have to live with all of it. And our father has quite the portfolio. Then there is everything he allowed to happen. Everything he could have prevented but knowingly didn't. Everything he did to you, to Anton, to me. All the hours in that basement. Our mother, let's not forget about her."

"He was good to her," Vitaly insists.

"But she's not here anymore. She hasn't been here for a long time, and that has left our father unmoored and lacking consolation. Why do you think he was so mean and so hard on us? Had Mom lived, he never would've treated us the way he did."

It's a hard pill to swallow, but Vitaly has to accept it. The facts don't lie. "There are moments when I can barely remember her face, you know?"

"Yet you resemble her the most. Your eyes have that tint of grey that hers had. Your hair's a tad darker, like hers, and your face, oh, Vitaly, it reminds me so much of her. If you find yourself forgetting, just look in the mirror. You'll see her right there, smiling back at you."

"Audrey, we never deserved you. You know that, right?"

There is pain in my brother's eyes. The pain of a brother who had no choice but to sit back and let our father hurt me, push and pull me in every which way that he saw fit. He couldn't protect me because had he stepped in sooner, the retaliation would've been downright bloody. "I could have been a better sister," I concede with a slight shrug. "I could've told you about my plans. Maybe then you would've known how to react when I left."

"Nah, Anton must've told you already that we kind of knew. It was a matter of when with you, not if. I could tell that you were emotionally exhausted. You'd literally checked out of the family long before you ran off. As angry as I was back then, I couldn't blame you, Audrey. Not even a little."

"How bad was it?"

"Oh, it was awful," he chuckles. "The old man fumed for weeks. He shot two of our house guards simply for being in the wrong place at the wrong time. I had to pay them both off just to keep things in the family. There were already plenty of rumors spreading about Papa flipping out and losing control. The last thing we needed were two body-guards with bullets in their legs to further cement that theory."

"I'm sorry."

"There's nothing to be sorry about. Like I said, I probably would've done the same if I were you," Vitaly says. "And that prick, Piotr. Wait till I get back to New York. He's all giddy again, thinking we're bringing you back so he can marry you. I cannot wait to sit him down and lay the law of the land on his ancient, wrinkly ass."

I can't help but smile. "How do you know his ass is wrinkly?"

"Do you have any idea what it's like to do a Russian sauna with these old fuckers? My God, Audrey, there are things I can never unsee, and there isn't enough vodka in the world to make me forget."

We laugh heartily. It's been a while since we've been able to just sit down and reminisce like this. The minutes fly by with memories that Vitaly and I pluck from the recesses of our tired minds—of us as children, of our mother, of the few good moments that we shared in the company of our father.

"What do you think Jason is proposing in there?" I ask my brother after a long silence. I can hear their voices from inside but I can't make out the words.

"Probably a deal that our father will have no choice but to accept." He glances down at the gun in his lap. "Lord knows he's fully aware of his only other option. I don't want to have to do it."

"I don't want you to have to do it."

He shakes his head. "Jason should've just ..." he trails off.

"Jason should've just killed him, yeah. I understand the sentiment, and I get it. As awful as it sounds, I honestly think we're allowed to feel whatever we want to feel where Papa's concerned," I say to my brother. "He's the one who backed us into this corner, Vitaly. We're simply protecting ourselves, our peace, and our future. If he cannot be reasoned with, what else can we do?"

"Except put a sick dog out of its misery, huh?"

"You knew this might happen," I remind him with a stern tone. "The minute you signed the papers, the minute you sat down with the other Bratva families, you knew this was a possible outcome. Papa doesn't relinquish control. He says he'll do it, but he doesn't know how because he lived his whole life trying to control every single circumstance, every single person within his reach. Letting go of that control means the very end of who he believes he is. That's why we're having these issues now. That's why he can't let go of me."

"I considered the possibility, but I just didn't think it would actually get this far, Audrey. Anton and I swear we tried to talk to him; we tried to reason with him."

"I did that for years before I left."

Vitaly lets a bitter smile sit on his lips. "And now I feel precisely the way you felt."

"Except you have the gun and the spine needed to pull that trigger. All I could do was run and hide."

"Yet you're just as brave," he says, giving me a long, affectionate look. "Mom would be so proud of you. You know that, right?"

I wonder what she might feel about all this as I subtly cradle my belly with both hands, an aching pang tugging at my heart. "I don't know, Vitaly. Everything seems so uncertain right now. There are things I could've handled better myself."

"She would want you to be happy," he says. "I want you to be happy. Anton wants you to be happy. And Jason is in there right now, doing everything in his power to make sure you get that freedom to pursue your happiness. That makes him a good man in my book, and Mom would agree. It's a shame she wasn't able to meet her grandchild."

"Yeah."

Tears prick my eyes. I would've loved to turn to our mother for comfort and advice during these trying times. "She would have been helpful today; I'll tell you that."

"I think, in a way, she is helping. Her life here on this earth was not without consequence. We are living proof of that, Audrey. We just need to make sure we live accordingly."

I don't know when my brother became so wise. Two years ago, he was still arguing with Anton over which fashion magazine cover model would be willing to screw them both on the same night. I guess life got real, really fast, after I left because the man sitting next to me now is not the man I left behind in New York.

Our mother would definitely be proud of Vitaly, though. I'm sure of it. To stand up to our father the way he just did ... hell, I think deep down, and despite the threat of death looming over his head, even old Grigori Fedorov is fucking proud of Vitaly.

My only hope is that Jason manages to talk some sense into him before it's too late.

Because Vitaly will pull that trigger.

CHAPTER 30

"I'm not sure what you can offer that might entice me," Grigori says, sitting uncomfortably in his wheelchair while I sink into the sofa. All this talk of shooting has depleted my energy reserves. It's been a long morning already. "You have nothing I want."

"Yet you're willing to talk to me," I reply. "And we both know it's not to buy time with Vitaly. Unless we reach a common ground, he will kill you."

"Don't you think I'm aware?" the old man scoffs.

I allow myself a broad, almost arrogant smile as I look at him, measuring every micro-expression dancing across his tired, drawn face. "Admit it. Deep down, you're proud of Vitaly. It takes a real set of balls to do what he just did."

"Mmm."

"Here's the deal, Grigori. You're not getting out of here alive unless we agree. Mind you, I could've just let Vitaly kill you, but I know it would pain Audrey deeply to lose her father, too, even after all the horrible shit you've done to her," I say. "Arkady Abramovic wanted to force his way into New York. Crazy, but that was not an impossible thing to do. It's only a matter of time before another Arkady tries to pick up where he left off. You might think it's a small possibility, but it's still a possibility, nonetheless."

Grigori gives me another sour look. "What's your point? My people can handle that. You heard my son; he's taking over. He'll deal with any other Abramovic stupid enough to try it."

"You need more than that. You need a branch here in Chicago, a Fedorov presence that is not too ostentatious but still visible enough to remind the Abramovic Bratva that you're not to be fucked with," I reply. "To that end, I offer a couple of my own properties. Buy them from me and set up a nice little office in Chicago. Use it for a legitimate business, something one of your kids can handle. Maybe a private kindergarten or a prep school. It would go a long way to garnering some favor with your daughter."

Grigori looks at me with slight confusion, but I can see a twinkle behind those cold blue eyes. I can almost hear the wheels spinning, the pieces falling into place as he processes my offer, one word at a time.

"The Abramovic Bratva won't question you, not at this point. After what happened to Arkady, they're in chaos. By the time they pull themselves back together, your business will already be established in Chicago. Legally. Irreversibly. They won't be able to do a thing about it. No funny stuff, though. I mean it. It has to be a legitimate, squeaky-clean operation. You do that and trust me, the Abramovic folks won't dare come near those properties.

You have eyes here, and they won't even consider charging at New York again."

"Why are you doing this?" he asks.

"Because it's a price I'm more than happy to pay if it gets you off our backs," I reply. "Audrey belongs with me. We're going to live the rest of our lives together and with zero ties to the Bratva. We're going to have a child together. We're going to raise our family in peace and harmony. Audrey deserves true happiness, my daughter deserves a mother, and I deserve a fucking happy ending after all the shit I've had to deal with over the years. The last thing I want is to fight you or anyone else ever again, and I feel like this is a decent deal for both of us. I give you something, you back off, Audrey; everybody's happy. And you get to live."

"I get to live."

"Yeah. Take my deal, or your own son puts a bullet through your skull. These are your only options, and I'm really trying to be a decent human being here, Grigori. Help yourself the fuck out."

He would love to jump out of that wheelchair and tear my throat out with his bare hands. I'll bet he's thinking about it, and he would absolutely try to do it, too, were it not for that femur I shattered. He is old and helpless, now more than ever. It's not a position he's accustomed to, and he is, therefore, incredibly frustrated. But the old Russian's survival instincts are still very much on point, forcing him to override his own pride and give me a sullen, tentative nod.

"What kind of properties are we talking about?" Grigori asks.

"I'll look through my portfolio and offer you three of my finest plots. Big and generously priced. I'll give you a nice discount for the bundle. Just to cover my original investment and legal expenses. I won't charge you for the renovations, the city hall approvals, or the last five years' worth of taxes," I tell him.

"Interesting," he mumbles.

"Don't be an idiot, Grigori. You know I'm not going to hand over prime real estate for free. Consider it pennies, though, compared to you getting to keep your life."

He thinks about it some more, his gaze bouncing all over the room. I'm guessing he's wondering about the bodyguards stationed around the house, judging by his persistent stare at the front door. He's likely positing what their reaction will be if he rejects my offer. I think they've already proven themselves loyal to Vitaly, though. There's no way out for Grigori—not anymore, not unless it's on my terms.

Ultimately, he lets a heavy, ragged sigh escape from his chest. "You drive a hard bargain," he says. "Three of your finest properties?" he confirms.

"Yes."

"Include The Emerald Residence among them, and you've got yourself a deal."

Audrey is selling her apartment. I'll lose about thirteen million dollars if I go ahead with this. Hell, it's worth it. Screw The Emerald. Peace for me and my family is priceless. Having Audrey by my side, happy and thriving, that alone is fucking priceless. I would sell everything that I own, everything, if it means I get to see her alive and free to do whatever she wishes with her own life.

With a broad smile, I get up from the sofa and offer Grigori my hand. "Let's shake on it, you psychopath."

"Watch your fucking tongue," he snarls, but he shakes my hand vigorously, sealing the deal.

I glance at the back door, eager to get my woman out of there. "Mind you, Grigori, if you flake on me at any given point, Vitaly will kill you, and nobody in your precious Bratva will object. I hope we're both clear on that."

"I know the kind of monsters I raised," he grumbles. "And I am a man of my word, Jason Winchester. You'll understand that soon enough."

"Good. We're on the same page then," I reply.

A minute later, I burst through the back door, prompting Vitaly to jump from his seat while I give Audrey a broad and confident smile. "Get your things, babe, we're going home," I say.

CHAPTER 31

It feels like a dream.

It's quiet and surreal, but it is happening. For the first time in what feels like forever, I am no longer haunted by demons from my past.

My father caved in to Jason's demands. What other choice did he have? I'm in the clear. My brothers and father will spend the next few days back in the hospital to continue their recovery, during which time their lieutenants will start sending memos across the whole of New York and Chicago.

I am not to be touched.

That is the first decree, and it seems like the Abramovic Bratva has already accepted that condition for a ceasefire. They will be pissed when they eventually find out that the Fedorovs have purchased properties in Chicago, but they won't be able to do anything about it. Jason made sure to inform the Feds about the deal as well. That way, neither the Abramovic nor the Fedorov clans will be able to do anything dirty on said properties unless they wish to unleash some apocalypse-grade RICO operation that would ultimately end them both.

I'll give my man credit; he played his cards well and then some.

We're back in Chicago, back at Jason's penthouse. Rita has also been given the green light to return. She and Lily will be joining us by Friday. We have the place all to ourselves until then, and there's a lot of catching up to do on so many levels.

A long, hot shower later, I find myself sitting comfortably at the dinner table before a delicious array of Italian food that Jason had delivered from one of his favorite restaurants. The TV is on in the den, the news chiming about recent developments in the investigation concerning the Abramovic Bratva. We're both watching with renewed interest as they confirm that the rifle used to kill Arkady has yet to be found.

"I'm sorry you had to do that," I tell him. "I know I've said it before, but—"

"It's okay, Audrey. I'll live with it. It may sound callous as hell, but I will sleep soundly, knowing that Arkady can't hurt you anymore," he replies, twirling pasta onto his fork. "I will also enjoy this food, finish this bottle of wine, and welcome every day that comes after with a smile on my face and a kick in my heels because we're together, and nobody will ever trouble us again."

"Are you sure?" I ask, doubt finding a way to mess with me as usual. "I mean, how confident are we that my father will stick to the terms of your deal and that he won't find a way to screw me over?"

"Vitaly and Anton are both watching him like hawks," he says. "The old man has been relegated to family functions and auxiliary votes for non-urgent situations only. He's got an army of bodyguards that will keep him indoors if he insists on being a dick about it. Gardening and reading are all he's good for. They even took his phone away."

"You're kidding," I gasp, my eyes widening with surprise.

"I am not," he chuckles dryly. "Something changed at that restaurant, Audrey. As bad as it sounds, I think that getting shot is the best thing that could've happened to Anton and Vitaly. It's as if they both snapped out of it and realized that it was time to force things into a different and better direction, with or without the old man's consent. They came into their own power the moment they almost lost their lives. And it makes sense. To me, anyway."

I shake my head slowly. "I still can't believe it, though. I am actually free, aren't I?"

"It's weird, isn't it?"

"A little, yeah. I'm used to constantly looking over my shoulder." I let out a sigh. "It's kind of sad, giving up The Emerald apartment, to be honest. But I would rather eat coal than live anywhere owned by my father."

"It's one of the reasons why I accepted his request to take The Emerald. In his mind, I think he figured he'd still retain some form of control over you."

"That's foolish. He, of all people, should know I'd sell in a heartbeat under those conditions."

"It doesn't stop him from trying. The man is desperate for control, even when he's not thinking clearly. But it no longer matters," Jason replies, adding more ravioli to my plate. "You need eat more, baby. There's a bun in that beautiful oven of yours."

My cheeks burn hot, a smile curling my lips. "Always taking care of me."

"And I always will," he says, his brow slightly furrowed. "Good God, woman, you're the love of my life. You're my soulmate. I went to hell and back for you. And right now, you're carrying our child. There's nothing I won't do... hold on, have some of this, too," he pauses to transfer several slices of fresh mozzarella cheese next to my pasta.

I can't stop myself from giggling. "You're trying to fatten me up. Stuff me like a Thanksgiving turkey, huh?"

"Honestly, you're a goddess at any size as far as I'm concerned, but I have to say, I can't wait to see that baby bump on you," he admits, reaching across the table to lovingly caress my face. "You look beautiful, by the way."

"Thank you."

"Relief looks good on you."

I am relieved. I can breathe. For the first time since I came to Chicago, I can actually take a deep breath and let it all out without fear. It's a peculiar sensation, but it's one that I will gladly get used to.

As the evening falls over Chicago's red skyline, I take in the glimmering city lights against the crimson sunset, a dash of gold stretching along the distant horizon. Just above, stars twinkle timidly as the moon rises lazily from the east.

Below, rivers of taillights pour through the city, people making their way up and down the roads, rushing to get home, to unwind and pop open a bottle of wine, to forget about the day they've had, and to welcome the night's soothing embrace.

The agitation of the past few days withers away, and I feel soft, almost limp, as I come out of the bathroom. The promise of a luxurious bed and the arms of my lover puts a smile on my lips, and as I walk into the bedroom, I find Jason standing by the window, buck naked in the semi-darkness of the night, gazing out in silence.

"I'm a tad overdressed, I see," I mumble, hidden beneath a pink satin robe.

Slowly, he turns around, the view of his chiseled buttocks replaced by a ravenous glower of one hell of an erection. My man is hard, waiting for me. I can only lick my lips as I approach him, closing the distance between us and losing my robe along the way.

"Fucking hell, Audrey, you look exquisite in this light," Jason says, his voice low and sexy, his lips parting slowly as I reach him.

My nipples tingle under his attention, but it's my mouth he goes for first.

He's hungry, and so am I.

"I've missed you," I whisper in between kisses before his tongue slips past and steals my words altogether. I love the taste of him. His dominant scent fills me to the brim and toys with my senses. The room is suddenly hot, my skin too tight, and my core ignited as Jason cups my breasts and squeezes, kneading them while his thumbs flick over my nipples.

He trails kisses down the side of my neck. "I'm never letting you out of my sight again," he groans softly, then playfully bites into my shoulder.

My hands wander, fingertips recording every inch of him. His sculpted pecs, the ropes of ab muscles, the inward dip of his hips. His cock, a magnificent sight in need of both my hands together to fully grasp it.

Instinctively, I get down on my knees and look up at him. Desire burns brightly in his eyes while a droplet of precum glistens on the tip of his erection. I lick it, welcoming the taste of him on my tongue. He twitches in my hands, and I suck him off—slowly, at first—just to get reacquainted with his girth.

But then I loosen my jaw and relax the back of my throat, letting him slide down and deep.

"Get up," he commands me, and I'm giddy with excitement. "You're up to no good tonight, Audrey. I'm not going to go easy on you just because we almost died again."

"Oh, no, baby, if anything, I need you to go hard on me. The hardest you've ever gone," I reply.

Jason turns me around and hugs me from behind, his lips tickling my ear while his heart thuds against mine. "Are you sure, my love?" he asks.

"I'm aching for you. Yes, please, a thousand times, yes." I moan and touch my breasts, fully aware of how much it turns him on.

"Fucking hell, woman," he gasps and pushes me closer to the bed. "Bend over, then."

Smiling like the devil, I do as I'm told. With my legs apart, I bend forward and hold on to the edge of the bed, feeling Jason's undivided attention scanning my body. His fingers explore my curves, tracing the lines of my spine and my hips.

I yelp when he smacks my ass. The delicious sting spreads through my buttock and sends heatwaves across my senses, setting my very soul on fire.

"Harder?" Jason asks.

"Yes, sir."

Again, he slaps my right cheek, and I damn near come in response, my pussy clenching as I struggle to stay on my feet. But then his tongue slides through my dripping wet folds, and a ragged moan escapes my throat. Damn, I won't last long at this pace. Energy gathers inside my core, balling into a veritable bomb. He won't need much to blow me apart.

He licks my pussy mercilessly. His lips close around my clit, and for the longest minute, he suckles on it, harder and harder as he listens to my panting and threaded moans, as his fingers dig into my flesh, spreading my buttocks so he can go to town.

"Don't stop, baby, I beg you..." I manage as his tongue is pressed against my clit.

I feel the climax quickly arriving. I fall over the edge of the world as he eats my pussy into a frenzy. I come hard, crying out in scattered syllables, my body rippling outward like an exploding sun. Everything turns white, and I can't see a thing. But I feel everything as Jason gets up and positions himself at my entrance.

His rock-hard cock tests me, and the tip glazed in my coursing arousal. He thrusts in, and I hold my breath, once again astonished by his gigantic size. I feel the veins along his shaft twitching inside me, my pussy instantly reacting as I wrap myself around him.

"I could do this and only this, forever," he whispers, then slowly pulls back.

"Don't leave me," I moan.

He rams into me. Hard. Swift. Decisive. Unyielding. I welcome the sweet sting of his invasion, a rhythm building up between us. "I can't leave you," Jason growls. "But I want to feel you, all of you. Touch yourself. Make yourself come."

"All over you?"

"All over me, darling."

The tension builds.

Sweat drips down our naked bodies. The sound of skin slapping skin with every movement. Jason's animalistic grunts as he grows bigger and harder inside me, as he claims me once again, and as he consumes me. I'm reduced to splinters of what I once was, surrendering completely, abandoning myself into his decadent feast.

He slaps my ass hard and fucks me like there's no tomorrow. It hurts so good as I apply more pressure to my swollen, tender nub. My breasts bounce joyfully as I come undone, screaming in sheer ecstasy while he shoots his seed deep inside of me. I hold him tight in my core, feeling him exploding, pulsating, melting within me.

Our bodies become one.

Our souls are forever bound.

It's our first night together since the nightmare ended. Jason kisses my cheek, breathing heavily as he holds me close. I come down from the clouds and open my eyes, realizing that it's not just our first night together since the nightmare ended. It's the first night of what is surely to be the rest of our lives.

This is what I've always dreamed of. Intense and passionate lovemaking. My best friend and protector is holding me close. My lover is bringing out the woman in me, over and over, until I can't even get out of bed anymore. My man runs his fingers through my hair as we plan for our future together.

"You're not just carrying my child in here," Jason says, his hand gently caressing my belly. We haven't moved from this position. I can feel him getting hard again while still inside of me. Moaning softly, I clench my pussy again just to get him riled up, and it works quickly, wonderfully. Before long, he's gliding in and out of me again, simply picking up where we left off. "You're carrying our future here, our lives. You're carrying love, Audrey. Our love."

"Our love ..." I repeat after him.

I am carrying our love. This child is proof that we belong together. That this was meant to be. And as the night unfolds and wraps itself around us, as Jason takes me away from reality, and we delve deep into the dark, hot recesses of our simmering romance, I welcome everything that the future holds.

CHAPTER 32

AUDREY

"Lily, go easy on the ice cream, honey; we still need to make room for dinner," Rita says as she and Jason's sweet, doe-eyed daughter share a chocolate and peanut butter ice cream bowl at one of our favorite cafes near Lily's school.

"It's Friday; cut the kid some slack," Jason chuckles, bringing over a bowl of mint chocolate chip ice cream for me. A smile dances across his lips as he joins us. "How are my three favorite ladies doing?"

"Oh, I'm good," Lily replies most casually, barely even looking at him.

She's too busy adoring a whole scoop of peanut butter ice cream, likely wondering if she can fit the whole thing in her mouth. "I know it seems tempting, Lily," I tell her, trying not to laugh, "but don't forget the brain freeze you got the last time you tried it."

"Yeah, but that was berry shorbet," she says, mispronouncing the word. "This is ice cream. It's different."

302 | K.C. CROWNE

"Okay, big girl, give it a go and prove it," Rita chuckles.

It's a beautiful day. One of those perfect late spring days on the greener side of Chicago. Lily's school is strategically positioned close to Armour Park, which means we often stop by for ice cream afterward. It's relatively clear this afternoon, and we get to bask in the sun and hang out without too many people cluttering our view of the field-house. It's nothing fancy, but it evokes a sense of peace that I absolutely cherish.

I love these routines that we've been forming.

Ice cream after school. Friday veggie dinners with Rita and Lily, the four of us talking about our week. Lily wants Jason to move her over to my school, but I'm actually negotiating a move to hers instead. It's a private school with so many opportunities for me to grow as an educator; I just couldn't refuse when Jason first suggested it.

Once a week, I get on Skype with my brothers, and we talk about recent developments. Our father won't talk to me—the old man is still licking his wounds. It'll be a while before he's a decent human being again, but I'm used to it. I don't even mind it as long as I have my life back.

"The news was quite dreary this morning," Rita says at one point.

"What do you mean? I've stopped watching TV since my father went back to New York," I shoot back with a dry chuckle.

But the frown on Jason's forehead has my humor fading quickly. "There's going to be a bit of a turf war between the Fedorov and the Abramovic clans," he says.

"That doesn't make any sense. I thought they were making headway with the negotiations."

"They were, but Arkady's younger brother is trying to stir the pot," he replies. "I doubt it will end well for him. Until then, however, he's kind of hogging the headlines."

"Why didn't Anton or Vitaly tell me anything about it?" I ask, suddenly worried that the routines that I've been building with Jason, Lily, and Rita might go up in smoke after all.

"I think they're trying to keep you out of it," Jason says. "But you don't have to worry about it, Audrey. You are safe."

I shake my head, quick to refuse such a prospect altogether. With trembling fingers, I grab my phone and call Vitaly, putting him on speaker as soon as he picks up. "What's up, little sister?"

"What's this nonsense about a turf war between us and the Abramovic family?" I blurt out. "It's all over the news."

Rita gives me a quick nod and discreetly takes Lily away from the table to give us some privacy.

Jason sits beside me, quietly listening while we bask in the sun. I gladly accept the scoop of mint chocolate chip ice cream he offers.

"Oh, that!" he laughs. "That's nothing. It's just for the media's blitz, I promise."

"Vitaly ..." Jason groans in frustration. "What the hell."

My brother chuckles with an almost sadistic delight. "I am so sorry. Anton and I figured it would keep the cops on their toes over there while we start our new businesses in

304 | K.C. CROWNE

Chicago. I spoke to Arkady's brother, Anatoly, and he was down with it. We put on a show for the newspapers, pretend we're missing a couple of people, threaten one another in public, beef around on Twitter and whatever, just to keep them busy."

"Good grief, Vitaly; I thought the Bratva was supposed to keep a low profile!" I snap.

"That's the old Bratva, sis. The new one has social media accounts and plenty of clout," my brother replies. "The public is loving it. And it's making it all the more confusing for the cops and the Feds. But I promise you, it's not real. You're safe, little sister. I swear."

"I could kill you," I say, shaking my head for the scare they just gave me. "Making me consider watching the news again ..."

"You could kill me, but then Anton would take over. Imagine that for a second."

Jason puts on a mock horrified face that Vitaly somehow assumes through the phone. "Yeah, I know. Terrible, right?"

"I hate you," I grumble, though he knows I don't really mean it.

"I never was the lovable type," Vitaly quips. "So! When will I meet my nephew, huh? What did the doctor say? Due date, anything?"

It's just like him to stir trouble and then pretend it's no big deal. I prefer these tiny jitters as opposed to the rains of pure hell that our father used to unleash upon us. Sure, I got startled mere minutes ago, but as my nervous system is soothed again, I begin to see the sense in building the Bratva

SEXTING THE SILVERFOX | 305
up in the online world. It's going to be incredibly confusing for the cops and the FBI, and my brother is right about that.

Not knowing what's real, what's fake, what's meant to go viral, and so on.

"I'm still about five months away," I tell Vitaly.

"You'd better name him after me."

Jason laughs. "That's going to be a no."

As the jitters subside and I once again readjust to the calm and tranquility of this new life with my new family, I realize that I need to come to terms with something. I may not be a part of the Bratva anymore, but the Bratva will always be a part of me. I cannot deny its existence, nor my blood ties, but I can tread carefully and make sure I am mentally prepared for whatever happens in the future.

My brothers may or may not survive this new age. The old-school Russians are still calling plenty of shots in New York. Some might perceive this online move as a sign of weakness. I can only pray and hope for the best. Maybe Anton and Vitaly will have nothing but smooth sailing ahead. But if the waters get choppy, I can rest assured that they'll find the best way forward.

"How's Papa?" I ask.

"Just as lousy as the last time you asked me about him," Vitaly answers with a flat tone. "He can't leave the house. I don't trust him yet."

"You can't keep him locked up forever, though," Jason warns him.

"I know, but for now, since he's still being a dick about everything, I have no choice. Once we cement the new businesses and we've got the peace treaties signed with Anatoly Abramovic and vetted by the rest of the Bratva, then I'll let the old wolf out. Until then, he's getting a taste of precisely the bitter medicine he shoved down our sister's throat. See how he likes it."

Vitaly may sound cruel but it does feel like just desserts.

After all the pain he caused, my father deserves a slice of the same torment he gave me. He needs to learn his new place in the family, and my brothers need room to breathe. Each of us is getting used to this new and different chapter in our lives. It is both scary and exciting, but for me, it's also exhilarating.

As I lean into Jason and welcome the warmth of his lips on my temple, I smile to myself, thanking the stars for allowing me to make it this far. Whatever comes next, we've got it handled because we have love and resilience, we have strength, and we have family.

EPILOGUE I

AUDREY

Five months later...

"He's perfect," Jason says as he stares at our newborn son with teary, wondrous eyes. He hasn't moved from his chair by my bedside since the nurse brought our bundle of joy in. "And you're a fucking queen," he adds. "Audrey, you're incredible."

I'm also exhausted. The epidural has worn off, and my whole body feels like a fizzling waterbed. My limbs are soft, and my fingers tingle slightly, but the mere fact that I'm holding my baby in my arms fills me with a whole new kind of energy.

"You're right; he is perfect," I reply, my heart filled with light. "Oh, God, Jason, I'm so scared."

"Scared?"

"What if I'm not a good mother?" I ask, my fears coming back to the surface after months of bubbling beneath. I've been holding this dread in for so long that I'd almost forgotten about it. But now that the baby is born, and I have no way of putting this genie back in the bottle, it's as if my mind is eager to become my worst enemy again.

Jason chuckles softly, pulling his chair closer to me. He leans in and plants a kiss on my forehead. His way of reassuring me, of reminding me that I'm not alone anymore. That I'm safe. "Are you kidding me? Audrey, you were made to be a mother. You're kind and patient, nurturing, and smart as a whip," he says. "Lily already loves you to the moon and back."

"She does, doesn't she?" I giggle, my cheeks burning pink.

"Audrey, you are already one hell of a mother to Lily, and you don't even realize it."

"Oh, Jason ..."

"I mean it. You've got this. And in case you forgot, we're in this together," he lovingly reminds me. "When you're tired, I take over. When you need a break, I take over. When you need to breathe, I take over. Even if you don't need any of the above, I'll still take over, just to make things easier for you. I'm his dad, and I intend to make sure our kids grow up with both parents firmly rooted beside them."

"That is reassuring, actually," I giggle softly while our baby stirs in my arms. I look down and giggle some more. "He looks like a raisin."

"An adorable raisin," Jason laughs.

Swaddled in white cotton, it's been mere minutes since our child has entered this world. He's tiny and pink-faced, his eyes shut, his cute, round cheeks still puffy and wrinkled. His little hands are clumped under the cotton, and he's still trying to get used to his new environment. "He's so quiet and sleepy. Was it the same with Lily?" I ask Jason.

"Oh, yeah. I thought we were blessed with the quietest kid," he says, fondly remembering Lily's first days of life. "Then all hell broke loose."

"How is she, by the way?" I ask.

"She and Rita are on the way," Jason says. "You went into labor so fast I didn't even have time to call anybody."

"Lily seemed excited to have a baby brother. I wonder how they'll get along."

"She'll be a good big sister, I'm sure of it," he replies, smiling. "She's old enough to understand a few things. I reckon the five of us will make a great team."

I give him a curious look. "So, Rita's down to keep working for us?"

"Absolutely. She said we should have more babies while we're at it."

I can't help but laugh. "Y'all need to give me a minute to catch my breath here first."

A knock on the door has both Jason and me looking up just in time to see Anton and Vitaly walk in, each of them carrying a huge bouquet of roses and lilies for us. They look different from the last time they were in Chicago, tanned and healthy, fully recovered from the gunshot wounds.

They're also sporting snazzy white linen shirts and slacks that make them look like hot surfer bros from the Californian coastline.

"I can't believe you two made it!" I quip.

My brothers light up when they see the baby in my arms.

"Are you kidding? We wouldn't have missed this for the world!" Anton replies, then proceeds to put both flower baskets on a nearby side table before he and Vitaly come closer to have a look at their nephew. "Holy smokes, Audrey, he's gorgeous."

"Looks like a raisin," Vitaly adds, raising a skeptical eyebrow that makes Jason and me laugh wholeheartedly.

"Bro, we all looked like raisins," Anton jokingly rolls his eyes.

"He's definitely a Fedorov. That nose ain't lying," my oldest brother says, then gives me a warm and affectionate smile. "Congratulations, little sis. You did it. We're proud of you."

"Congratulations, Jason," Anton adds. "Bet you he's going to be a handful."

"Let me guess, the Fedorov children were all handfuls," Jason replies, joining in on the banter.

We've been so worried and stressed about the whole Bratva ordeal, and we're still settling into what we like to call a normal life. Jason is the reason I smile more, he's the peace I've always wanted, and I do my best to reciprocate, but even I can tell that he sometimes succumbs to the fear of potentially losing me and the baby again. I can only imagine what it felt like when Dad told him that Arkady had taken me.

"You know it," Vitaly says. "Anton used to stick his fingers into every socket in the house."

"I only did that a couple of times; don't be so dramatic," Anton replies, then whips up his signature deviant grin. "But then I started using a fork. Total game changer."

Amidst the laughter and the joy, the jokes and the heaps of fun that we're about to deal with alongside countless sleepless nights and dirty diapers, I feel myself detach from the scene as if my spirit is hovering somewhere just above, watching them. My brothers are chucking puns and revealing embarrassing childhood memories of us. Jason laughing with one hand resting over mine. Me reminiscing and wondering about the future.

"Audrey?" Jason's voice pulls me back into my body.

I glance down to see a diamond ring sparkling in front of me. "What the..." I mumble, somewhat confused, while Anton and Vitaly stifle hard chuckles.

"She was not paying attention," Anton says.

"Are you serious?" Jason laughs as he holds up the ring for me.

"Oh, wow, wait ... what?" I manage, trying to pull myself back to reality.

Jason takes a deep breath. "Will you marry me? I had a whole speech prepared, but then you went into labor and ... well, here we are."

I need a moment to wrap my head around this. The ring is stunning. The diamond is huge, crowned with tiny sapphires on white gold. It's delicate, but it also stands out without being too ostentatious. The kind of ring he knows I'll gladly wear even while working with messy, chocolate-covered five-year-olds. My heart starts galloping as my brain finally catches up.

"Oh, my God ..."

"Audrey, I love you. I never thought I'd meet someone like you, let alone get to build something so extraordinary together," Jason says. "I need to make an honest woman out of you, however. I plan on spending the rest of my life making sure you are happy, loved, and constantly evolving to always be the best of anything you ever wish to be, baby. Marry me and make me the luckiest man in the world."

"Jason ... yes, absolutely yes!" I immediately reply.

He slips the ring on my finger. I'm briefly hypnotized by the light that bounces off the diamond and splinters into thousands of tiny, colorful shards just before Jason swoops in to kiss me. He pours all of his love into it, our lips trembling, our breaths faltering, as we join our hearts as one. Vitaly and Anton cheer in Russian and English with equal enthusiasm until I'm forced to shush them.

"You'll wake the tiny demon," Vitaly gives Anton a nudge in the ribs, nodding at our still-sleeping baby.

"His name is Edward," Anton corrects him. "We only call him demon if he ever sets the curtains on fire. I thought we agreed on that." He gives Vitaly a sly grin.

This is perfection.

It is more than I ever expected. And whenever I think about how Jason and I met, how we got swept up in that sizzling storm, clothes flying everywhere, secrets unraveling and damn near destroying us, I find myself feeling thankful.

Exhausted but thankful.

The best is yet to come. I know it.

EPILOGUE II

AUDREY

They say time flies by when you're having fun, but the same can be said for a first-time mother trying to navigate her new life, her new family, and a blossoming career as an educator for one of the best private kindergartens in the city—possibly the state of Illinois, altogether.

A year has passed since everything changed.

Since Vitaly took over the family business.

Since my father was forced out of the Bratva altogether, having to step into his retirement with a chip on his shoulder and a sour look on his face.

Since Jason and I moved in together. Our son is a year old, and as expected, he is practically an atomic yet adorable little demon. My brothers weren't too far off with their theories. But Lily and Rita make a formidable team in helping Jason and me with raising Edward. He's not a true handful, though he's not the easiest kid, either. I guess that's his appeal because I love every day that I get to be in his life, good or bad.

There's so much that I'm still learning, but Jason has been true to his word. He looks after us. He juggles his businesses and his family with exceptional tenacity, setting a brilliant example for me to follow, as well. I love him more and more with each passing day. I can no longer imagine a life without him, and that can be scary at times—especially on the eve of our wedding.

We agreed to keep the ceremony small. Only our closest friends and family have gathered at the Wayside Chapel. Rita and Lily are my beautiful bridesmaids in matching pink dresses. Vitaly and Anton will walk me down the aisle. They kept arguing over who would give me away, so I ultimately gave up and asked them both to do it.

My heart is stuck in my throat, the wedding jitters doing quite a number on me. I'm standing outside the chapel's ornate wooden doors. Inside, my future husband awaits, along with the officiant, the wedding party, and the guests. Among them are former Army buddies of Jason's. Their presence makes my brothers more nervous than the bride.

"Feds, so many Feds in there," Anton sighs, running a hand through his hair.

"You look dashing," I say, trying to soothe his frayed nerves.

"What if it's a trap? What if they plan to arrest us as soon as you say, 'I do,' huh?" he replies, giving me a panicked look.

Vitaly jokingly smacks him over the shoulder. "Cool your heels, Capone. It's a wedding. Our sister's wedding. What the hell?"

I would laugh if I weren't so anxious myself. It's a beautiful place, quiet and simple, yet elegant and welcoming, surrounded by lush gardens and blessed with all the spring sunshine that Mother Nature has to offer.

I picked out the perfect dress for this. The Regency-style corset hugs my full figure without suffocating me, adorned with fine pearls and silver thread, while the skirt and the sleeves flow freely in pure white silk, the hems lined with floral-themed lace. I opted for flats since no one can see my feet anyway. Besides, I plan to do plenty of dancing at the reception tonight, so the last thing I wanted was to wear myself out before we even got to the venue.

My brothers look particularly handsome in their Armani suits—elegant, dark blue jackets and pants in stark contrast with their white shirts and black bowties. They would've had a fine career in modeling on New York's most prestigious fashion runways had they not been born into the Bratva.

"Cut him some slack," I tell Vitaly. "He's nervous, too."

"We are not under investigation," he reminds Anton. "They're just Jason's friends."

Anton shrugs and gives me a childlike pout. "You know, you can still marry Piotr, if you want. I could hook you up. At least then we'd keep it all in the Bratva."

"I will end you," I shoot back.

"I'm kidding," Anton laughs. "Gosh, you are gorgeous..."

He takes a moment to admire me while Vitaly hands me my bouquet of white roses. This is it. The threshold we've all been trying to get to for quite some time. The ceremony marking my passage into a new and better life. I'm leaving the Fedorov name behind for good and becoming a Winchester.

"I still think you should hyphenate," Vitaly sighs deeply. "Audrey Fedorova-Winchester... it has a nice ring to it."

"Except I'm trying to keep a low profile regarding my Bratva ties, remember? We agreed on this months ago," I say. "Granted, I am sorry to bid the name farewell ... sort of."

Anton chuckles dryly. "Shut up, you couldn't wait to sign the marriage certificate."

"So, I can marry Jason, obviously!"

"Yeah, right..."

"Now, now, don't be sour," Vitaly tells Anton. "She will always be a Fedorova to us, brother. We all know that."

"Through and through, huh?" Anton smiles softly, brotherly love beaming from his big, blue eyes. "Mom would be so happy for you, Audrey, so happy."

I nod slowly, wishing she could be here with us. In a way, she is, though. She is present through me, through my brothers. She never truly left us, and she never will. And it's the best that I can hope for, at least in this lifetime. Vitaly glances at the door just as the sound of the organ playing announces that they're ready to receive the bride for the ceremony.

"Come on, sis. We've got this," Anton says as he and Vitaly flank me and offer me their strong arms. "Time to give you away."

"Just don't tell Jason we like him too much," Vitaly adds. "We want to keep him on his toes in case he ever steps out of line with you."

I'm close to bursting out of this corset with sheer laughter when our father's voice startles all three of us. "I'm interrupting, little zaika."

"Holy …" I freeze for a split second.

Slowly, my brothers and I turn around to find Grigori Fedorov standing before us.

"Quiet as a mouse," Anton whispers.

We didn't hear him approaching. Somehow, he got past the security detail that Anton posted at the chapel's main entrance. We thought the old man had stayed in New York. It's not like we forbade him from the wedding; he just never responded to any of our invites. He's been too busy grouching over the whole takeover, so we figured he wanted to sulk alone in his room back at the Fedorov mansion.

Yet here he is, wearing a neatly tailored grey suit and a silver bowtie, his white hair combed and his skin glowing. He looks a lot better than the last time I saw him. Vitaly said he'd gone on a diet. It's doing wonders for his skin and outward appearance; I can say that much for him.

"Papa, what are you doing here?" I ask with a trembling voice.

Part of me is terrified that he's come to ruin my wedding day. I wouldn't have put it past him. He can be so bitter and vindictive. But the look on his face speaks of something else —a warmth I haven't seen in so many years; it feels downright foreign.

"Little zaika, I've been anything but a decent father to you, especially in recent years," he says, constantly stealing wary glances at my brothers. "I wouldn't know where to start with the apologies and making amends, but I figured you would like me to walk you down the aisle. It's a father's duty, after all."

"Are you serious?" Anton gasps. That gets him another nudge and a shush from Vitaly. "Ow. Dude ..."

"I am serious," our father declares, keeping his chin up. "It is the least I can do now. I cannot change what I've said and done. I cannot take it back, and frankly, I think apologies and amends might be useless at this point, anyway. I do not expect you to want me in your life, nor will I insist on the matter," he adds and takes a deep, shuddering breath. "But your mother would never forgive me, even in the afterlife, if I don't step up now and do the right thing."

"Papa ..." I manage, tears quick to fill my eyes. I'm conflicted, yet I cannot seem to find the words to send him away. Maybe I should. He has caused me so much trouble and so much pain. But he doesn't expect me to forgive him. He knows that all too well.

I can see it in his eyes. The torment. The regret. I doubt he'll ever utter a real apology. This is the closest he'll ever get to one, and I would not be true to myself if I didn't accept his token of peace. I've always dreamed of having my father at my wedding—a wedding with a husband of my choosing, that is. Not Grigori Fedorov's.

"Will you let me walk you down the aisle, little zaika? It would be my privilege. You have chosen a great man as your husband, and I wish to honor you both."

All I can do is nod slowly as Vitaly and Anton step aside. Papa offers me his arm. A smile tests my lips as I take it. For so long, I've wanted my father to see me, to really see me for who I am. I dare not dream too wild a dream here, but I'm starting to think my wish is finally coming true. Grigori Fedorov sees me as who I have always been. His daughter is an independent woman with dreams and ambitions of her own.

And he is ready to accept and cherish that.

"All right then," I mutter. "Giving you the benefit of the doubt, Papa."

"I will not disappoint."

As Anton and Vitaly push the chapel doors open, the organ music pours into the lobby with "Here Comes the Bride." As my father walks me down the aisle, as the guests rise and collectively gasp at the sight of him, the sight of us together, I know I've made the right choice. As Jason sees me coming, as the sun shines in his beautiful hazel eyes, glowing with love and raw emotion, I know we're on to something wonderful here.

He gives my father a slight frown as Papa gives me away, but the old wolf doesn't seem bothered in the least. He just responds with a curt nod and steps to the side as Jason takes my trembling hand in his, our hearts thudding like horses at a race.

"And so it begins," he whispers.

The officiant opens the good book, flipping to his preferred page. Silence falls heavily around us, and all I can hear is the promise of a wonderful life ahead.

The End

Made in the USA
Monee, IL
20 November 2024